Tales of a Jilted Hypochondriac

By Tracy H. Tucker

Copyright © 2012 Tracy H. Tucker
All Rights Reserved

This book, or parts thereof, may not be reproduced in any form without permission.

For all permissions, please contact the author at tracyhelentucker@gmail.com.

Disclaimer:
This book is a work of fiction. Names, characters, places, and incidents are either the product of the author's imagination or used fictitiously, and any resemblance to actual persons, living or dead, business establishments, events, or locales is entirely coincidental.

Any trademarks, service marks, product names or named features are assumed to be the property of their respective owners and are used only for reference. There is no implied endorsement for using one of these terms.

This book is dedicated to...

My husband Owen, for his technical (and loving)
support throughout this long process,
and for always being a sounding board—
without sounding bored

Authors Jessica Park and Christopher Smith,
for their advice and encouragement

Angela, Holly and Gail,
for giving feedback
during the book's beginning stages and beyond

and for my daughters, Chelsea, Chloe and Caleigh,
who have made motherhood a wonderful journey

Table of Contents

CHAPTER ONE: Breathless
CHAPTER TWO: Heart Failure
CHAPTER THREE: Malignancy
CHAPTER FOUR: Man(ick)
CHAPTER FIVE: Metastasis
CHAPTER SIX: Numb
CHAPTER SEVEN: Loss
CHAPTER EIGHT: Rabid
CHAPTER NINE: *Blurred vision*
CHAPTER TEN: Septic
CHAPTER ELEVEN: Headaches
CHAPTER TWELVE: MS
CHAPTER THIRTEEN: Bad Blood
CHAPTER FOURTEEN: Matters of the Flesh
CHAPTER FIFTEEN: Toilet Trouble
CHAPTER SIXTEEN: Small Lumps
CHAPTER SEVENTEEN: Stagnant
CHAPTER EIGHTEEN: Attention Deficit Disorder
CHAPTER NINETEEN: Off Balance
CHAPTER TWENTY: Bitter Taste
CHAPTER TWENTY-ONE: Hard to Swallow
CHAPTER TWENTY-TWO: Hyper Tension
CHAPTER TWENTY-THREE: S.O.B.
CHAPTER TWENTY-FOUR: Tongue in Cheek
CHAPTER TWENTY-FIVE: Susceptible
CHAPTER TWENTY-SIX: Flutters
CHAPTER TWENTY-SEVEN: Rash
CHAPTER TWENTY-EIGHT: Pregnant Pause
CHAPTER TWENTY-NINE: Seeing Red
CHAPTER THIRTY: Growth
CHAPTER THIRTY-ONE: Sniffles
CHAPTER THIRTY-TWO: Anti-dote

RECIPE FOR JILTED HYPOCHONDRIAC:

Start with one 42 year old female, marinated in
naiveté.
Add generous dollop of kinky,
sprinkled with deceit and shock.
Distract with chocolate. Shake until unrecognizable.
Leave in kitchen overnight.

I KILL ME:

Tales of a Jilted Hypochondriac

CHAPTER ONE: Breathless

I could think of two big reasons why this threesome wasn't going to work: her boobs. When my husband of nineteen years told me he wanted to "spice things up a bit," I was envisioning sex toys... spanking... chocolate-covered penis. The kinkiest thing we had done thus far was Richard tying me to the bedposts with the silky belts from my bathrobes. We'd had a code for him to untie me if I started to freak out. The code was me saying, *untie-me-right-now.* So when he first proposed the idea of a playmate, I was shocked. I mean, who *did* that, anyway? Certainly, not us. He was an insurance salesman whose specialty was planning for a secure future. I was a high school English teacher in the next town over. We lived in the wholesome Green Mountain State. And we were *parents*—which was something Eleanor Wilkinson definitely was not, as was evident by her breasts.

They were truthfully too big to be called "perky." Thing One and Thing Two were, for lack of a better term, up and out. My breasts, on the other hand, were not only small (32 B minus) but had turned into saggy, limp skin sacs with droopy areolas and indifferent nipples from two years of nursing babies. So it was very much *un*appreciated that my husband not only felt the need to invite

6

someone to join us under the covers, but someone with a cup size further along in the alphabet than mine.

It had all started with a trigger point. Richard had been complaining of his upper back muscles being tight, and since I knew he'd been under a lot of stress at work, I got him a gift certificate to a local spa. Eleanor, a transplant from England with what Richard called a "killer accent," was his massage therapist. After about four sessions of seeing her, Richard mentioned that someone at the office had engaged in a threesome, and then said what did I think of that. I said a twosome was more than enough for me, and the conversation had ended. The morning after his sixth massage, he told me over breakfast (while the girls were upstairs getting ready for school) that he thought he might like to try a threesome, and what did I think of that. I had stirred my coffee a bit too vigorously so that some of it slopped over the sides of the mug and onto the table. I had not known what to answer, and thought it wise that I refrained from my initial response of *what the FUUCKK?!* After a few moments, I whispered (so the kids wouldn't hear) why didn't we just watch some good porn instead?

That's not what I'm talking about, he snorted. *I feel like we need to really shake things up here. Make it exciting again.*

Aren't I enough for you? I asked. I didn't understand this; we had had sex three times last week, and I'd gone down on him every time. Even when he hadn't showered immediately before.

I need a change, he had answered. *Sorry, but I'm just being honest.* He had looked me in the eyes when he said that.

That was when I got scared. And I said, *okay.*

Eleanor stopped taking Richard as her client once the three-way had been arranged. His trigger point had dramatically improved, while I found myself dealing with thoughts of another type of trigger. But I would do this, act like a Big Girl. I would do it for Richard, and for us. We would have this one-time *ménage á trois,* it would jump-start our marriage, and afterwards, maybe on our twenty-fifth wedding anniversary, we would be at the point where we'd shake our heads and laugh and ask each other, what the hell were we thinking?

We planned it for a Saturday night, at a nearby hotel. Richard and I would check in first, and then he would text Eleanor once we'd gotten settled in the room. Our daughters—Lily, thirteen, and Carli, nine—were having sleepovers of their own (G-rated, unlike ours) at friends' houses. Ground rules, which I established independently of Richard, included no penile penetration with Eleanor, only with me—condoms were far from foolproof, and I didn't want to risk any STDs. Richard had hesitated at that until he saw the look on my face and nodded hastily in agreement. I told him he could receive oral sex from Eleanor (I was willing to give up that job), and he could return the favor, although I would shudder whenever I'd picture it. My last rule was that I would only do what I felt comfortable with when the time came, whether that be participant, coach, cheerleader, or spectator.

It was taking me longer than I'd anticipated to choose an outfit. Conservative was obviously not a fit for a situation like this, but I didn't want to slut it up, either, because then Eleanor might expect certain things from me. I'd had no prior lesbian experience, except for a very minor stint in college, and that didn't count because all the girls on my floor were doing it.

Richard had gotten angry with me for taking so long to get dressed. "Christine, just PICK something, for God's sake! You're just going to take it off, anyway. We're supposed to be at the hotel in twenty minutes."

I snapped at him to stop *rushing* me, couldn't he see that I was keyed up about this, and he should be goddamned GRATEFUL I was doing it at all. This whole thing, it was completely foreign to me—almost incomprehensible. But so was losing Richard.

I finally decided to wear my newest pair of jeans and a plain, cornflower-blue top with a deep V-neck, one of Richard's favorites because it showed off my eyes. September nights in Vermont were cool, so I wore a thin white tank-top underneath. After stressing over my hair (I decided to wear it down and loose) and my makeup (a quick smoothing of liquid foundation, hastily-applied mascara and under-eye concealer), I told Richard I was ready. This was, of course, a lie.

I packed a small bag with a toothbrush, toothpaste, two pairs of underwear, and the black negligee Richard had bought for me to wear tonight. I did not bring a change of clothes for the following day. Richard had somewhat reluctantly agreed that we would not spend the night with Eleanor—in my mind, this would have been much too intimate. I wanted it to be sex and nothing more. After it was over, I wanted to be able to go back to our own bed, our children, our *lives,* and move on.

We were getting close to the hotel. My heart had been banging against my chest for the better part of an hour. I felt lightheaded and fluttery. My God, what if I was to hyperventilate and pass out?

Richard would be furious. *Hypoxia: a deficiency in the amount of oxygen reaching body tissues.* Mild cases would only cause inattentiveness, poor judgment (I definitely had that, given what I was about to do) and uncoordinated movement, but I knew that severe cases resulted in complete unawareness and could even progress to a comatose state. My breathing reflex could actually *stop,* and if this persisted, brain death was inevitable. Would Richard and Eleanor still do it without me?

I turned my head toward my husband. He appeared relaxed, serene. "Richard. How do I look?"

He glanced over at me and then returned his gaze to the road. "You look fine."

I sighed. I did not want to look fine. I wanted to look heart-stoppingly beautiful.

"Stop worrying. It's going to be a very sexy experience for us. Memorable. And it says something about our relationship that we can trust each other enough to do this."

We? This did not feel like *we.* And as far as what it "said" about us: I was silent, while Richard was speaking loud and clear.

As we pulled into the hotel parking lot, my chest began to constrict. A sort of buzzing—the feeling, not the sound—in my fingers. Hyperventilation syndrome. It was an old friend, but an annoying one who occasionally scared the crap out of me. I inhaled deeply, pushing air into my belly, and exhaled slowly. *In 2-3-4, out 2-3-4.*

Richard put his hand lightly at my back as we walked to the front desk, each of us carrying a bag. I hadn't seen what he had packed, and for some reason this was unsettling. "Reservation for Richard Bacon."

The desk clerk smiled at us as if we were a

happily married couple, handed Richard the key card and directed us toward the elevator.

We did not speak as we rode the elevator to the fourth floor. Richard took his cell phone from his coat pocket and began texting. I opened my mouth to say I thought he would wait to text her until we got to our room. He apparently did not want to wait. I closed my mouth and instead studied his slender build, the wiry, closely-cropped sandy hair just beginning to gray. Would Eleanor, in a show of passion, run her fingers through it, teasing out the tight curls as I often did when Richard and I kissed? I took deep breaths of the elevator air, which seemed in short supply. *In 2-3-4, out 2-3-4.*

Richard slid the key into the slot (why did that have to seem sexual?) and opened the door. The room had, as expected, a king-sized bed. The drapes were partly open; I went to the window to pull them closed. I felt Richard's eyes on me and turned around.

"She should be here in a few minutes. Are you okay?"

I stared at him.

He cleared his throat. "It'll be easier once you get some alcohol into you. I brought some wine."

You think of everything.

"Eleanor recommended the brand. You'll get a kick out of it."

Everything, except me.

The hotel room suddenly felt too small for us, and our guest hadn't even arrived yet. I told Richard I needed to use the bathroom, went inside with my bag and closed the door. I put my hands on the counter to steady myself and took a deep, rattly breath as I studied my reflection. I was grateful that people told me I looked younger than my age of forty-two; I had thick hair, slim hips, good teeth. Eleanor was in her early 30's. What would she think of me? And more important, why did I care?

As I brushed my teeth, I contemplated how one might commence a threesome. In the business-casual style with introductions all around, handshakes, smiles—then strip? Or a more leisurely approach of wine, innocuous conversation, maybe some nervous laughter, tentative kissing—then strip?

Voices. I would soon find out. She was here.

I could not breathe. Shallow, desperate gulps of air. *Acute onset of shortness of breath.* I knew there was a condition to warrant this—besides a husband and his massage therapist waiting for you to come out of the bathroom so all three of you could take your clothes off.

"Christine?"

Pulmonary embolism. That was the condition, and a high risk of mortality to boot.

"Honey?"

God *damn* it! What was I going to do if I couldn't breathe? I was expected to be doing *heavy* breathing in a few minutes, and here I was sounding like a fucking Chihuahua in a steeplechase.

Richard's voice again, a bit louder this time. "Eleanor's here."

I prayed that my voice would sound bright, enthusiastic, like it did when I was trying to get my students to read a book I knew they'd hate. *My students.* My God, if they knew.

I told myself to get ahold of myself. *Bright, enthusiastic.* "Okay!" I managed. I reached for the tiny bottle of hotel mouthwash. My breath might have been shallow, but I would make goddamned sure it was fresh. I swished and spat, then decided I did not want to taste medicine-y and reached a trembling hand to get a cup of water. Another glance in the mirror. My hair looked flat. I flipped my head upside down, cursed myself for forgetting a brush, and raked my hands through my hair. Looked again at my reflection and decided I was too pale. No blush in my make-up bag (I was so unprepared for this night, in many ways). I pinched my cheeks hard, for color, and opened the door.

The first thing I saw was Richard beaming. The second and third things I saw were boobs. Eleanor's boobs. And I knew that between my Chihuahua breaths and her Saint Bernard breasts, this threesome was going to the dogs.

CHAPTER TWO: *Heart Failure*

I pulled my eyes off Eleanor's rack, which proved challenging since it took up a good percentage of her. She was very attractive. I did not want to admit that. Blonde, of course, with a chic, sleek, angular cut that was longer in the front and tapered toward the back. She had high cheekbones shaded a perfect rose (she'd apparently remembered to use blush), and full, glossy lips. Her blouse, deep violet with a plunging neckline edged with beads, looked silky and expensive. She wore a black skirt embossed with swirling flowers which matched her top, and black high-heeled pumps.

"Hallow, Christine," Eleanor said, her shiny lips parting to reveal perfectly white teeth. Her voice was warm, like melted butter. There was no competing with that accent; the sexuality it gave her was undeniable. My friend Stella used to joke about hearing anyone—male or female—with an accent. The second this person would start speaking, her automatic response was, *pardon me while I take off my clothes*. How ironic.

My tongue felt stiff and leathery. I could only produce the word "hi." She extended a hand and I shook it. Her skin was cool, smooth...everything about her was cool and smooth, while I felt sweaty and frumpy. I hated myself for not curling my eyelashes, or putting on lipstick, or dusting my face with bronzer; my summer tan had long since faded to my pale fall skin. And I should have dressed more for the occasion—like a slut. This wasn't a soccer game, for Christ's sake! I might as well have worn a turtleneck and mom jeans.

I felt a sharp pain in my chest. Left side, not good. A few seconds later, the same pain. Stabbing. Perhaps it was indigestion from dinner. But it was very possibly a heart attack. Oh, *God*. What were the symptoms women had? I consulted the medical dictionary which had pushed its way to the front of my brain and flipped open to "H." *Although women, like men, report chest pain or discomfort as their most common heart attack symptom, women are more likely to experience a burning sensation in their upper abdomen, lightheadedness, nausea, shortness of breath and sweating, and often back or jaw pain.*

Richard was smiling as he looked back and forth at Eleanor and me, as if this were a playdate and he was a proud dad. I felt dread begin a slow, torturous spine climb. But I had agreed to this.

All the shallow breathing had dried out the insides of my cheeks and turned them cottony. My mouth made a clacking sound. "It's nice to meet you, Eleanor," I managed. I waited for her to say, *please, call me Ellie*. She did not. I decided the word "haughty" came to mind to describe her—not *hottie*, as I am sure Richard wanted me to think.

"And it's AP-so-loot-lee LOVE-lee to meet you as well, Chris."

Using my nickname, without seeking permission. Too familiar. The urge to flatulate inflated within me, like a giant balloon. Now that would be a turn-on. *Ohh RICHard, she's positively CHAHming!*

"Richard's told me a loht about you."

Nausea. Jesus, I was going to throw up. I sucked in little gulps of air. My skin felt prickly, like the start of a cold sweat. Richard went to the chair where he'd put his bag and unzipped it. "I brought the wine Eleanor recommended. Very appropriate for the occasion." He grinned as he held up the bottle.

I leaned closer to read the label. *Ménage á Trois... California Red.*

"Appropriate, huh?" he chuckled.

"Yes," I nodded. "Because *ménage á trois* is the French term meaning 'threesome,' and that's what we're here to have. A threesome. So the name of that wine is very appropriate."

Richard regarded me with the cool detachment of a principal dealing with an unruly pupil. He set down the bottle on the dresser and reached in the bag for the corkscrew and wine glasses. He had brought our nicest glasses, wrapped in kitchen towels. From our kitchen, in our house, where we could have been right now, eating ice cream in front of the TV.

He opened the wine and poured. My hand was trembling as I took my glass. As expected, Richard made a toast ("to a memorable evening"), and we clinked glasses and drank. We stood until it became awkward and then sat down, Eleanor and me in chairs and Richard on the edge of the bed.

The next order of business was putting our phones on silent, like when you're at a performance. Only *we* were the performance. I didn't like doing that, because what if the kids tried to call. But then I remembered I did not have children in this scenario.

A second glass of wine for Richard and Eleanor. I declined; I wanted to keep semi-sober, and if I needed to be rushed to the hospital for a possible heart attack, alcohol would interfere with the other medications I would undoubtedly be given. Richard and Eleanor sipped and chatted amiably with one another and with me; I smiled and nodded as the pain sliced through my chest.

And then it was time. I would have preferred a parting handshake, perhaps a European kiss on both cheeks and leave with Richard—with my dignity and marriage intact. But my husband had other ideas. He cleared his throat and set his glass down on the nightstand. Eleanor smiled knowingly and winked at me. *Winked,* as if we were in on this together.

"Well," said Richard, a smile flickering on his lips. "Can we get started?"

I sat rooted to my chair. "Can we turn off the lights?" I asked in a small voice.

"Just one," my husband answered. "I want to be able to see."

I clicked off the lamp beside me. Eleanor rose from her chair and moved to stand in front of me. My face was burning. She held out her hand, and as if in a dream, I took it and stood up.

I detected the scent of French vanilla. Her eyes were very green. She was wearing purple mascara. "So are you...bisexual?" I whispered.

Eleanor laughed, a high, tinkly sound, like wind chimes. "You are positively aDORable, Chris." She led me over to the bed, my steps heavy and slow, to where my husband was sitting. "Let's get to know one another better, shall we?" she said softly. I started to tremble. Richard, just inches away, drew in his breath.

She turned to face me, her back to Richard. I tried not to think of him looking at her ass. Still holding one of my hands, she wrapped her free arm around my waist and began to kiss my neck. She was so *uninhibited.* Weren't Brits supposed to be conservative? I did not know what I should feel, so I felt everything. Fascination, disgust, arousal, fear, timidity, horror. And chest pain, worsening with every kiss. What would the ambulance crew think, when they inevitably were called to come resuscitate me? I would be unconscious and therefore unable to explain, but I hoped Richard would have the good sense to tell them this was a business meeting. And they would think, *monkey business.*

I stood, frozen. Eleanor put her mouth near my ear and whispered for me to relax, let myself enjoy it. I looked at the ceiling, the drapes, the silent television, the unremarkable print of two sailboats hanging on the wall, and then down at Richard, who had put his hands on Eleanor's hips. My heart thudded wildly. Her hands were in my hair now as she kissed my cheeks, forehead, eyebrows, and all around my lips. There was the sound of heavy breathing, and I couldn't tell if it was Eleanor, or Richard, or me.

Just when I thought she was going to kiss me on the mouth, she turned around to face Richard and put her hands on his shoulders. He was still sitting on the bed, staring up at her, and his face looked so *hungry.* Like a starving man at an all-you-can-eat buffet. Watching this rendered me incapable of movement, and I stood like granite with my arms hanging stiffly by my sides.

Eleanor bent down slightly and began kissing Richard. She was kissing my husband as I stood and watched. Something inside me leapt up in utter indignation, and I was just about to set it free when she turned around to me. Her actions were so smooth, so seamless, it was almost as though she had rehearsed this whole scene—or she'd had plenty of prior performances.

Her mouth was on mine. I tasted wine and

lipstick, felt her hand on the outside of my shirt, groping my breast, and I wondered in shame if she knew how much of it was really just padding.

I was becoming more lightheaded with each passing second. And another symptom, in my back. *As a prelude to a heart attack, women often experience upper back pressure that feels like squeezing.* I opened my mouth against Eleanor's to announce that I was dying, when I realized the pressure I felt *was* from squeezing: Richard's arms, tight around me, with Eleanor in the middle. We were making an Eleanor sandwich.

She pulled away from me, her impressive chest heaving, and went to Richard for more kissing. He began to unbutton her blouse while I stood unsteadily. So this was how a threesome went: taking turns. First her, then him. Give a little, take a little. Sharing. I had decided it was too...*crowded,* for my liking.

"Take off your shirt, Christine," he mumbled, his mouth still on his massage therapist.

He was helping her to take her clothes off, while I had to go it on my own? This stung a bit. I did as I was told and crossed my arms in front of my chest, shivering and waiting.

Richard slid the now-unbuttoned blouse off Eleanor's shoulders. It cascaded to the floor in a soft, flouncy heap to reveal her lacy, ivory bra. She gave a little sigh (complete with an accent) as he unzipped her skirt and tugged it down rather unceremoniously. I felt a small burst of satisfaction that it seemed to catch on her hips, but this was quickly squelched when I saw she was wearing a matching ivory thong. And looking fantastic in it.

I could not help but stare, bug-eyed, as she reached behind her and deftly unclasped her bra strap to unleash the beasts. Richard was staring, too, pride all over his face—as if he'd been standing next to God when Eleanor-to-be went through the tits line and God asked him, *how big do we want these fun bags?*

Mount Eleanor was speaking. "Lie down, Christine."

Keeping my arms across my chest, I forced myself to get on the bed. I suddenly felt very chilled, and nausea was making a comeback. *This will soon be over, girl,* I told myself. *Just a little while longer, and then you can go back to real life.*

"Now your pants, Chris." I could hear the urgency in Richard's voice.

"Let's not keep OLL the fun for ourselves, Richard," chided Eleanor. She smiled at me, as if she was doing me a favor, and crawled up the bed until she was hovering over me. My heart slammed against my chest as I felt her fingers at the top of my pants. Unbutton, unzip, off. As easy as 1-2-3.

"Good guhl," she murmured. "You are ray-lee, ray-lee beautiful, Chris." She leaned over to kiss me again.

I could not move, did not protest when she gently rolled me over onto my side so she could unhook my bra. Did not say a word when she slid her tongue in my mouth and cupped my breast in her hand. This was not me, I was not here. I was vaguely aware of Richard yanking his shirt over his head and stepping out of his jeans, and that was when I became the most self-conscious: not only for myself, my body, but *his*. What if he couldn't perform in front of her? What if she was amused by the size of his penis? On a good day, I'd call it mediocre. Plus, he had a very, very hairy ass. Had she seen it during one of his massages? Maybe she thought it was masculine. I just thought it was hairy.

Richard was moaning as he climbed on the bed with us, which heightened my embarrassment. This was a sound that only his wife should hear. But he, like Eleanor, was completely uninhibited, while I shrunk in on myself like a patient at the proctologist's. Eleanor moved over to make room for Richard (more sharing). It was then I noticed he had something in his hand. A scarf. One of mine.

I asked him what he was going to do with that scarf.

He was breathing heavily, leaning over me, his penis poking at my thigh. "I want to blindfold you. It's part of my fantasy."

I started to protest and then Eleanor whispered in my ear. "It's very eROTic, Chris, to not know what's going to happen next, until you feel it. You'll see." Then she laughed. "Actually, you *won't* see, but you WILL understahnd. Just *troy* it."

It was two against one. I let him tie the scarf around my head and did not complain that it was too tight, even though it was. Soon I felt hands and mouths on me, and I could not tell whose was whose. Sometimes there was a pause and groaning, and I knew this was when they were touching each other. My heart rate soared as I realized that he could be having sex with her, right now, and I wouldn't know. They could even be pointing at me and *laughing* silently, and I wouldn't know. A scarf had not been part of the plan. In fact, *I* had not been consulted about any of this. They had set this up, and Richard had led me to believe I was able to make ground rules, when really, *they* were in charge.

I wanted my life back. I started to sit up but was abruptly pushed back down. French vanilla scent, so I knew it was Eleanor. Shock and fear crept into my voice. "Stop!" I felt her hands release me. I tore the scarf from my eyes to see the two of them kneeling on the bed, naked and bewildered, faces flushed, hair disheveled. They looked like a couple.

Another pain in my heart. "I'm sorry," I said, hating myself for apologizing. "I can't do this anymore. I thought I could, but I can't. This was all an awful mistake." I gathered up the bedspread to cover myself. "This is not me. And Richard," I said, looking at him, "I don't believe this is you, either."

I addressed Eleanor, who was now sitting back on her heels, her arms folded across her breasts. The color in her cheeks had faded. "I want to apologize for wasting your time. But I really can't do this. I hope you understand." Managing a half-smile, I added, "I think this is his mid-life crisis," and my voice was almost tender.

I glanced at my husband who was sitting on the edge of the bed, staring at the wall.

"Richard, I would really like to go home now."

As the three of us began to silently pick up our clothes, I knew that somehow, he believed I had failed him.

CHAPTER THREE: *Malignancy*

It had been a week since the failed threesome. That night, on the way home in the car, I had apologized over and over, until Richard had exploded. "ENOUGH!" he barked, in a harsher tone than I thought the situation warranted. "I don't want to hear another word about it. And I'll never ask you to do anything like that again."

I told myself this was his way of apologizing. I had to believe it.

Unlike last week, this Saturday night showcased our normal routine. Richard, Lily, Carli and I were leaning over the island in the kitchen, sharing pizza, a big bottle of root beer and a bag of barbecue chips, all of the above in between texting. Carli pulled a long string of cheese from her pizza slice and let it dangle over her mouth as she tipped her head back to eat it.

"Don't do that," Richard told her. "That's not good manners."

She pouted and comforted herself with a swig of soda.

This was a bit out of the ordinary. *I* was the one who usually commented on the kids' manners (or lack thereof); Richard was always much more lenient. I noticed he seemed particularly antsy tonight and kept shifting his weight from side to side, as if he was uncomfortable. I hoped he wasn't going to need another massage.

"I'm sleeping over at Julia's," Lily announced. "We're gonna skype with her cousin from England."

England. I snuck a glance at Richard. He was

chewing intently, staring down at his plate.

"Julia's lucky," Lily continued. "She gets to go visit her every year."

While your father and I had our very own piece of England right here.

"That's cool," I said.

"Yeah. Are we going to Florida this year?"

I started to say "yes" when Richard answered for me. "We don't know yet."

Carli chimed in, dismayed. "I thought Mumma said—"

"Your mother and I still need to discuss it."

This was news to me; the last time I'd asked him about it, he said he was looking into airfare. Lily wiped her mouth with a napkin and let out a satisfyingly loud burp. Her father glared at her. She shrugged and grinned. *"Excuse* me. I'm gonna go get ready. Can I have a ride to Julia's? And can we go to Universal this time?"

I left it to Richard to respond. He remained silent.

"Dad?"

"I said your mother and I still need to discuss it. Get your stuff and I'll take you to Julia's." There was an edge to his tone. Lily got the hint, gave me a *what-is-HIS-problem?* look and headed upstairs with Carli at her heels.

Richard folded up the pizza box to take it into the garage. "Tell Lily I'll be out in the car."

"Okay." I busied myself with crunching up the paper cups and throwing them away, feeling apprehension take root and begin to grow. Last Saturday night had been rocky, to say the least, and this one wasn't looking like smooth sailing, either.

I picked up my phone and texted Lily her father's message. She thundered down the stairs moments later, blowing me a kiss on her way out the door. After Richard returned, I decided, I'd ask him if we could discuss the threesome. It had become the elephant—or the Eleanor—in the room syndrome. We would start there.

The telephone rang as I was loading the dishwasher. I went to the machine to check the caller ID. Kevin Curtis. The name was vaguely familiar, but I couldn't place it.

"Hello?"

"Hello...is this Christine?" A woman's voice.

"Yes."

"Hi, Christine, it's Gail Curtis...my husband works at the agency with Richard."

"Oh...yes, hi." Now I remembered.

"I'm calling because..." Her voice trailed off.

"Hello?"

"I'm here...sorry. It's just that it's hard to say this."

The blood began pounding in my ears. My voice hardened. "What is it?"

"Well, I found some...pictures. On my husband's computer, when I went to use it, and he told me about them."

"What pictures?" I was in the horrific place of needing to know this very second what she was talking about, and never wanting to hear what she was going to say.

"Pictures of you with a...blonde woman. You were blindfolded, so I wasn't sure you knew you were being photographed."

I sank to the floor. My voice faded to a whisper. "No. No, I didn't know."

Her voice was very gentle. "I'm so sorry to tell you this, Christine. I was very upset with Kevin for having the pictures. He said Richard had emailed them to him. I just wanted you to be aware of it."

"Thank you," I said. "For telling me."

"Of course. If it makes you feel any better, I made Kevin delete the photos."

"Thank you," I repeated. I hung up the phone. *He had taken pictures.*

The pizza I had eaten wanted out and was insisting on the uphill route. Richard would be home soon; Julia lived only about ten minutes away. Had others seen the photos? Richard had several good friends at the office. They'd go golfing, fishing, drinking together...what if they were all in on this? This insane, never-should-have-happened, incredibly private event! And there were pictures of me doing it!

I gagged on these thoughts until I could keep them in no longer. I ran to the bathroom and vomited, just as I heard the doorknob turn.

Winston, our yellow Lab who had been snoring on the family room rug, lurched to his feet and stretched. Nothing was different about this night for him; his dad was home, and it was his duty to greet him.

I stood trembling in the kitchen as my husband closed the door behind him. Winston trotted over and pushed his nose against Richard's hands to be petted. Richard unzipped his jacket and slipped off his shoes, not wanting to dirty the house. He looked exactly the same, and I marveled at this, given what I had just learned.

"I got you some Funny Bones," he said, putting the package on the counter.

I stared at those snack cakes, and there were two things running through my mind. #1, *he took pictures of me naked and shared them,* and #2, *I will never be able to eat Funny Bones again, and goddammit to hell, because I used to really like those!*

Richard looked at me expectantly, like why aren't you saying thank you?

"I don't want any goddamned Funny Bones," I hissed. "We need to talk."

He appeared startled, then quickly regained his composure. "Yes. I agree."

Winston barked, sitting at the pantry door. We had pretty much ruined him as a puppy by giving him a cookie whenever he came in from outside. He had changed the rules over the years to include any human who came in meant he deserved a cookie, or anytime he sat at the pantry door meant he deserved a cookie. Pretty much anytime he wanted, he got a cookie.

Winston snapped up his treat, wagging his tail at me appreciatively. He had drooled on the floor, and I stepped around it as I entered the family room. Richard followed. We both sat down.

"Carli upstairs?"

"Yes," I said, and with that realization came another one: I was not going to be able to scream at him like I wanted to. I could not keep it in any longer. I was seething with rage, burning with humiliation, glorious in my pain. "I want to know why the fuck you would take pictures of last weekend and email them to your friends."

His face was expressionless. I had to give him credit for that one. He hesitated before speaking. "I don't know what you're talking about."

"Save it, Richard! Gail Curtis called me. She saw the pictures on Kevin's computer. Saw *me,* naked, in the fucking threesome! What the *fuck* were you thinking?" I leaned closer so that we were only inches apart. Punching distance. Eye-gouging

27

distance.

His calm demeanor infuriated me. "I don't know, I guess it was a turn-on. I wanted to show the guys at work, because we'd been talking about it. It didn't mean anything."

I was incredulous. It meant *everything!*

"*Why?*" I scream-whispered. Spit flew from my mouth and onto his cheek. "How *could* you do that to me—humiliate me like that?"

"I'm sorry. Really, I am. You know what assholes men can be—they wanted proof. Listen, I wanted to talk to you tonight, too. I haven't been completely honest with you."

There was *more?*

"This whole thing, it's a symptom of a bigger problem. I'm not happy, Christine. And just so you know...it wouldn't have mattered if you *had* been into the threesome. It was unfair of me to ask you, because at this point, it doesn't even matter."

"What do you mean, 'at this point?'" I said, awestruck. Fear had overtaken fury for the moment.

His voice was gentle, like Gail's had been on the phone. "I've gotten to the point where I can't do this any more, Chris. I've been going through the motions for a long time now. I just haven't been able to tell you."

Until now.

"Like I said, there's a bigger issue here. My wanting to do the threesome was like trying to put a bandaid on a melanoma."

I gripped the couch cushion. I had to ask. "Are you sleeping with Eleanor?"

He shook his head. "No. And it isn't so much about wanting someone else as it is not wanting *this.*"

Was that supposed to make me feel better?

"We could have gone to counseling," I whispered.

He smiled ruefully. "I know. But my heart wouldn't have been in it."

*What you really mean is, your heart wouldn't have been into **me**.* The son-of-a-bitch didn't even want to give us a chance.

Winston barked at the pantry door again. I was struck by how everyday events such as this would still occur, no matter what. The dog would get cookies, the refrigerator would keep things cold, I would go on breathing.

"I'm sorry. I can't do this anymore."

I had used those exact words last Saturday night.

"I think it's best that I stay at a hotel tonight. I'll be back in the morning before Carli wakes up, and we can talk to the kids. All right?"

"Get out," I said hoarsely. "You want out, so just get the fuck out." And then the weight of this was upon me, like how I'd always imagined the bad-news phone call from a doctor would feel: *you have a massive tumor, it has spread, and it is inoperable.* The blackness which began in my heart seeped out, spilling into the very core of me—incurable, and hopeless.

CHAPTER FOUR: Man(ick)

The tears started in the car, on the way to see Hank on Sunday afternoon. He had been my friend since high school, a comedian who worked as a pathologist to pay his bills. Because of his medical background, Hank had the dubious honor of being my go-to guy whenever I'd scare the crap out of myself with some awful disease, especially under times of duress. I did not envy him for the near future. Looking at him—his bulky frame, closely-cropped hair and square, masculine jaw, you'd think *hetero,* but when he opened his mouth, you discovered he was as gay as the day was long. Given his rugged appearance and teddy bear personality infused with razor-sharp wit, Hank had impressive fan clubs in both sexes. If you were a gay man, you wanted to be his lover. If you were a woman or straight man, you wanted to be his friend (and secretly, his lover). Plus, he gave the best hugs—which I really, really needed right now.

Richard and I had told the kids in the morning, once Lily returned from her sleepover. We had a family meeting in the family room to discuss the dissolution of our family. We did not mention the D-word and instead used the term "separation," although it was clear my husband had made his decision. The girls had stared first at me, then at their father, stunned, Carli looking as though it might be some big joke we were playing *(no, kids, we really aren't going to split up! Just kidding!).* It soon became clear we were telling the truth. Lily's mouth tightened into a thin line. Carli drew her legs into classic yoga/meditative position *(oh, to be flexible again!)*, her eyes wide and bewildered. I noted the unblemished, creamy-softness of her face and cursed all the zits yet to come. I ached to touch her cheek, but if I did so, I would crumble. I had to stay intact, solid—mind over matter, mother over marriage.

Richard hugged first Lily, then Carli. "I love you both," he said. "And I will always be your dad. We will get through this." He said this calmly, with the look of a man at peace with himself.

Lily mumbled she was going to take a shower and headed for the stairs. Carli sat quietly, contemplating her father's words, then asked if we could have pancakes for breakfast and were there chocolate chips to put in them. I said yes to both questions, and ran in the bathroom to throw up.

Now I was pulling into Hank's driveway, blubbering like a woman whose marriage was over. He answered the door before I could knock, pulled me inside, and wrapped me in his arms. I inhaled the scent of his Gio and sighed. I loved how he wore that cologne, even on a Sunday.

"I won't ask how you are, pumpkin, because I already know."

"Thanks," I sniffed, my voice muffled against his shirt. "Is James here?"

"Went to visit his 'rents for the day. So I'm alllll yourrsss. Be gentle with me."

I followed him into his Mexican-style kitchen. It was splashed with vivid reds, brilliant oranges and warm yellows, with ceramic suns, crescent moons, and colorfully-patterned lizards adorning the walls. And it was immaculate, as usual. There wasn't any room inside me to hate him for his housekeeping and decorating capabilities, so I tucked that away to save for later.

We sat down at his high-top table. Hank took the roll of paper towels off the holder and handed it to me. "All out of Kleenex, sorry. Can I get you a glass of wine?"

Wine. *That night.* "No, thanks. If I start, I'm afraid I won't be able to stop."

"Understood. Water, then." He took out a bottle from the refrigerator and handed it to me, smirking behind his geek-but-chic Ray-Bans. "So...will you be leaving your teaching job for a porn star career?"

He had just added a whole other layer of stress. I slapped his arm, horrified. "Jesus Christ, that is soo not funny. If those pictures ever got out..."

"Did Richard take care of that, at least?"

"He said he'd emailed the photos to two people at work, and made them promise not to forward them to anyone else. And I made him tell them I found out, and to delete the pictures immediately. Supposedly, one of his friends already trashed them. I have to hope that's the end of it."

"Well, hopefully you don't have anything to worry about, then. Just try to put it in the past."

"Believe me, I do not want any reminders of that night. I feel so fucking *humiliated* to have been exposed like that! I just keep going over and over it in my head."

"It's a good thing you're not obsessive," he teased. "And it's too bad you weren't able to at least enjoy the experience." Hank's face took on a thoughtful expression. "You know, I was in a threesome once."

"Seriously? When?"

"Back in college, with my roommate and his

32

girlfriend. Of course, I have since become infinitely wiser, and would now have the good sense to make it an all-male team. No vaginas allowed. But a good Manwich...mm mmm *mmm!*" He winked at me. "Now back to you. Has Richard moved out?"

"He took some clothes and said he'd get the rest of his stuff in the next few days." The malignancy within me began its slow, cold spread. "This is so surreal, Hank! I don't even know what to feel. I hate him, but I still love him, and I hate myself for that. I could never trust him again after what he did, but there's a part of me that wants him to come home."

"I understand. I'm sorry, chicky. It sucks. How did the kiddos take the news?"

"It's hard to tell. Better than I thought, probably because half their friends' parents are divorced. But it's all so new...it'll take time for them to get used to this."

"And for you, too, my dearest."

I ripped off a half sheet of paper towel and blew my nose. "Richard, however, is already used to it. The asshole was so goddamned *calm* telling them. As if he was perfectly fine with it!"

"Because he is."

"It just flowed right out of him, like he'd *planned* this whole talk."

"Because he had."

Hank was beginning to seriously piss me off, mainly because I knew he was speaking the truth. "And did I tell you about the Funny Bones?"

He clasped his hands dramatically. "Ooooh, bones! Now we're getting somewhere!"

"The SNACK cakes. He bought me some last night, even though he was planning to tell me he wanted a divorce."

He raised an eyebrow and pursed his lips. "The creamy center didn't make it any better? Funny, it always does for me."

I burst into giggles while Hank watched, bemused. I did not think I would be able to stop laughing, until I thought of how odd it was. A tiny ache took root in my chest and began to spread and grow. Suddenly, I was bawling. Hank's face shifted into mildly concerned. *Inappropriate display of emotions.* Schizophrenia. That was what he must be thinking. And I was paranoid that he was thinking this: another symptom. My God.

"Christine," he soothed. "You are all right."

I took a few deep breaths. I was not convinced. Maybe it was manic-depressive disorder. Or an old-fashioned nervous breakdown. I ripped off another piece of paper towel.

"You're all raw on the inside. This is very understandable."

I blew my nose. I always hated doing that in front of someone, even Hank; I wanted to have a mirror handy to see if I had any BIVs (Boogers In View). "How did this happen? He wasn't like this when I married him. He used to be more caring, and sensitive. But now, he seems cold. And he's made everything all about him."

"I would say little Richard had larval tendencies."

Larval tendencies? What was he, a caterpillar? A worm—now, *that* I could understand. But a caterpillar...those black and rust-colored fuzzy ones were cute and harmless. Definitely not Richard.

"What I am saying," Hank said, a slow, sad smile crossing his face, "is that your husband did not turn out to be what you thought or hoped he would be. Instead of a Monarch, you got a moth."

"Correction," I said with a laugh, "I got the moth's asshole." I paused. "Do they even have assholes?"

"I don't know," Hank answered quietly. He studied me, and his face was so kind and familiar that I began to cry again.

"I didn't want a moth's asshole," I whispered.

"I know, honey." He reached out and patted my hand. "No one does."

"So what do I *do?*"

"You go on. You do it for those precious girls, and for you. Lean on your family and your big gay friend until you're stronger. Get counseling if you need it. Be Christine the mom for now...Christine the woman can rest up for a while. She'll be waiting when you're ready to get out there again. You are a sexy, beautiful woman, and you're stronger than you think."

I stood up to hug and thank him. What I wanted to add was, *thank you for being my friend. Thank you for opening the door so quickly today, and thank you for letting me use your paper towels. Thank you most of all for telling me I am sexy and beautiful.*

We chatted for a little while longer before I walked to his foyer. I opened the door to the outside, and stepped into my new life.

CHAPTER FIVE: *Metastasis*

The malignancy spread as the telling began. My parents lived three hours away, but being retired (Mom as manager of a fabric store, and Dad from a car dealership), they drove up the day after I called. I thought it best that my parents didn't know their little girl was photographed naked making out with a woman, so I just told them (truthfully) that Richard had decided he didn't want to be married to me anymore, and left. My father, who never swore and rarely hugged, said, "That bastard!" and held me tight. My mother clutched the cross hanging around her neck as she cried, saying Richard was being selfish and cruel, and how could he leave such a nice family. I don't know, I said. But I think it's a mid-life crisis.

Mom put her hands on my shoulders and looked me square in the eye. Then she pulled me close so that my face was squashed up against her ample bosom. She spoke into my hair, loudly so I would be sure to hear what she was saying. "HE...DOESN'T...LOVE YOU. HE... DOESN'T... CARE." I liked my take on it better.

It may have been foolish, but I believed that if anyone could have prevented Richard from hurting me, it would have been my mother. She was formidable, a towering, glowering amalgam of loud and proud, close-cropped gray hair sprayed into submission, silver bangle bracelets and heavy jangly earrings in a state of perpetual tremble. She wore just enough Estee Lauder White Linen to be disarming, but beneath that lush fragrant scent was a steamroller in heels.

My mother had always thrived on bolstering the misfortunate, on championing the downtrodden. When it came to her only child who had been stomped on, her giddiness was almost palpable. She brought a tote bag full of self-help books on divorce, grief, nutrition, single parenthood, raising teenage daughters, and perimenopause. The books were already highlighted and studded with post-it notes. The only ones that seemed to be missing were on topics that intrigued me the most: breast augmentation for the over-40 crowd, and new trends in masturbation.

She also brought me a desktop calendar. It was not blank. Mondays, Wednesdays and Fridays were to be my exercise days, as indicated by the bold black **WORK OUT!** at the top of the squares. At first, I thought the type of exercise was up to me, until I noticed the small asterisk and looked at the bottom of the calendar for the key. Mondays were treadmill days, Wednesdays were for weightlifting and walk the dog (the "W's" were highlighted for easy memory recall), and Fridays were reserved for yoga or Pilates. Saturdays were marked *major housecleaning* and Sundays were *laundry catch*-up days. On Thursdays, I was supposed to get together with a friend for dessert. *Every other weekend was marked Mom and Dad here!* The exclamation point did not go unnoticed.

I continued telling people. I'd always begin the conversation the same way: *I have some bad news that's probably going to shock you.* And then I would inevitably start crying, and the listening party would say something like, "Christine, what is it?" in this very frightened voice. That would be the point where I'd feel like this was all a bad dream, and it was so very strange to be telling people something this awful about my life. I had always been envied: married to my college sweetheart, two beautiful girls, a nice home...we could have replaced one of those families on advertisements for photo Christmas cards. The people in those ads didn't even know each other; they got paid to pose and look like the picture-perfect family. The woman was undoubtedly a bitch because she couldn't eat anything fattening, the guy was surely an arrogant asshole, and the kids' real parents were probably stage parents who pushed them too much. My Christmas card picture, however, had featured the real thing. At least, I'd thought it did.

Stella, my former soccer teammate from high school, had been through her own divorce. She had since remarried and moved south to Brattleboro. "It gets easier," she told me on the phone, from 145 miles away. "Just wait and see. You'll get used to it."

"But how do you get used to sleeping alone, and waking up alone?" That was the worst. I had loved sleeping with a man. It felt was so warm and safe. We always slept the same way: both of us on our right sides in spoon position, me behind him with my left leg wedged between his legs, my left arm draped over his waist. I would press my nose into his neck, inhaling the comforting husbandy scent of him. And we would sleep.

Stella paused for a few seconds before speaking. "You don't get used to it," she said. "That's the hardest thing."

When my mother heard I was having trouble sleeping, she promptly went out and bought me a body pillow. It was blue and gold with suns, moons and stars, very celestial. I laid it on Richard's side of the bed with one end on his pillow, and snuggled up next to it. I draped my leg over it, pressed my nose against it. It smelled like polyester, not husband. A body pillow did not have a heartbeat I could feel. It didn't snore softly. And it didn't have a penis.

I hadn't known I would miss a penis this much. I found myself stopping by on a regular basis to visit Hank, especially when James wasn't around—for Hank's friendship, of course, but also for his penis. I'd hug him tightly, sometimes pressing my lower half against his at just the right angle, and hoped he didn't notice. But his brain, his knowledge, was what I continued to need most. During one phone conversation, I voiced to him my newfound concern that my fear of death might actually cause it. What if there was a tumor hidden somewhere inside me, which I created just by thinking about it?

"If that were true, you would've been dead a long time ago," he replied. I could hear the smile in his voice. "Listen, sweetheart, I'd love to talk more about your impending death, but I have some people I have to diagnose with cancer. I'll call you later?"

"Okay!" I said. I hung up the phone and cried fresh tears for all the people who were just living their lives, and wham, out of the blue, the bad news. And I was one of those people.

I told our dental hygienist at my next cleaning appointment that my husband had walked out on me. It was challenging speaking with someone's fingers poking in and out of your mouth, but I persevered. Her eyes widened above her purple mask. "That *asshole!*" she murmured, and then looked around to make sure no one had heard. "The next time he comes in, I'll make sure to jab him. By accident, of course." I smiled. She was so nice.

I made sure I told my closest colleagues at

school before the students arrived so I could go in the bathroom to splash cold water on my face and reapply makeup. Since we were very close, I shared with them the intimate details. They were stunned. Fitzy, the history teacher, stared down at the conference table, his face frozen with not knowing what to say. I felt a bit sorry for him; he was male and therefore also suspect. Jess, who taught math, was my closest friend at work. She was usually very good at giving advice, but this was out of her realm of solving for x (or in this case, *ex*). She looked past me into the hallway as she gathered her long auburn hair into a ponytail and gave the elastic a vicious twist, her eyes brimming.

"So what're you gonna *do*?" Fitzy said, finally.

Jess snorted. "You mean after she kills him?"

"I'm going to call an attorney," I said. "He's filing for divorce." That D-word. I shuddered. "Can we talk about something else?"

Jess squeezed my shoulder and changed the subject to next week's Parent Night. "Are you going to beg for things you need for the classroom?"

I nodded; I did that every year.

"I think I'm going to ask for tampons," Jess mused.

We looked at her.

"They're *expensive!*" she said.

"How about Pamprin?" Fitzy offered.

"Yes," Jess said. "I could phrase it like, anything *you think I could use for my period.* Because that could include chocolate."

"Maybe you could tell them to keep track of your menstrual cycle on their calendars at home," I suggested. "You're usually pretty regular. And it would benefit their children."

Fitzy leaned forward, his blue eyes

narrowing. "Does this mean I can ask for condoms?"

At this reference, my schizophrenia kicked in and I burst into tears. Fitzy looked bewildered. "I can't have sex anymore," I sobbed. "And I miss it."

"Of course you'll have sex again," soothed Jess. "You'll have sex again, and it will be better than before. Just think of how exciting it will be to get to know someone physically. After all those years with the same person...you get to try out a new penis! It'll be like getting a new car."

I contemplated this. In my mind's eye, I could see my Caravan driving away: the bulky Loser Cruiser pockmarked with dents and riddled with rust. Visions of Mercedes and Porsches danced in my head. Sleek models with lots of power. Hmmm.

"So are you gonna be okay?" Fitzy looked at me anxiously. "The kids are going to be coming soon."

"And hopefully, so is Christine," grinned Jess.

I gave a wan smile through my tears.

"Now," said Fitzy, leaning in toward me conspiratorially. "About these pictures..."

Jess looked horrified. "Oh my GOD, Fitzy."

His blue eyes widened. "Can't a guy ask a simple question?"

"Even if I had them," I said, "I would never, ever show you." He could be truly disgusting at times. But he did have a penis.

41

CHAPTER SIX: *Numb*

The freshmen always loved my class on Halloween, mainly because we didn't read or write and ate junk. I devoted the day to scary storytelling and candy corn. We'd pull the shades in the classroom and shun the ever-present fluorescent glare overhead in favor of the less-invasive, deliciously eerie glow of a handheld flashlight (candles would set off the smoke alarm). Huddled on the floor in a corner, the kids would press themselves together in "fear" (any excuse to touch each other), and we'd let the scary stories carry us to a dark and evil place, till the bell would ring and remind us we were already in one.

It was Melissa's turn to tell her scary story. She shifted a little held the flashlight under her chin, giggling nervously. I raised my eyebrow as a friendly warning to settle down. She gave an apologetic smile and began. "Well, there was this kid, and he got into this elevator, and there was this really fat woman, and she kept like STARING at him, and he got all freaked out, so he pushed the button for the THIRTEENTH floor..." (here she paused dramatically) "...and the elevator like wouldn't STOP, so he pushed the button again, and the fat woman kept looking at him, and then SHE pushed the button, and the elevator stopped between floors, and she just kept looking at him." Dramatic pause. "It was really freaky."

Silence. Rachel, a gentle soul, said generously, "Wow, that was pretty creepy."

"Who wants to go next?" I asked brightly. I

was getting scared by these stories, but for all the wrong reasons.

Real fear surfaced later that afternoon, on the way to meet with my attorney. The only thing I knew for sure was that I had to fork over three thousand for the retainer fee, and that this woman was supposed to be good. As instructed, I brought an accordion-style folder stuffed with Richard's divorce complaint, bank statements, last year's tax information and a pay stub. I couldn't fill a pocket to hold what I'd dreamed for my future: a newspaper clipping of our 50th wedding anniversary, postcards from trips taken after we'd retired, photos of shared grandchildren. This is what I wanted the judge to see. What I wanted *Richard* to see.

Anticipating the whole divorce process had put me under tremendous strain. I would try to find comfort wherever I could get it. In chocolate, of course: attacking a pint of delectably gooey Ben & Jerry's Phish Food, or pouncing on the few stale chocolate chips I'd find in the back of the cupboard. Comfort in the vibrating shower head, especially on TurboPulse. Comfort in wrapping myself in one of the kids' sleeping bags at night (I would feel *held*). And comfort in rather strange and silly things, like the fact that my attorney's last name sounded strong: *Garrison*. I had a feeling, though, there would be little comfort in this first meeting with Madeline Garrison. A sense of doom began to grow as I entered the building. This was the legal beginning of the end of my marriage.

Madeline's office was on the third floor. I walked up to the receptionist's desk, smiled bravely and gave her my name: *Christine Bacon*. It struck me that I wouldn't have that last name much longer. This was one thing I would be glad for him to take back. Trimming the fat, so to speak.

Ten minutes after I'd settled myself into one of the straight-backed chairs, I looked up to see a woman in a gray jacket and skirt. Her dark brown hair was pulled back in a large clip with pieces falling around her face, which made me feel a bit less intimidated. She was tall and leggy and reminded me of a Thoroughbred. Her glasses were small, black and rather cat's-eye, the type you never would have worn in seventh grade, but when paired with an attractive forty-ish face made a person look intellectual and sexy at the same time.

She smiled and shook my hand. Firm grip; good sign. I followed her into her office and she closed the door behind us.

"So your husband filed for divorce." A statement, not a question.

"Yes, I—he—left me." I sat down at the big oak table and began to empty the contents of my folder.

"I'm sorry." Her apology sounded a bit too automatic. She reached into her drawer for a yellow pad of paper. "Let me explain the process. There are four main issues..."

I pulled a piece of paper from my folder and began scribbling.

"...parental rights and responsibilities, spousal support, property division, and attorney fees. Since your husband filed, you may either file an answer or your own complaint. Both of you will complete a child support affidavit. In about a month, you'll have your first court appearance with the case management officer, unless we reach a temporary agreement and file a certificate-in-lieu."

These were unfamiliar terms. But this was only the start, and if I expected to get through it, I'd have to be tough. Suddenly, I became aware that my lower left leg was cramping. I shifted in my chair and uncrossed my legs.

"Before I go any further," Madeline Garrison said, "I'll need to get some information from you."

I nodded, leaning down to massage my calf.

Brushing away a stray piece of hair from her yellow pad, she wrote *Christine Bacon* in flowery cursive letters and asked me my Social Security number. I recited it, still rubbing my leg. Funny, it had never stayed in spasm for this long. Muscle cramping was a sign of something serious. The dread thickened. I racked my brain.

"Your husband's name?"

"Richard Bacon," I said, my voice cracking. My calf was feeling very tight. I stomped my foot, a little too hard. Curious, Madeline glanced up from writing. "My...my foot's asleep," I explained, adding, "I hate when that happens!" to lighten the mood.

"Do you know his social?"

Oh God. I knew what this could be. *The earliest symptoms of amyotrophic lateral sclerosis, or ALS (also known as Lou Gehrig's disease) include twitching, cramping, or muscle stiffness.* This was ALS. There could be no other explanation.

"Do you know Richard's social?" she repeated.

"Dick," I corrected. "I like to call him Dick." I stomped my foot again. Still crampy. I squeezed my calf, hard, as I told her his number in a wobbly voice.

"Are you all right?"

"Yes," I replied. *No,* I thought. *I am not all right! I have ALS! I am going to die a slow and horrible death, and I'll be aware of every painful second, because this disease leaves your intellect intact!* I had known someone in town who had died of ALS. It had been awful to see her go from being a vibrant, active woman to a shell of a person in a wheelchair, who near the end was making only guttural sounds. Her children were in their early twenties and ended up taking care of her. But my children wouldn't be old enough to take care of me. They would end up going to live with their strong and healthy father, while I laid in my own excrement, drooling on myself!

I began to cry.

"I know this is difficult for you, Christine. But you'll get through it. You're certainly not the only one this has happened to." Madeline gave me a rueful smile, reached in her drawer and set a box of Kleenex on the table.

I glanced at her left hand. A silver wedding band and an impressive pear-shaped diamond engagement ring. She was all set. Her husband would never leave her; she had brains, money, great legs and smoldering eyes. Behind those glasses was most likely a wildcat in the bedroom. She probably *initiated* threesomes. And she was an attorney, for Christ's sake. If they divorced, she could take him for all he was worth, and he knew this. He'd never leave.

I began to resent her. My calf muscles were screaming. The thought of my impending death made me cry harder. Madeline didn't seem to mind. "Take all the time you need," she soothed.

Was she going to charge me for the time I took crying? This was enough to suppress my tears. I took a deep and shaky breath. "Okay," I snuffled. "I think I'm fine now. I'm sorry for making such a fool of myself."

She waved a jeweled hand at me. "Don't

apologize. Now, to get back to the information I need. What's his line of work?"

"He's an insurance salesman."

"How long have you been married?"

"Nineteen years."

"And you said he left you."

"Yes," I said, straightening. "After he humiliated me." My ALS seemed to have subsided for the moment. Madeline looked up, mild interest on her face. And then I plunged. Lawyers knew all about confidentiality, after all. "He took some compromising pictures of me naked, without my knowledge, and emailed them to his coworkers."

Now Madeline's interest was more than mild. "That sounds like an invasion of privacy. And grounds for a lawsuit."

I hadn't considered that. My attorney was looking at me eagerly, hungrily. I could almost see the dollar signs flashing in her head. But I also realized that if I wanted to pursue this, there would be more exposure of me. The context of the photos would have to come out. The judge, the court reporter, the bailiff, the clerk—and quite possibly more people—would see the pictures. And, of course, there would be the inevitable comparison of Eleanor's melons with my raisins. It would get ugly. As much as I wanted that Dick to be held accountable for what he did, I did not want ugly.

"No...I'm not going that route," I said. "Just the divorce." Which I hadn't even wanted.

Madeline looked disappointed from behind her sexy glasses. "I'll just make a note of it," she said coolly, and scribbled on her paper. I strained to see what she had written. Probably, *who would want nude photos of Little Ms. Chestless?*

Madeline asked about the children and their

ages. I cried again when I said their names. We talked about the marital finances, if I would be able to keep the house, how much I could expect in child and spousal support. She gave me instructions on how to complete my financial statement and asked what I would prefer in terms of parental contact, warning that Richard might seek shared residence.

My heart dropped into the vicinity of my ankles. "Shared residence? You mean, he'd want the kids to live with him part of the time?"

"Yes. The week-to-week schedule is quite common."

"But I couldn't let that happen! My kids wouldn't want that."

Madeline nodded. "I understand. I just want you to be prepared."

My calf began to tighten up again. "How long does this whole process take?"

"That depends. Hopefully, you'll come to an agreement and won't need to go before a judge."

"And if we can't agree?

"Then you're looking at a court date of at least a year. At <u>least</u>. There's your motivation." She looked at her watch. "Let's discuss the matter of my retainer, and then we'll be done for today."

As I watched her close my file folder to signal the end of our appointment, I discovered the paralysis in my calf had worked its way northward, to my heart.

CHAPTER SEVEN: Loss

I began to regard the bathtub as a sanctuary. There really was nothing special about the tub; it was your standard, fiberglass, ivory-colored model with a textured floor so you wouldn't slip. Nothing glamorous, especially with the streaks of mildew on the shower curtain liner, and the clumps of hair I always had to be the one to scoop out. But once daily baths became a ritual for me, my tub had never looked better.

Lily and Carli went to dinner with Dick twice a week. While they were with him, or after they had gone to bed, I would retreat to the bathroom. I'd take the philodendrons and German ivy from the window and place them along the side of the tub: a poor woman's tropical paradise. My mother had bought me lavender-scented candles (for relaxation, because HE...DOESN'T...LOVE ME) which I would set in between the plants. I'd run the water, hot enough to make me turn pink, add the bubble bath which was sure to give me a vaginal infection, and sink into my frothy haven. In the tub, nothing could touch me—except, of course, streams of water from the strategically-placed shower massager, if I was so inclined. Behind the shower curtain, I was somehow protected—held and soothed by the warm water. It was rather like being in a womb.

On this cold November night, I was looking particularly forward to my bath. I had a mediation scheduled at the courthouse after the holidays, and the idea of having to see Dick's face in close proximity was almost more than I could bear. Since he'd moved out, I'd only seen him from a distance when he would drive in to pick up the girls. So far, I'd been able to keep him behind glass: on the other side of my window and behind his windshield. I was grateful for this, although I would have appreciated it even more if the glass on his car had been tinted. Or riddled with bullets. That also would have worked.

Lily and Carli had been gone about an hour. It was a school night, so they would be home soon, but I had enough time for a bath. I settled myself into the tub, cupping my hands underwater and pushing the bubbles back and forth in a rhythmic motion. I scooped a handful of foam and spread it across my breasts, smoothing it over my belly. My stomach seemed flatter than it had before. I leaned forward to look down at my legs. My God. Where was the fat? Everybody's legs looked a little meatier in sitting position, and I'd always had extra padding. Why had this changed?

Easy, girly! I told myself. *This isn't necessarily a bad thing. Your pants are fitting more loosely, and that's good. Your ass has never looked better.* But this kind of weight loss in such a short period of time wasn't healthy. I had noticed having to pull my belt tighter, and now my legs were thin. What if I kept losing weight? What if I couldn't stop?

Trembling, I lay back in the water. I scoured my brain for comfort. If I continued to waste away, I could always go to the hospital and be fed through a tube. This realization cheered me a bit. I had only a little while until my children returned, so I would do my best to enjoy my bath. I closed my eyes. I could picture the nurses hovering over me as I lay in the hospital bed, hooked up to an IV. The nurses would take care of me; they would not let me die. The water held me close, and I began to drowse.

"Christine? Are you up there?"

I'm almost done, I thought sleepily. *Just a few more minutes.* I struggled to open my eyes. It was almost as if I was really hearing Richard's voice. My gaze drifted from the tendrils of steam curling around the faucet to the full-length mirror across from the tub, blurred with condensation. Foggy mirror, foggy mind.

"Chris."

That voice. Richar—Dick's voice. For real.

"Chris?" A more impatient tone.

I lurched to my feet, splashing water onto the bath mat and almost falling out of the tub onto the tile. Dick was in the house.

I grabbed a towel from the shelf and wrapped it around me, shivering. My teeth were clacking together. He called my name again. I grabbed another towel, twisting it around my hair turban-style, so it covered my ears to muffle the sound of him. We emailed; we did not speak to one another. He knew this. But now, the way he said my name! Like nothing at all was wrong.

"Christine, I know you're up there." (Pause.) "I just wanted to tell you I planned to take the girls to my parents for dinner tomorrow night, since it's my father's birthday."

I did not answer. I put my hands over my ears and squeezed, hard, to block out the sound. I would not listen. I could not. After about thirty seconds, I let my arms drop to my side, my muscles aching with the effort of keeping that voice away. And then I saw the doorknob turn.

I lunged for the door, slamming it as it began to open. I twisted the lock and backed away from the door, shaking uncontrollably. It felt as though my bones were rattling. I would not make a sound in case my children were listening, but inside my head I was screaming. *Get out of my house, you bastard!*

I did not move. I waited. Tremors racked my body. Then, very faintly, I heard Dick's voice again, inches from the door. *"Bitch,"* he said softly. And then I heard him walk down the stairs.

I stood, frozen, until I heard him say goodbye to Lily and Carli. A moment later, Carli was outside the bathroom door. "Mumma? Are you coming out?"

No, I am not, my darling. I am going to stay in the tub until the water shrivels me up and carries me away down the drain. I don't want to do this anymore.

"Yes, in a minute."

She hesitated. "Wasn't it weird that Daddy came upstairs? I don't know why he did that."

"Me either," I said. "I'll be right out, sweet pea. Start getting ready for bed."

"Okay," she answered. There was relief in her voice. This she could do; this felt normal.

I dried off and draped my towel on the rack. He had called me a bitch. I wasn't the only one who saw my spouse differently. Somehow, I was not the same to him, either.

In the tub, the remaining water gurgled its death knell and was silent. I left the bathroom, completely drained.

CHAPTER EIGHT: *Rabid*

December 25th was two weeks away, and that meant a scramble to grade papers so there would be no red pens staining my vacation. It meant lugging boxes of decorations from the basement and cramming every inch of available space in my kitchen with craft fair snowmen I'd paid too much for. It meant playing Christmas music during lunch at school until Fitzy complained he felt like he was going to shit tinsel. And it meant a visit to the local tree farm, crowding into the little cabin with the other (intact) families to listen to tinny holiday music and drink cups of watery hot chocolate before shelling out $45 for a sap-leaking, back-breaking, needle-shedding symbol of holiday joy. My mother had decided I should get the tree as the sole adult so I could feel a sense of independence, and then my father, acting as understudy, would play the role of spouse and help me set it up.

This year would be Dick's and my first Christmas as separated husband and wife. Did Hallmark make a tree ornament for that? I could think of a few designs. Maybe a naked bride, and a groom holding a camera phone. There could be a big bruise under the groom's eye from where the wife slugged him. Or, a wedding ring split in two with a busty British massage therapist holding the pieces. There could be a big bruise under the massage therapist's eye from where the wife slugged her. The word *separated* always conjured up the image of a dismembered torso, with limbs scattered nearby. It felt pretty much like that.

But separated or not, Christmas was coming, and I was determined to make it a good one for the kids. My mother had stressed the importance of keeping traditions alive to attain some level of normalcy. I was proud of myself for taking the girls to see *The Nutcracker* as we'd always done as a family, and even prouder that I did not allow my gaze to linger too long on the well-endowed crotches of the male dancers. In addition to *The Nutcracker*, one of the most important traditions was the trip to the tree farm. This was what I kept in mind as the girls and I tromped through mucky brown fields to find a tannenbaum worth fighting over.

"Where's all the snow?" Carli wanted to know. "Christmas is supposed to be white."

Christmas is supposed to be a lot of things. "We still have two weeks. I'm sure we'll get some," I said, lacing my voice with optimism.

"We might not, though," Lily responded. I threw her a *don't start* look, but her head was turned toward a family cutting down a tree. A father, mother, son and daughter. The father was tall and handsome and smiled a lot. He'd probably gotten laid last night. The mother was petite and adorable in her fuzzy red hat and matching mittens. Even the tree was perfect: gargantuan, majestic. They undoubtedly had cathedral ceilings and a huge window in which to display the tree. They'd load the tree with expensive ornaments and drape it with hundreds of tiny white lights—they wouldn't use colored ones. But they would proudly display the popsicle-stick-and-glitter stars the kids made in preschool. You could just tell.

Carli ran ahead to a tall evergreen. She undoubtedly had tree envy after seeing that family's selection. "How about this one, Mumma?"

I shook my head. "Too big." I glanced over at Lily, who was standing with her hands jammed in her pockets. "Come on, Lil...help us find one."

She dipped her chin into the collar of her coat. "I'm cold."

"Well, then, let's find a tree and we can go."

"Why didn't we just get a fake tree?"

I could feel my jaw begin to tighten. Why was she making this so difficult? We'd never gotten an artificial tree. We always came to this tree farm. Couldn't she understand I was just trying to keep things the same? I forced myself to use my best I'd-throttle-you-if-I-could-but-I'm-your-teacher voice. "Because live ones are better."

"But once you cut them down, they aren't alive anymore. They're *dead*. So we're really bringing home something we killed." She looked immensely pleased with herself.

I stared at her. I could hear the son of the Perfect Family asking politely if they could go get some hot chocolate. "Of course!" his perfect mother replied. "That's the best part!"

"Come on, Carli," I said. "I feel like killing something."

I trudged to the next row of trees. "Do you girls see anything you like?"

Lily rolled her eyes and shrugged. Carli ran to a rather sparse-looking tree. "How about this one?"

"That one's not full enough, honey." I turned to see a couple in the next row standing by their selection. They looked like newlyweds. The wife stood back as her husband cut into the tree with the bow saw. Her eyes were glowing. There was something sexy about a man cutting down a tree: even a stocky guy with glasses like this one. He was probably going to get laid tonight. We stood watching him work the bow saw with quick, even strokes. The tree began to tip.

"Timberrrr..." I called. Lily and Carli looked at me like I had three heads. "That's what they say," I explained, "when they've cut down a tree and it's falling and they want to warn people."

Carli was puzzled. "Why don't they just say, 'look out, there's a tree falling?'"

I gritted my teeth. "Because that would take longer to say. They want people to get out of the way quickly."

Carli was undaunted. "You could say it fast. Like 'lookoutthere'satreefalling.' Kids might not know what 'timber' means."

"WhatEVER!" Lily exploded. "Just shut up!"

"LOOK," I hissed. "We are getting a goddamned Christmas tree."

The girls gaped at me.

"We're getting <u>this</u> one." I pointed to the tree closest to me.

"But some of the needles are orange," Carli said hesitantly. "And it's not very big."

"It's perfect," I snapped.

Within minutes I was sawing away at the trunk with vicious cuts. *Goddamned--sonofa--BITCH!* The tree was mine. It began to lean. Breathing hard, I gave it a shove, looked at Carli and yelled, "Look out, there's a tree falling!" Lily rolled her eyes. Carli stared at me, unblinking.

We headed back for the cabin with the murdered tree, me in front holding the trunk, Carli at the other end, and Lily in between. We did not speak. Suddenly, a black and white cat darted in front of us. Carli twisted around to look and dropped her end of the tree. "Mumma, look! He's so cute!"

We put down the tree and I walked to the next row where the cat had disappeared. "Kitty-kitty-kitty!" What was he doing on a tree farm? The owners leased the property but didn't live there, and the closest neighborhood was some distance away. It must have been a stray. I continued searching.

"MOM!" Lily called. "Can we go?"

"In a minute," I yelled back. "I'm trying to find him. He shouldn't be out here."

I moved between the trees, taking slow, careful steps. Black tail with a white tip, snaking back and forth. He was huddled under a tree. I crouched down, hoping no one would come down this row and scare him off. I reached for him very carefully. Lily yelled my name again just as my hand came in contact with the stray. He whipped around to face me...*shit!* I felt his needle-sharp claws sink into my wrist, in the space between my glove and coat. He bounded away through the brittle yellow grass.

I met up with the girls near the cabin. "Where's the cat?" asked Carli.

"He took off." Gingerly, I pulled back the edge of my coat sleeve to reveal the scratch. There were two half-inch gouges, deeper than I'd thought, and very red.

"Did he bite you, Mumma?" Carli leaned forward to peer at my wrist. "It looks like teeth marks."

Now I was unsure. What if he *had* bitten me? If he was a stray, there was no telling what diseases he could be carrying. Toxoplasmosis, or cat scratch fever, or...*rabies*. Jesus, Mary, Joseph and the Wise Men, he could have rabies!

I gave Lily a little push in the direction of our car. "I need to pay for the tree. Take your sister to the car and I'll be right out."

"But can't we have some hot chocolate?" Carli asked.

"No."

"But that's the best part!"

We are not the Perfect Family! "No," I repeated, "we don't have time. I have to get home and put something on my wrist." I would wash the wound with antibacterial soap and hot water, and use hydrogen peroxide. Then I'd put some of that bacitracin ointment on it. I could call my doctor (or even the vet) and get some more advice. I would be fine.

Upon arriving home, I tugged at the ropes holding the tree on top of the van and wrestled the conifer to the ground. After I'd plunked it in a pail of water and leaned it against our garage wall, I raced to the bathroom to tend to my wound.

"Mom," Lily called from downstairs. "Dad's here."

I opened the medicine cabinet and scanned the shelves for the peroxide bottle. What if we'd run out? Ah, there it was. I pressed it to my chest. *Thank you, thank you, my brown disinfectant friend!*

"Mom." Lily's voice sounded sharp. "Do we have to go with him?"

I turned the hot water on and squirted some soap on my wrist, working it into a lather. "Isn't he taking you shopping?"

"I don't want to go."

Carli piped in. "Me neither. I'm tired."

"Well, go tell him."

"We already did. He says we have to. Will you go talk to him?"

I hesitated. Was I ready for this? Maybe it would be a good thing to force myself to see him, before the mediation. Perhaps I could spread some holiday cheer, wish him a Merry fucking Christmas.

"Yes," I called back. I could do this. I shook the water from my wrist and patted it dry with a washcloth. I'd have to continue my disinfecting regimen after I'd spoken with Dick.

Approaching his car, I steeled myself. He rolled down his window, his cheek muscle twitching.

"They don't want to go with you today," I said. "They're tired. We just came back from getting a tree."

He stared at me. "They can rest at my apartment."

The sound of his voice made me want to leap out of my skin. It scraped my ears like the tines of two forks colliding. The wind lifted my hair and I jabbed it behind my ear. I took a deep breath. The sleeping tigress in me, wanting to protect her young, growled. "They'd rather rest here," I said. "In their own house."

The muscle in his cheek twitched again. "The girls have two houses now."

"But this is their *home,*" I said. "There's a big difference. You're living in a two-bedroom apartment. It's not the same. *You're* not the same," I added, folding my arms across my chest. The December air was biting, but I was determined not to let him see me shiver.

His lips drew into a thin line. Like a worm. "People change, Chris. You should give it a try. Just remember that the 'poor Mommy' role isn't very becoming."

I struggled to call forth the image of Hank, who would be flashing me a *keep your cool, pumpkin* look right about now. "It's no secret I've been in pain, Richard."

Dick leaned forward. I could smell coffee on his breath. "Well," he said softly, nastily, "a good mother would be stronger."

No one was going to criticize my motherhood. I was the only one who could do that. The tigress attacked. I slammed my hand against the side of his car, hard. "You and your goddamned angry face!" I spat out the words. "You look like shit."

"Have *you* checked a mirror lately?" His eyes were blazing.

"I just got a CHRISTMAS TREE," I screeched. "It was muddy!"

I looked over at the house. Lily and Carli were standing in the window. I wondered how much they had seen, or heard. I took a step closer to his car and arranged my thumb and forefinger in the most offensive hand gesture known to a man: the demonstration of length. "You are THIS BIG," I said, and walked away. Merry fucking Christmas.

"Are we going with him?" asked Carli, when I came inside.

I shrugged, unzipping my coat. My hands were shaking. I could feel Lily's eyes on me. "I don't know. I guess I'll leave that up to you."

"Come on, Carli," said Lily. "He'll be pissed off if we don't. We can come back after dinner." She grabbed their down vests from the mudroom closet and handed one to her sister. I opened my mouth. I knew I should say something, like, *don't use the word 'pissed' around your sister. Or, thank you for making things easier by going. Or, if you're really tired, stay home!* Before I could choose, they were both out the door. Carli turned around to blow me a kiss.

I could not bear to watch them leave, so I decided I would go upstairs to continue the disinfecting process. I couldn't risk infection.

The doorbell rang. Most likely one of the kids—maybe one of them had forgotten something, or Carli wanted an extra hug. I waited at the bottom of the stairs. No one came in. I went to the door.

It was Dick. What the hell could he want? I opened the door, arranging my face to look disinterested.

He would not look me in the eye. "Do you have your insurance card?"

What was he talking about?

"I backed into your car when I was turning around in the driveway. I'll call my insurance company in the morning and make arrangements to have it repaired." His face was stony, unflinching.

He had hit my car. I had the sudden urge to slap a blood pressure cuff on him for fun, just to get a reading. Instead, I went to retrieve the card from the purse and handed it to him silently. His mouth twisted when he said "thank you." It looked like it almost killed him. Had we not hated each other so much at that moment, we could have laughed. Hard.

But of course there would be no shared humor. No making love under the Christmas tree, no waking up extra early on Christmas morning to make the kids pancakes with red and green M & M's. There was now only separation—between Richard and me, our girls and their parents, dreams and reality. I highly doubted Hallmark could capture that in an ornament.

CHAPTER NINE: Blurred vision

He opens the bedroom door, and I roll onto my back at the sound. I am wondering why he's coming to bed so late. What has he been doing? Watching the History Channel, probably. No matter, he's here now, and I have been waiting for him. He moves silently toward me, and I reach out my arms. He lays on top of me, comfortably weighty. I bury my nose in his neck: Old Spice aftershave and a hint of Dove soap. He puts his mouth on mine. His kiss is hard and insistent. I know he will not want eye contact, but I try anyway, pulling back to stare at him. His eyes are cold amber. They briefly meet my gaze and then close. Something moves beside me. It is a little girl, and she is saying she's had a bad dream. "Go tell your mother," I mutter. "Can't you see I'm in the middle of something here?"

And then he leaps onto the floor. Triumphant, he points at me. "YOU are an unfit mother," he says. I scrunch up my face at him. I beg your pardon! Weren't we just about to make love? And what's this about unfit?

"I am not unfit. I've dropped two pants sizes," I answer. "And I've been toning up."

He shakes his head, disgusted. "You are unfit to be a mother. She's going to live with me."

No!! I lie there, frozen. The little girl whom I now recognize as Carli reaches out and brushes her fingertips against my cheek. "Goodbye," she says softly.

I reach for her hand, which for some reason

became my cat's tail.

No longer sleeping, I breathed hard, pulse thudding. Mr. Bean, my orange tiger, looked at me with startled green eyes. I must have grabbed him in my dream. I gave him an apologetic chin rub and he laid back down on the bed, purring in forgiveness. Beanie was the only one in the family who probably didn't miss Dick one bit, having taken up residence on his pillow.

And speaking of cats, the rabies scare had passed. After posting flyers in the neighborhood near the tree farm, I received a phone call that the stray cat was actually a pet who was up to date on vaccinations. I could be sure of this since I had obtained permission to contact the veterinarian for confirmation. Crisis averted.

I craned my neck to see the clock. 5:32, about a half hour before I usually got up. Back in my old life, if Richard and I were awake a little bit early, he'd insist on a quickie before we both left for work. *Let's get the day off right,* he'd say. And I'd joke, *what you really mean is, let's get YOU off right.* He'd roll me onto my side, thrust about ten times, and climax. It always amazed me he wanted to get there so quickly. I always considered my orgasms to be the fudge center of a very gooey and delicious chocolate cake: a sweet and satisfying end to a delectable experience. But Dick had liked shoving his fork straight to the center.

Lying here alone (except for Mr. Bean), I was painfully aware it would be a while—perhaps a *long* while—until I shared my bed with someone else again. It was almost incomprehensible that I would have to get to know another man in that way. And Dick would be sharing his body with someone else, too, if he hadn't already done so, revealing his body secrets: the thin white scar on his chin from when his older sister hit him with a tennis racket (accidentally, but I was still grateful). The tattoo of the guitar and the letters *JH* in tribute to Jimi Hendrix on his upper bicep. The skin tags in his armpits, the freckles on his penis, the coarse, curly hair covering his buttocks. We used to joke about that...I'd stroke his lower back, and my fingers would travel down to his butt, pretending to be entangled, and I'd say, "help me, I'm lost, help!" in this tiny, high-pitched voice. That would always make him laugh. I wondered if future women would ever make a comedy show about the hair on his ass. Probably not.

Later that afternoon, it was less about the hair on his ass and more about the pain in mine as I sat at the mediation beside my attorney. Dick (at least I assumed that dark shape was him; it was as though he was in my blind spot) sat across the table with his lawyer, a pudgy, 30-ish man who looked the part in his straining navy jacket and conservative blue tie. But I had a strong suspicion that after hours, he'd plunk himself in his recliner with a Michelob and a *Girls Gone Wild* DVD. Madeline introduced me to him, making sure to announce me as Christine *Kellen* Bacon. He extended his hand. So this was how it was done. We were going to act like grown-ups, be civil. I shook his hand. Sweaty, as expected. I studied him more closely. He looked familiar. He smiled at me, a little nervously, sucking noisily on his breath mint. *Altoid*, I thought. *I will call you Altoid.*

"I'm sure she'll be here any moment," Madeline reassured, referring to the mediator.

Dick and I both nodded, saying, "Okay," and cleared our throats simultaneously. I wanted to drive my foot into his crotch for him daring to be in sync with me. Couples did that.

Altoid began to chew on his Altoid and addressed Dick. "So, you ever pick up the guitar any more?"

Dick cleared his throat again. "No. Not since college."

His attorney smiled, shaking his head. "Aww, that's too bad. You were good, man. Could have had yourself a musical career."

Guitar? How would he know...and then I remembered. Altoid had gone to college with us, and for a time had played bass in Dick's band.

Something was different since the last time I'd seen Dick. My God, he was wearing hair gel. He had actually spiked his hair. It looked as though gerbils had used his head for an amusement park. I flashed back to his rock band hair, his sexiest body part. When we first started dating, my mother thought he was a bit too wild, too uncouth for me. There was absolutely no need, she said, for his hair to be that long. At my (via my mother's) urging, he trimmed it for our wedding. After he started his insurance job, it became shorter still. Conservative. Respectable. Until neither of us really remembered how it used to curl damp and thick and glorious when he'd play.

"You ever keep in touch with the other guys?" Altoid continued.

"Not really," answered Dick, shifting in his seat. " I guess we've all moved on."

"We used to pack that bar downtown...Luna's. I remember there'd be people lining up outside, waiting to get in. Really too bad you didn't stick with it."

Dick—whom I could now refer to as *Slick* due

to the gel—shrugged. "It was good while it lasted. But sometimes, you just have to move on to bigger and better things," he added, leaning back in his chair. He looked steadily at me.

Son of a bitch! I curled my toes inside my shoes and forced myself to look at Dick/Slick again. I wanted to desensitize myself to his face. I studied his long nose, the chicken pox scar on his right cheek. He had retrieved a piece of gum from his pocket, and I watched his jaw work. Razor stubble on his chin, a hint of oiliness to his forehead. I was pleased to see he looked a little older.

Altoid sucked his mint. Slick snapped his gum. They made a fine pair.

The door opened, and in blew a tall, heavyset woman with hair bleached to the color and texture of straw. She held a large, well-worn pocketbook under one arm and a dog-eared, white notepad under the other, which she promptly slapped on the table. **BACON - *Mediation*** was scrawled at the top in loopy script. "Sorry I'm late," she huffed. "Shall we get started?"

Two and a half hours later, I watched her check the box marked *Unfinished in Mediation*. We had been able to agree on only a couple issues. Visitation would remain unchanged. Slick did not want to pay spousal support, despite my attorney stating firmly *(good girl, Madeline!)* that I would not be able to afford the mortgage without it. Altoid responded by saying that Slick would let me have the house in place of any alimony, to which Madeline argued that the house wouldn't be much good if I couldn't afford to pay for it. The conversation went around and around in this type of circular fashion. Like a ring. I glanced down at my finger where my wedding ring had been. A faint white line was all that remained. Surprisingly, Slick was still wearing his. I wanted to yank it from his finger—drag it over his knobby knuckle so it gouged into his flesh—and then shove it on the tip of his threesome-seeking penis. It would have fit.

I realized everyone was standing up. I pushed back my chair and rose, rather unsteadily. A wave of nausea moved through me, and I fought against the tide. Madeline must have noticed my vulnerable state because she gave me a hard look. I stared back at her to let her know I was all right. Her face looked out of focus. I blinked, twice. She was still blurry.

What was going on with my eyesight? I blinked again.

Madeline motioned for me to follow her. I was only too glad to oblige; the room felt oppressively warm. I could feel Slick's eyes on me. I hoped he was looking at my ass.

"Give me a call next week," Madeline was saying. "We can talk about possible proposals."

"All right," I said. My voice came out in a whisper.

Madeline gave me another hard look. "Do something for yourself this weekend."

"Okay," I answered meekly. People said that to me all the time. *Do something for yourself.* What the hell was I supposed to do? In the past, doing something for myself would mean make time to be alone. I already had plenty of that.

I blinked again, alternately widening and narrowing my eyes. Why didn't everything look sharp and defined? I muttered *thank you* to Madeline and brushed past her to get to the stairs. I had to get home to look up my symptoms. If I could still see.

67

*****

"Hi, Mumma." Carli greeted me as I walked in the door. "Mr. Bean threw up."

My heart was beating wildly. It had been a difficult drive home with my compromised vision. "Can you clean it up, please? Mumma needs to get on the computer for a minute." Out of the corner of my eye I could see (although blurrily) Carli frowning.

"Lily's using your laptop. And I don't want to clean it up."

"Then throw some newspaper over it and I'll get it later," I growled. Where was it in life's rule book that mothers had to be on puke patrol? Wasn't it enough that we wiped noses and bottoms, and unclogged the toilet?

"He threw up in the family room," Carli added helpfully. Her tone had softened, sensing my mood. "How was your meeting?"

"We relived your father's musical career." I went to the bottom of the stairs. Mr. Bean materialized and curled himself around my leg, purring. I wanted to drop-kick him. I could hear Lily clicking away. "Lily! Why aren't you using your own computer?"

She called back to me distractedly. "It's dead, and there's something wrong with my charger."

I thundered up the stairs and was outside her bedroom door, surprisingly fast for someone who might be going blind. "I need to use it. *Now.*"

I pressed my ear against her door and could hear her mutter very softly, "Jesus *Christ.*" I opened my mouth to reprimand her, just as she opened the door and handed me the laptop.

I didn't want to waste any more time.

Stomach churning, I hurried back downstairs. My eyes still were not focusing properly, no matter how much I blinked. I told Carli to go see what was on TV and headed for the privacy of the study.

Carli called after me. "Aren't you going to take your coat off?"

I glanced down. I hadn't even unbuttoned it. "I'm cold," I said, a little more nastily than I'd intended. "Please go watch TV."

I googled the term "blurred vision." Trembling, I scanned through the possible causes. I was going for brain tumor but seemed to be coming up a little short. This was unexpected. I squinted my eyes and stared at the computer screen. Here was something: *Grave's Disease*. Symptoms: *weight loss without dieting*. (Check.) *Palpitations, rapid heart rate*. (Oh, yes, as in the present time.) *Increased appetite*. (Not really, although the bag of Fritos I ate the other night might disagree.) *Tremors, nervousness, sweating, breathlessness*. (My God, could this *be* any more me?). *Heat sensitivity*. (The mediation room had felt stuffy.) *Irritability* (a/k/a the bitch factor, an ongoing symptom).

I continued reading. Grave's *Disease can cause inflammation of the eyes, swelling of eye tissue, and protrusion (bulging) of the eyes...some patients may develop lumpy reddish thickening of the skin in front of the shins called pretibial myxedema*. I recoiled in horror. Holy Mother of Christ, who would want to date anyone with big bug-eyes and ugly shins? I started to cry. The words on the screen swam in front of me. My eyes were getting worse—right before my eyes.

I grabbed a tissue from my pocket (I had wanted to be prepared at mediation) and gently wiped away my tears, not wanting to contribute to any swelling. There was one section I hadn't read yet: *Complications. If the patient does not receive treatment, Grave's Disease may cause an increase in heart rate, which may result in further heart complications, and in severe cases, death.* **Death!** I had found it.

Sniffling, I went into the kitchen for the telephone and called Hank. He answered on the fourth ring, a little breathless. "Hey."

"It's me."

"Of course it is. How's your Lou Gehrig's?"

"It's doing all right," I blubbered. "But I think I have Grave's Disease."

He snorted. "You picked *that* one? That's not fatal. You must be slipping."

I became a bit indignant. "Well, it says it *can* be fatal."

"So can calling a friend when he's in the middle of some really good sex."

"I'm sorry," I said. *The son of a bitch, having sex before dinnertime! And bragging about it.* "I was just at my mediation, and my eyes got all blurry."

"You're fine. Go clean your contacts. I have an impatient penis to tend to."

After I hung up, I took off my coat and sat down at the table. Carli was there beside me, laying her head on my shoulder. A good deal of my future was cloudy, but this much was clear: I was still a mother. I was still me. I wrapped my arms around Carli, and held on tight.

CHAPTER TEN: *Septic*

It was D-Day: the day of dread, doom, division...divorce. I supposed I should have been thankful that mine would be a rip-off-the-bandaid kind, taking only six months as opposed to the horror stories I'd heard of some dragging on for years. Somehow, though, it was hard to feel grateful.

I had decided to go into school for the morning, as it would keep me busy. Fitzy said I was crazier than a shithouse rat for not taking the entire day off, but I had to keep busy. Keep normal. Keep me. The wife was soon to disintegrate, but the teacher could stay strong and solid.

Several days ago, I had bought a new outfit for court, knowing full well I wouldn't ever wear it again. I was going for that conservative-yet-sexy look. Something the judge would approve of, yet certain to make Slick regret the reason we were in court. I'd decided on a silky black top with three-quarter sleeves and a black skirt covered in delicate white flowers. The skirt had a mind of its own and would alternately cling and swish at will. I liked that. The night before, I'd had my hair highlighted with deep auburn and strawberry-blonde streaks. My hairdresser had shown me how to get the tousled look I'd always wanted, with some mousse and strategic scrunching. Slick had always liked my hair straight without anything in it, claiming that hair products were too sticky and smelled weird. Yet he had become a gel-er. Well, two could play that game.

My Short Fiction class was the first to see my

new look. The girls commented first. They were a sweet bunch, enough into the fashion scene that they'd notice if I'd changed the brand of my mascara. "Mrs. BACON," they breathed. "You look so cool!" I was pleased, but needed a male perspective (even if it came with pimples). I turned to Luke, who was staring at me.

"Did you do something different to your hair?" he asked, almost suspiciously.

I smiled. "Yes. What do you think?"

He continued staring, narrowing his eyes. "I'm trying to decide if I like it or not."

I opened and closed my mouth. The girls standing next to me shifted uncomfortably. Who would say something like that? Hadn't his parents taught him any manners? I moved closer, breaking that fragile teacher-student barrier, so that we were inches apart. I could hear him swallow. "Luke," I said, pleasantly, "take a good look. See how my hairdresser layered it a little, so it would have more body? She put in two different colors, so it has *dimension*. See?" I tipped my head and parted my hair in a few different places to show him. He needed to know.

"Yeah," he said. "I see. It looks good."

I wasn't buying it. "Do you *really* think so, Luke? Because just a second ago, you said you were trying to decide. What changed your mind?"

"Well..." he paused. His eyes widened and his nostrils flared slightly. He looked over at the group of girls and raised his eyebrows.

"Lowlights," one of them whispered.

He turned back to me and snapped his fingers in triumph. "Lowlights. That's what it is. The lowlights."

I glared at the girls. "Don't HELP him. He

needs to learn about being tactful. Who knows what that means?" They all stared at me blankly. *"Somebody get a dictionary!"* I shrilled. They scrambled.

Cassie found the definition first, knowing enough to look up the root word. "Tact," she read, "a keen sense of what to say or do to avoid giving offense; skill in dealing with difficult or delicate situations."

I pointed my finger at Luke, who was trying desperately to make eye contact with someone—anyone. "TACT," I said sternly. "Remember that."

He nodded. I noticed the other students staring at my hand. It was trembling. I folded my arms across my chest. Maybe I should have taken the whole day off.

I gave the class the reading assignment for the day and checked the clock: 9:02. I would only be married for another four hours. What would it feel like—the actual moment of divorce? Would the grief be as deep as the joy in the moment when the minister says, "You may kiss the bride?"

The room felt too small. I had to get out. I pushed back my chair and walked unsteadily toward the door. I could feel the kids' eyes upon me. "Bad morning," I apologized. "I'll be right back." Luke gave me a half-smile. I felt a twinge of regret. I shouldn't have held that Y chromosome against him.

Fitzy and Jess were in the teachers' room across the hall during their free period. Knowing I had a class, they were surprised to see me. "I had to get out of there for a little while," I explained. "They're silent reading, anyway. They'll be good."

Jess nodded and motioned for me to sit next to her. Fitzy flashed me a smile and gave Jess a poke. "So finish the story."

Jess raised her eyebrows in a classic *let's-talk-about-this-later* warning. Instantly, I became interested. "What is it? What were you talking about?"

She frowned.

"Tell me," I insisted. "It'll take my mind off this afternoon."

Jess shook her head. "Believe me, *you*, of all people, don't want to hear this."

Fitzy snorted. "Tell her. She'll just bug the shit out of us if we don't."

I looked at Jess expectantly. She sighed. "All right, but don't blame me if you flip out. Somebody who works with my brother got this paper cut, and it got infected. Three days later, he was in the hospital...it turned septic. The fourth day, he was in a coma, and the fifth day, he died."

Why the hell did she have to go and tell me that? As a teacher, getting a paper cut was a common job hazard. But I'd never imagined it could lead to *death*. Until now.

"So, what were his symptoms?" I asked casually. I had to go about this in just the right way, or I'd never get the information I wanted.

Jess shrugged. "I really don't know."

Bitch. "Yes, you do," I said. "You just don't want to tell me."

She rolled her eyes. "Why do you do this? You're just torturing yourself."

I waited.

"For God's sake," Jess snapped. "The skin around his cut got all red and streaky. He started feeling sick when it got into his bloodstream, but he didn't go to the doctor till it was too late. End of story. You satisfied?"

"Yes," I said meekly.

"You going to have some time for yourself after the hearing?" asked Fitzy, changing the subject to something equally as horrible.

I nodded. "My parents are coming up for the weekend to help with the kids."

Jess looked at the clock. "I better use the bathroom before the kids come back. I've already peed twice this morning." She leaned in to me, her eyes widening. "Maybe it's BLADDER CANCER!"

I was unfazed. "Try ovarian. The tumor could be getting really big and pressing on your other organs."

"Or maybe her bladder's just the size of a Sweet Tart," Fitzy offered.

Jess bent down and wrapped her arms around me. "Good luck. Call me later. And watch out for sharp paper."

I rolled my eyes at her, but inside I was filled with gratitude. She always knew how to handle me.

*****

Three hours and forty-two minutes later, I was sitting in the ground floor of the courthouse, outside Courtroom Three... trapped in the bowels of the great judicial beast in the final throes of digestion, waiting to be shat out. I was having intestinal issues of my own, the threat of diarrhea roiling inside me. There was a strange and unpleasant odor, somewhere between mildew and dirty feet. Or it could have been my soon-to-be-ex-husband. Dick was sitting diagonally from me across the hall, talking with his lawyer. He was wearing a tan jacket, ivory shirt and a pale green tie. I didn't know that jacket and tie.

The dread which had been lying dormant

inside of me began gouging at my insides until I felt myself go hollow. I had to clench my jaw to keep from shrieking. *Richard! I don't want to do this. Please, let's try counseling. Think of Lily and Carli, Richard!* Please.

He would not look at me.

"Christine?"

I faced my attorney. My eyeballs were stinging.

"How are you?" she asked.

Stupid question. "I've been better."

Madeline smiled ruefully. "I'm going to go in the conference room with Richard's attorney for a few minutes before we start. Will you be all right out here?" She tilted her head in Richard's direction.

I nodded. If the looming divorce hearing became too overwhelming, I could always think about heart disease. Or leukemia. I hadn't used that one in a while. And there was that poor guy with the septic infection. I could check my hands for cuts.

"Things are running according to schedule, so that's good." Madeline reached out to lightly touch my arm. "The actual hearing is very quick. It probably won't take more than fifteen minutes, if you can believe it."

Fifteen minutes to dissolve a twenty-five year relationship. How efficient. I looked over at Richard and met his gaze. He quickly looked away.

"You should feel good about being able to stay in the house. And to be able to have the girls with you most of the time. Richard could have gone for shared residence." My attorney looked at me almost disapprovingly, as if I was supposed to be looking at the positive side. I felt like beating her senseless. I blinked savagely.

Madeline gave a little sigh. "I know this isn't

what you wanted. I'll be right back." I watched her walk down the hallway with Altoid at her side. They were chatting like old friends.

How incredibly cruel to have Richard and me sitting only yards apart, the air so excruciatingly thick with anticipation I could have choked on it. My armpits felt sticky. Waves of heat tumbled through me. *Sweating is often a sign of an impending heart attack.* I stood up and walked partway down the hall, away from Richard. Then I walked back. Towards him.

My skirt clung to my legs like a timid child. Why hadn't I sprayed the hell out of the Static-Guard can? And what was I thinking, heading directly for my soon-to-be ex-husband? No one was stopping me. I wasn't stopping me.

HAIRY ASS, I scolded myself. *Think of his hairy ass.*

Richard had his chin cupped in his left hand, staring down at the floor. As I drew closer, he looked at me. His eyes narrowed and he brought his hands to his thighs. I glanced down at those hands: the squared-off nails, the dry skin around the cuticles. The hands I had held, squeezed, kissed, the hands that had patted our dog, carried grocery bags, held our babies...now no longer mine.

"Richard—"

"Please don't make this more difficult, Christine."

"I just...I just wondered something." I searched his face, looking for some glimpse of regret, sadness. Anything. My voice was a whisper. "Are you still in there?"

"Yes," he said, flatly.

There was no comfort in that. I stood there, rooted to the floor, like in those bad dreams where

77

the boogeyman is chasing you, and you are trapped in the horror of the moment. The sudden reappearance of Altoid saved me. Altoid...breath mint...lifesaver. I felt a wild urge to laugh, but Madeline, walking briskly toward me, quelled it. I noticed that her dress hung obediently at her knees, with not the hint of static cling. It figured.

The courtroom door opened. A rather rotund bald man who looked like he could be someone's grandfather stepped into the hallway. He was wearing a uniform: white shirt, black pants. The bailiff.

"Bacon versus Bacon?"

Altoid and Madeline said, "Yes."

My heart began to gallop. *His ass. All that hair.*

"You're up," the bailiff announced.

We weren't talking just a little hair. The thing was covered.

I had always envisioned a courtroom would look far more imposing, with paintings of portly, red-faced justices frowning down on litigants. There were no wall hangings, but there was a stern-looking judge in a black robe, and microphones, and tables marked "PLAINTIFF" and "DEFENDANT," and a witness's chair. It was a real courtroom. And I would be getting a real divorce.

My stomach rumbled and cramped. I prayed for my bowels to be patient. My heart fluttered and pounded, skipped and throbbed. A sharp pain attacked my midsection and headed north. I would have traded my children for a TUMS.

My mouth spoke the words I needed it to while my mind went into rewind.

"Christine Kellen Bacon."

If you don't kiss your lovely bride, I certainly

will [laughter from the guests].

"Nineteen years."

But I can't sleep, Richard. I just want to look at her! I couldn't wait for the nurse to bring her to me so I could feed her. Her eyes are the brightest blue in the middle of the night. She stopped nursing to look at me when I talked to her. I wish you could have been there.

"Two daughters. Lily, and Carli."

Careful, don't spill Daddy's orange juice! Do you want me to carry the tray? Let's see if he's awake yet.

"Irreconcilable differences."

Don't you ever want to just talk? About us, I mean. Not the kids, or work, or the house, but us.

The bailiff yawned and shifted in his chair, his arms folded comfortably across his ample belly. The judge commended us for working out our issues. And then he signed the paper that would cut so deeply.

Afterward, in the parking lot, Richard and I prepared to get in our cars, which happened to be closer than either of us wanted. We stared at each other in that strange and impossible moment. Stared at each other as two people might do when they think they may have met at one time, long ago. Richard opened his mouth as if to speak, and then closed it. There was absolutely nothing left to say.

CHAPTER ELEVEN: *Headaches*

It began above my right eye, just about the time my parents walked in the door. A stabbing pain, *pinging* at me. Brain tumor. I braced myself.

My mother waved her meaty arms, bracelets clanging together, and started to cry. "Oh, Christine," she said. "You don't know how good it feels to be here to help you!"

Piiing. My voice sounded muffled with my head squashed against her chest. "Thanks for coming, Mom."

"Hello, Chris," my father said, clearing his throat. I leaned in for a quick hug, respecting his discomfort. There was one time in my childhood where I remember him holding me—*really* holding me. I'd been having trouble sleeping (and therefore, so was he). I had snuck into his room and stood beside his bed. I'd said his name very lightly, fearful he'd wake up, yet hoping desperately he would (did I mention I was a junior in high school?). After my third visit, he finally dragged himself out of his bed and came into my room. "Chris," he said, his voice ragged with fatigue. "Would you please just go to sleep?"

"Dad," I said, starting to cry. "I'm trying."

Without another word, he sat down on the bed and took me in his arms. Dumbfounded, I laid my head against his shoulder. Years later, I could still remember the cottony feel of his white Hanes t-shirt against my cheek and the faint, not unpleasant scent of perspiration. I could still recall the essence of my Dad: comfortably rumpled. Safe. *There.* We sat like that for a long time. And then I slept.

Dad's face relaxed and brightened as Lily and Carli barreled into the room. "Well, look at these two! All grown up!"

"A little *too* grown up, I think," said my mother, frowning. "What is that you're wearing, Lily?"

"It's a cami, Mimi."

"A what?"

"A *cami.* Camisole."

My mother looked hard at me. "They're wearing lacy underwear?"

Lily giggled. "Everybody is."

"Lil," I said, "why don't you put Mimi and Poppa's suitcases in the guest room?"

My father waved a hand at her. "Don't you bother with that, honey. Your grandfather's old, but he's not *that* old."

Oh, good. I'd insulted him, and it hadn't even been five minutes.

"Christine, how are you enjoying *Real Simple?* " Mom looked at me almost suspiciously.

Ping. Lily stole a sideways glance at me. She knew that the magazines, which I'd been receiving for the past four months, were still wrapped in plastic. I kept them in the bottom drawer of the computer desk. My life was too complicated to take the time to read about how to make my life simple.

I smiled at Lily, and then at my mother. "It's a great concept." At least that was sincere. My mother *hmphed* at me and followed my father into the guest room, her navy slacks swishing, heels clacking importantly against the floor. I always felt decidedly frumpy in her presence, my sweats and t-shirt contrasting with her smart Coldwater Creek pantsuits. As assertive and commanding as she was, however, she was a paradox, my mother. From as far back as I could remember, my mother had been pretty much scared shitless of everything. In my mother's eyes, every activity could lead to death. If I was invited to a friend's camp, the boat ride would result in drowning. Driving at dusk meant death, because this was the time of day when moose lumbered across the road and caused fatal car accidents. Going sledding? You'd hit a tree. Ferris wheels were dangerous, since the orange jumpsuits who put them together were either past, present or future convicts who were too drunk or too high to notice the leftover screws on the ground after they put the ride together.

Pimples, too, were fraught with danger. Squeezing them, especially in what my mother labeled the "area of death" (the border around your nose), might cause the infection to travel into the bloodstream and inevitably to your brain. I distinctly remembered being in the throes of puberty, standing in front of the mirror and finding a hideous-looking zit near my nose. My heart hammering, I popped it—and waited to die.

Even fairy tales could be lethal. I received an early lesson in censorship when my mother blackened over the line about Little Red Riding Hood hiding in the oven. So it was really no wonder I had learned to fear every freckle, blemish, cough, bump, lump, tingle, bruise, and hiccup.

Richard hadn't known how to deal with my anxieties. He'd either ignore it, or tell me to call Hank. Once, during one of our marital ruts where we barely spoke and didn't touch, I had been terrified I had leukemia, one of my old standbys. I had begged Richard, who was watching

Sportscenter, to feel the lymph nodes in my neck. He shrugged and gave his usual response. "Go get it checked. I'm not a doctor."

"But you're my husband," I said. He had rolled his eyes and absentmindedly poked at my throat as I leaned over him. "You're fine," he said. "I'm not worried." I had wondered, then, exactly what he meant by that.

And now the pinging in my temple. I'd never had such a bad headache. Relentless, and aspirin hadn't helped. I hoped it would go away soon, especially since I was meeting Hank and Stella for dessert. Stell was here visiting her sister and was seven months pregnant with her first child after years of trying. I couldn't wait to see her—couldn't wait to touch that belly swelling with life, and promise, and *hope*.

My parents took over dinner preparations, a welcome reprieve for me. My mother fussed over the salad, adding chopped walnuts and black olives and cheese she'd grated herself. Although it was early spring, Dad cooked turkey burgers outside, grousing about the condition of the grill. Lily flitted back and forth between kitchen and back deck, fetching a spatula and spices, cooking spray and slices of cheese, with Winston at her heels. Carli set the table, folding napkins into triangles and placing handmade namecards in front of each person's glass. Mimi had brought a package of colored tissue paper and pipe cleaners, and showed Carli how to create ruffly, three-layered flowers. I felt a pang of guilt (and another ping in my temple) for not doing more crafty things with my daughters. I was sure that idea had come fresh from the pages of *Real Simple*.

"Have another burger, Christine," my mother

urged. "You're looking thin. Isn't she looking thin, Bill?"

I still hadn't had much of an appetite, and since I was getting dessert, I declined. My head pinged again. I would try caffeine. I went to heat up a cup of water for tea.

"Don't stand in front of the microwave," my mother warned. "You'll get cancer."

When I returned to the table, Carli had a question for me. "Mumma," she asked, making the sign of the cross, "what does this mean? Kristen says she does it in church."

My mother stopped chewing, her fork halfway between her mouth and the plate.

"It's the sign of the cross," I said, shifting in my chair. *Ping. Ping-ping.* I hadn't given my children what you'd call a real strong religious upbringing, and my mother was always quick to point this out. "Christians make that sign."

"What are Christians?" asked Carli, wrinkling her nose.

"Oh my Lord," my mother murmured.

"People who believe in Christ," I said, a little too sharply. I hoped that would be the end of it.

"Who's Christ?" Carli wanted to know.

Jesus Christ, she doesn't know who Jesus Christ is. My mother reached for my father's arm and made a low moan. I knew that inside, she was screaming.

A grin spread slowly across Lily's face. *"Jesus* Christ, Carli? That ring any bells?"

"I know JESUS," Carli retorted. "I just didn't know he had a last name."

Lily was enjoying herself. "Do you know who the Pope is?"

Carli pouted.

84

"He's like the head of the Catholic religion," Lily continued. "He lives in the Vicodin."

"VATICAN," I corrected loudly.

My father put his hand up in protest, defending Lily. "Pope John Paul probably did live in the Vicodin, at the very end."

"This needs to STOP," my mother wailed. "Christine, I would be more than happy to look into some area churches and see what they have for Sunday School programs. These children—"

"I know," I said. "I should be taking them to church." *Ping-ping-pingpingpingping...* My God, this headache was really starting to scare me. It felt as though I had a woodpecker behind my eye. What if it was a tumor, pressing on my optic nerve? Or an *aneurysm*. I hadn't thought of that. That was even more probable than a tumor. An aneurysm just waiting to burst and kill me, right there in front of my parents and my children. I fought the urge to make the sign of the cross.

"I have to go." I stood and picked up my plate. "Thank you for dinner. I'm supposed to meet Hank and Stella in a few minutes."

My mother was wearing her classic *we're not done talking about this* face. "Before you go, Christine, your father and I have some exciting news to share with the three of you." She beamed. "We've sold our house and are moving to be here with you."

Ping-ping-
PINGPINGPINGPINGPINGPINGPING...

"This way," my mother continued, "we can be here to help you and the girls out in any way we can. What was it that Hillary Rodham Clinton always said? *It takes a village.* That's the beauty of us being retired!"

Lily smiled broadly and Carli jumped up,

squealing, to hug her grandmother. I grinned weakly at my father as I stood up. I would not deal with this right now. I would meet my friends, and then I would return home to my pagan children. I would crawl into bed, bunch up the pillows around me and sleep in the middle, my arm draped over Winston and my head pressed against Beanie. If it was a good night, I would cry for only ten minutes. Like it or not, this was my life. Real. But not simple.

CHAPTER TWELVE: MS

"So you're officially Ms. Christine Kellen now," said Hank. "How does it feel, slut?"

"It feels weird, bee-yotch," I answered. We were sitting in a booth at Riley's restaurant, waiting for Stella to arrive. Owned by our high school classmate Todd, Riley's was famous for its thick milkshakes (banana chocolate chip a popular flavor), clam baskets, delectable onion rings, and overpricing of all of the above. Riley's was also known for its schizophrenic decor. Yvette, Todd's wife, was fond of decorating according to her moods. If things were going well, she'd display chubby-cheeked ceramic figurines: smiling cheerleaders and seasonal sports figures with huge blue eyes and tiny dots for pupils, all hand-painted by her mother. During a stretch of bad marital relations, the statuettes were replaced by leering clowns in silky, jester-style costumes. Todd loathed the clowns, and Yvette knew it. Tonight, Riley's was resplendent with wicker baskets of bright plastic flowers, nylon-and-wire butterflies and ceramic baseball players. Had I been in charge, I would have sent in the clowns.

Hank brushed a few stray crumbs off our table and separated the two wayward Sweet & Lo from the stack of sugar packets. "So are you relieved, or depressed, or what?"

I shrugged. "Both." Richard had been out of the house for six months. And now that separation was final. There was a dull, heavy permanence about it. "It feels like I've had a refrigerator dropped on me. Only more flattening."

"It's going to take time to feel whole again, dear."

To my chagrin, I started to cry. "I don't want to do this anymore," I said. "I really don't. I want to be able to go home tonight and get into bed with Richard, the Richard I married, and I want to have everything be—"

"Now, now," Hank murmured, reaching across the table to squeeze my arm. "It'll be all right, Ms. Kellen."

I sniffed. My hand felt all tingly. That was strange; usually it was my foot that fell asleep. I put my hand under the table, wiggled my fingers and made a fist. It felt almost...weak. And here came my mental medical dictionary, barreling in and slamming itself open to **M**. *Symptoms of multiple sclerosis vary depending on the location of affected nerve fibers. Signs and symptoms may include numbness, weakness or paralysis in one or more limbs; brief pain, tingling or electric-shock sensations...*

"What's the matter?" Hank was staring suspiciously at me.

"Nothing."

"Don't play innocent with me, miss. What's going on?"

Why the hell did he always know? "It's my hand. It feels weird."

Hank sighed. "Chris, can't you just let that go? Just for tonight? You need to try to relax, and forget about everything."

Something inside me crumbled. This was my *life!* How could you forget something you had to live, every minute, every hour, of every day? "Oh, I'm sorry," I said. "I didn't realize I could just

88

FORGET about everything. I wish you'd told me sooner so I could have saved myself a lot of pain."

Hank opened his mouth to say something (either comforting or snide; I couldn't tell), but was interrupted by the arrival of Stella. "There she is! Oh my stars, look at her! Would you *look* at that belly!"

I swallowed the self-pity clogging my throat. Stella. Her dark hair, usually parted on the side and touching her shoulders, was swept into a stylishly-messy bun. Wisps of it had escaped and framed her face, which was, despite the cliché, absolutely *glowing*. She had always been pale-skinned, but there was a healthy pinkish tint to her cheeks now. Her eyes were soft and dewy. And her gorgeous round belly. No billowy maternity top for Stella; she was pregnant and proud in her clingy pink top.

Hank and I took turns hugging her. I put my hands on her belly and let them linger there until we both started to cry.

"Pregnancy definitely agrees with you, Stell," I said.

"And divorce agrees with you," she winked. "You look GORGEOUS. I love your hair with those highlights and lowlights!"

I felt my mood begin to lift. Yvette could keep her clowns in storage.

"It is so great to be here with you guys," said Stella, easing herself into the booth. "I'm so glad I came!"

"And I'll bet you're happy to have driven here, too," Hank grinned. We giggled like the fourteen-year-olds we were on the inside. This was how we had talked since high school. Example: when Hank's partner had a business trip out of state, the question would be, Did *James get off okay?* And the answer: *Yeah, and his plane left the airport, too.* Juvenile, yes, but that was the whole point.

"So catch me up." Stella started to open the menu, then rolled her eyes and put it behind the salt and pepper caddy. Like Hank and me, she knew it by heart. "Have you slept with anybody yet?"

I could feel a blush darken my cheeks. "The divorce was final two days ago."

"Well, what the hell are you waiting for?"

I sighed and rolled my eyes. Which hurt my head. Probably the residual headache from a couple hours ago. Or, it was another symptom of MS: *Impaired vision, often with pain during eye movement.*

"Well, I just remember when Daniel broke up with me after four years. I went without sex for like six months."

I nodded. I was all too aware of what that felt like.

"I was hornier than a three-peckered billy goat."

I grinned in spite of my multiple sclerosis. Stella could be sophisticated, but she also had this surprisingly perverse side which surfaced from time to time. Like when she used to visit Ninny, her grandmother, and would draw male genitalia in the dust on Ninny's coffee table. Nin had very poor vision and couldn't see the penises, but Stella always got a charge out of thinking about Nin's better-sighted friends stopping by and getting an eyeful.

Stella continued. "There was this guy who worked as a cashier at the grocery store, and he was adorable. Or maybe he was butt ugly. I don't remember. He used to flirt with me whenever I'd go in. He was young—had to be oh, ten years younger than me. Maybe even fifteen. Anyway, there I was, majorly horned up and el desperado. So I asked him out—you know, just for a drive after he got done work."

"A *drive?*" Hank snorted. "That's not *too* obvious!"

Stella raised her chin. "I told you, I was desperate. So we get in the car, and we drive like 100 yards to the Staples parking lot where it's all vacant, and we start making out. And when I come up for air, I say, 'I feel like Mrs. Robinson!' And he goes, 'Who's that?'"

"JEE-zus, that's awesome," Hank said, dabbing at his eyes with a napkin. We had been loud enough to make the people in the next booth jerk their heads around to see what teenagers were shrieking. It felt good.

The waitress appeared. She was about our age. A little overweight, unnaturally blonde hair, dark circles under her eyes. Her nametag read "Jenny." She probably had been pretty in high school, the type of girl voted "best smile." I quickly glanced at her left hand. No ring. I wondered if she was a "Ms.," too. When I was in elementary school, the teachers who had kids call them "Ms." were mean and fat. Comforting thought.

"The usual, right?" Stella looked at us for confirmation. Hank and I both nodded. It would undoubtedly be complicated for poor Jenny, but we'd do it anyway. One of our favorite pastimes was to try to get out of paying full price for a menu dessert by putting together our own fabulous concoction. This usually involved a sundae and something on the side.

"We'll each have a small sundae with cookie dough ice cream and hot fudge," said Stella. "And a brownie on the side, heated."

Jenny started to scribble down the order and then looked up, her brow furrowed. "Did you know you can get the—"

"Brownie Supreme. Yes, honey, we know," interrupted Hank.

"You see," I explained patiently, "we went to school with Todd, and we therefore enjoy screwing him."

"In the figurative sense, of course," said Stella.

"Of course," I agreed. "We'd never want to do it in the literal sense. We're just trying to get out of this as inexpensively as we can."

Jenny smiled nervously. "Okay!" she said, taking our menus. "I'll bring you some waters and your desserts should be right out."

We watched her walk away. "Poor thing," sighed Stella. "Anyway...let's get back to Ms. Kellen here."

Now what the hell was my forearm doing? It felt all tight, like a cramp. I began to breathe faster. *As the disease gradually worsens, muscle spasms, slurred speech, vision loss and problems with bladder, bowel or sexual function may develop.*

This definitely felt like a muscle spasm. And I'd had to pee all the time lately. Diarrhea, too—like I couldn't get to the bathroom fast enough. My God. Why hadn't I seen this before?

"Chris. I'm talking to you." Stella tapped her finger on my placemat.

Occasionally, mental changes such as forgetfulness or confusion occur. What were some of the other symptoms? I couldn't remember.

"Have you been sleeping okay?" she asked anxiously.

She was going to make a wonderful mother. I

wobbled my hand in the so-so sign. "I've been dreaming a lot. Like last night, I had this weird dream that Richard—I mean, Slick— was standing beside my stove, stirring this pot of boiling water, and when I got closer, I could see he had this turtle in the pot, but it didn't have its shell anymore...it was just sort of writhing around, all pinkish-red, and he looked at me and said, 'I took the liberty.' And I said 'you sure did take the liberty, you son of a bitch!'"

Stella and Hank looked at each other with raised eyebrows.

"Wow," breathed Stella. "And I thought my dream about feeding the baby under the table like a dog was weird."

"So who's the turtle?" Hank asked knowingly.

I made a face at him. "You're a pathologist, not a shrink."

"I did a psych rotation in med school," he huffed. "Seriously, who do you think the turtle is?"

I curled up the edges of my placemat and began making little rips to fringe it. "Well," I said, "I think it's me."

"Exactly." Hank beamed.

"But why a turtle?"

"Because think of how helpless and raw and vulnerable a turtle is without its shell—or in your case, without clothes. God," he said, shaking his head. "That is just the COOLEST dream, Chris."

"I'm glad my pain is entertaining for you," I said.

Stella asked me how Richard was starting off as an ex-husband.

"Well, besides the fact that he's been paying his child support late, is now coming up with excuses of why he can't take the kids and feeds them

TV dinners and Mountain Dew when he does have them—all of the above just to piss me off—he's fantastic."

She covered her face with her hands. "I can't believe you have to deal with this. At least tell me the kids are doing well."

The kids. How were they? They seemed all right, but truthfully, I couldn't be completely sure. It was hard enough for me as an adult. I would try to get them to talk about it, but Lily would brush me off with a terse "I'm FINE, Mom," and Carli would make me squirm when she'd ask me if I ever hated her father. Now there was a question.

"Well, Lily wants to move to California, become a professional surfer and never get married."

Hank nodded approvingly. "Smart girl."

"I'm worried about her. She's social, but she has this introverted side and she doesn't anybody in. She's online all the time, and I wish she'd do other things. I was thinking maybe sometime you could give her a little scrapbooking lesson?" Hank was also an amateur photographer and turned vacation pictures into works of art.

He grinned. "I'd love to get her started. We'll have her addicted in no time. It's better than heroin. Won't cost you any less, but no track marks."

"Thanks," I said, and turned my attention to Stella's pregnancy. I wanted to change the subject to something more pleasant—a promising new life rather than a failed old one. "How's our future president doing in there?"

"Oh," she sighed, "I guess I can't complain. But I will. I keep having contractions all the time."

"Braxton Hicks," I said, and smiled. I refrained from sharing my pregnancy war stories,

94

even though it would have allowed me to bask in the memory of that glorious Battle of the Bulge, which had ended all too soon. Overall, my pregnancies had been thankfully uneventful. And growing a baby had kept my hypochondriasis at bay. Which reminded me.

Maybe this weird feeling in my hand was caused by the same disease that made my foot fall asleep at my attorney's a few months ago. I'd had that same prickly feeling a couple times since then, on both sides of my body. So if it wasn't MS, it could be some other neurological disorder. Terror moved in, found a seat inside me and made itself uncomfortable. *I discovered I was frozen in my chair. As the disease progresses, paralysis may develop.* Jesus, Mary and Joseph, this wasn't fear paralyzing me. *Paralysis* was paralyzing me.

Jenny appeared with a tray of desserts: frilly towers of whipped cream, aromatic fresh brownies. I could not even move my mouth to thank her, to smile. I felt myself begin to slide down into that recognizable abyss, down and down, where I knew it would be cold and dark, but which had become more familiar to me than my face in the mirror. I knew I should instead be grateful for this time with my two best friends, for having *laughe*d, but I let myself slide anyway. And hoped someone would pull me back up.

Hank pointed his ice cream-dripping spoon at me and said sternly, "Ms. Kellen, you need to get laid."

Stella nodded. "Absolutely. Get on some matchmaking sites. E-harmony. Match dot com."

"Or," added Hank, "join Facebook like I keep telling you, and then you can search for former classmates you wish you'd had sex with in high school."

I managed a smug look. "No Facebook. I'm too busy living my life to post it." I forced myself to pick up my spoon and dent the perfect white tower of cream. "I just want to *kiss* someone. There was this guy at Baskin-Robbins the other day who gave me two huge scoops of World Class Chocolate, but he only charged me for a single. I had all I could do not to lean over the counter and plant one on him."

Hank raised an eyebrow. "Would tongue have been involved?"

"Of course. But he was about nineteen."

Stella squealed. "Even better, Mrs. Robinson!"

"Mrs. BASKIN-Robbinson," I corrected, and giggled. Then, inevitably, tears. "My God, what is WRONG with me? You'd think *I* was the one who was pregnant."

Stella's eyes were large and shining. "Oh, honey," she said. "I am so sorry."

"Don't take this the wrong way," I cried, "but I really hate you right now. I hate you, because you're just beginning."

She reached across the table and touched my arm. I stared at her hand. At the bright gold of the wedding ring, at the blue veins, enlarged by pregnancy, snaking beneath her skin. My veins had looked like that, too, when I had been pregnant. And married.

"But Chris," she said softly, "you're just beginning, too."

We ate. I told Stella I was sorry for telling her I hated her, and she apologized for thinking I was a bitch for saying it. Jenny came over with our check. Hank grabbed it eagerly. "Did we screw him?"

We all hovered over the slip and drew in our

breath. Jenny waited, peering over our table. I knew she was on our side.

"My GOD," Stella moaned. "I can't believe this! This cost us more than if we'd gotten the Brownie Supreme!"

"No effing way," I said, amazed. Maybe Todd was onto us.

Jenny sighed. "Well," she said, gently. "Sometimes in life you're the screwer, and sometimes you get screwed."

Didn't I know it.

CHAPTER THIRTEEN: *Bad Blood*

So it had been decided. My divorce, which at first felt very much like an ending, was really a new start for me, according to Stella. I was grateful, even though a tiny part of me still hated her. But yes, I was beginning, too. I would give birth to the new me. And what better time to begin than in the springtime? Everything was fresh: budding and even bursting with new life, from the baby maple leaves trembling on their branches to the stunning red cardinal darting from shrub to feeder with his wife. Though his partner was plain, he looked like the type to fly the straight and narrow. I just knew.

The divorce had given me wings. I was OUT THERE. I was ready to soar, to fly headlong into the wide open sky with my wide open dreams. I knew there was someone else waiting for me—a new friend, lover—husband, even. I would take quick but fabulous fantasy trips to see him. He was, of course, magazine cover-gorgeous, with a shock of jet black hair wild to the eyes but silky to the touch. I would twist locks of it around my fingers as I'd pull his head in to meet mine. When I kissed him, he tasted of peppermint. And when I needed a little air, he would let me catch my breath without continuing to thrust his tongue toward my tonsils like someone else I used to know. His eyes were pale green and reminded me of sea glass. He was broad-shouldered and muscled; you could even see the outline of his pecs under his shirt, which was truthfully a little tight for good taste. He was brazen and bold with others, but fiercely tender with me. He would look into my eyes when we made love. And he would hold me when I'd cry. I loved him for that. And one of the best things of all: there was not a single hair on his ass.

Unfortunately, these thoughts of Mr. Ultimate were not keeping me warm as I was making the kids' lunches for school. I felt a bit chilled *(hypothermia? thyroid disorder? lupus?),* tired *(chronic fatigue syndrome? fibromyalgia? mononucleosis? anemia?)* and a bit achy...which I learned, after my early morning internet research, was a symptom of a slew of illnesses, both common and exotic. Hepatitis and scurvy were two of them, although I felt I could safely rule out the latter since I wasn't a sailor in the 1500's. No on Psittacosis, because it involved bacteria from pet birds. Leptospirosis was a possibility, though, since it was an infection caught from animal urine. African Sleeping Sickness, spread by bites of the tsetse fly, intrigued me especially since it resulted in death without treatment, but even I had to admit that was a little unlikely.

I wasn't the only one low on energy this day. Lily sluffed into the kitchen, yawning and bleary-eyed. Winston, lying on the tile, lifted his head and thumped his tail at her.

"Good morning," I smiled, opening the refrigerator.

She frowned at me. "Don't pack me an orange, Mumma. I hate those stringy white things on it. And after I eat one, my fingers smell like an *orange.*"

"All right, an apple, then."

She scowled. "Whatever."

She needed to be told it was springtime. I pointed toward the front yard. "LOOK out there,

Lily. What do you see?"

She glanced out the window. "Mud."

I sighed. She was young. She didn't know. "I mean IN the mud. Bursting with new life."

She looked again. "You mean those little purple and yellow flowers?"

I beamed at her. "Yes, those little purple and yellow flowers! Those are called *crocuses*. Aren't they beautiful?" This was a good day in motherhood. I was showing my daughter ebullience for life, and I was also working in a little lesson on gardening.

"I guess," Lily shrugged.

I watched her walk to the dishwasher, yank it open, take out a bowl and plunk it on the counter. She opened the cupboard under the bar for the Honey Smacks and shook the box until the cereal spilled over her bowl.

"Crocuses are the first flowers of spring," I said.

"Why are you telling me this?"

I looked at her face and studied the dark smudges beneath her eyes. Her skin looked too pale, almost translucent. I went to the cupboard for the bottle of chewable vitamins and set it in front of her. "I don't know, I just think springtime is rejuvenating. I wanted to celebrate it with you. I feel like—like a *crocus*."

"Mom, just STOP. That is so *retarded.*"

"Lily, please don't use that word." My teacher voice.

"Okay, then, that is so *mentally challenged.*"

Now it was my turn to frown. I didn't appreciate her wintery mood.

"I'm not going with him anymore," she stated flatly.

I looked up from writing Carli's lunchbox

note.

"With Dad," Lily said. "I don't want to go with him."

"Why not?"

"He does dumb stuff with us—stuff *he* wants to do, like go to music stores and look at guitars. And there's nothing to do at his apartment. He still hasn't gotten internet, so we can't even get online."

Ah, there was the real issue. Social isolation. "Well, I'll speak to him the next time he picks you up. And maybe you can ask if you could invite a friend to go with you."

Lily snorted. A few Smacks tumbled from her mouth. "Yeah, I'm sure my friends want to go to his crappy apartment." She paused. "I think he's got a girlfriend." She tipped her cereal bowl to her mouth and drank.

I felt myself wilt, slipping back in the winter of my discontent. A deeper chill wrapped its icy fingers around my spinal cord and started to squeeze the springtime out of me.

"You do?" I made my tone light, casual. *Crocus. Think crocus.*

"Mm-hmm. It sounded like it, the way he was talking on the phone."

I stiffened my shoulders. They felt so *tired*. If, in fact, I was anemic, it could be a sign of something serious. Iron-deficiency could be at the root of it, yes, but I dismissed that thought. Because anemia could also be caused by leukemia.

"*Mom.* Did you hear what I said?"

"Yes, I did."

She waited.

"Well," I said cautiously. "Your father and I are divorced, which means we are both free to see other people. And from the sounds of things, he started first." Smiling face, upbeat tone. This unknown disease and Richard were not going to get the best of me. It was springtime.

Lily relaxed and shrugged. "Yeah, apparently."

I felt little arms around my waist. Carli, pressing her face into my side. "Apparently what, Mumma?"

I bent down to hug her. "Apparently, you are going to be late for school if you don't get going. Have some cereal."

As I straightened, my shoulders felt fatigued again. My thoughts catapulted into the doctor's office. I would roll up my sleeve and extend my arm for the needle. I would be brave. The nurse would draw blood, and then they would send it to the lab for a quick reading. It might take fifteen, twenty minutes. I would sit there and continue to be brave. The doctor would knock and open the door. He would smile at me, gently, and then deliver the news. *You were right, Ms. Kellen,* he would say. *You are anemic. Your white blood cell count is abnormally high. We think it's because of leu...*

"Can you make cinnamon rolls?" Carli was holding the Pampered Chef deep dish baker that had been on top of the stove.

Lily turned from dumping her bowl in the sink. "Oh, I forgot to tell you...don't use that thing. Beanie sprayed in it."

The joys of owning an old male cat. I took the baking dish from Carli and sniffed. Unmistakable. Remembering the leptospirosis, I hastily set it back on the counter and went to the sink to scrub my hands raw. The smell shoved me into the reality of the moment. The rumpled hair of my youngest daughter, the dribble of milk on the countertop, the little purple and yellow flowers outside my window, straining to reach the sun. And cat piss.

Leukemia might end my life, so I needed to hurry up and begin it. And if my ex-husband could move on, I could, too. I would search for my gardener, someone who would help me to grow and bloom, but who would recognize the fragility of a new flower just starting to poke out of the ground.

If I was lucky, he'd have a long cultivator.

CHAPTER FOURTEEN: *Matters of the Flesh*

I am riding in the back seat of Richard's Impala while he drives. He is laughing and this bothers me, because he is supposed to be desperately unhappy now that we're divorced. We drive to a seedy hotel where he disappears. I meet a man in black leather, who for some reason I believe to be my friend, although his face is hidden in shadow. He's leaning against a motorcycle with a helmet in his hand and talking with Lily, who has appeared out of nowhere. He asks if he can take her for a ride. I'm hip, so I say, sure! You have a helmet and everything, go for it! Lily is thrilled I am so at ease with this. She smiles at me, hops on the back of Shadow Man's bike, and they are off—going a little too fast for my liking, but I'm cool, I can deal. Humming, I turn around, and there is Fitzy, who looks at me sternly and says, "Did you really just let her leave with that man?"

I panic. What is wrong with me? How could I have let her go? I grab my phone and call her. A calm male voice answers. "You're calling to see how long I'll have our little girl, right?" Horror renders me speechless. "I'll have her as long as I want," the voice continues pleasantly. A scream tries to work its way up from the very depths of my soul, but my voice is a whisper. "You had a helmet," I say weakly, "and you were supposed to be my friend."

*****

"You were in my dream last night," I

104

informed Fitzy at lunch.

He looked at me slyly. "Really?"

"It was a *scary* dream."

"Too big for you, huh?" he grinned.

Jess reached into the candy jar and threw an M & M at him. He caught it, popped it in his mouth and turned to me, opening his arms wide. "I'm telling you, Christine, one night with me and you'd be sleeping like a baby. No more of these goddamned dreams we have to keep hearing about."

"I'll keep that in mind."

He winked at me as he got up from the table and strutted into the hallway. "You do that. I've got to go take a dump."

I watched him leave. He did have a rather nice ass. He had mooned us once after school, so I knew it was slightly hairy. But only slightly.

Jess was watching me. "Don't you even think about it. I'd kill you first." She readjusted the elastic holding her ponytail and stretched her arms toward the ceiling, arching her back and yawning mightily.

"Tired?" I asked.

"Uh huh. Busy weekend. I went shopping for—" She snapped her fingers and pointed at me, her brown eyes wide. "I can't believe I forgot to tell you! I saw your ex this weekend. With some woman."

Fluttery feeling in my chest *(premature ventricular contractions...possible causes: cardiomyopathy, myocarditis, hypoxia and heart attack).* "What did she look like?"

"Blonde. With big ta-tas."

I took a deep breath. Casual, nonchalant. I...didn't....CARE. "Where did you see them?"

"Target. Shopping in the seasonal section."

A faint throb in my lower abdomen. *Pelvic*

pain at the beginning or end of menstruation can be a sign of ovarian cancer. "So what did they buy?"

Jess reached into the refrigerator for a bottle of water. "Mmm...I'm trying to remember."

"Well, was it like beach towels, or lawn chairs, or what?"

"I think they said they were looking for a big cooler to go camping."

Camping? Richard had never wanted to go camping. When I'd suggested we try it, he had told me he didn't think the kids would want to. "Too buggy," he had said. "Too much work."

And then something else occurred to me. "Wait. What do you mean, 'they *said?*'" I gave a little laugh. "It almost sounds like you *talked* with them!"

A pause.

"Jess?" My voice sounded shrill, like I'd just discovered one of my best friends had had a conversation with the two people who'd ruined my life.

"Chris," she sighed. "The divorce is final. Did you really think he'd stay single? He can date other people, and so can you. Why would you even care?"

My face began to burn. I may have said the same basic thing to Lily, but coming from Jess, it just sounded wrong. "What did you do, shake her hand and say, 'nice to meet you, your tits are spectacular?'"

Jess put her water bottle on the table. "For Christ's sake. He's turned into someone else. He's not even what you want anymore. Someday, maybe you'll be grateful he left you."

"Oh, right!" I laughed. "Thank you for divorcing me. Thank you for fucking up my life."

She looked down at the floor, shaking her head. "You're going to have to work on getting rid of this anger, or you won't heal."

"Well, maybe you could work on being loyal to your friends!" I was shaking all over now, my teeth chattering.

"Hey, hey," she said, and took me in her arms. I sobbed into her chest for the *tenth? hundredth?* time. "I wasn't being disloyal! I just got cornered. I said hello, and Richard made some comment about looking for a cooler, and I said 'oh' and mentioned I was shopping for my parents' anniversary gift. Then I got out of there."

"You actually said the word 'anniversary?'" I said into her chest.

"Yes. I did that on purpose. And Richard looked uncomfortable." She pushed me away from her and looked down at her shirt. "If you got mascara on me again, I am going to be so pissed off."

"I've been wearing waterproof," I said, sniffling.

"Good. You're free next period, right?"

I nodded.

"So am I. We're going to do some online research. Come to my room."

I had to make a trip to the bathroom first. I studied my face in the mirror. Blotchy, as I knew it would be. I took my compact from my purse and dusted powder over my cheeks and nose. And then I felt an itch on my left buttock. I reached down quickly to scratch, hoping no one would open the door and see my hand in my pants. It felt like something was there. Like a pimple, or bug bite, or...I froze. Could it be?

I turned back to the mirror, pulling my pants down just enough to see the top of my buttocks, and looked over my shoulder. A tiny bit of blood had appeared where I had scratched. My worst fear had been realized. It was the mole.

I knew the cancer brochure by heart. The heading, KNOW CANCER'S SEVEN WARNING SIGNALS! The word CAUTION down the front in blazing red. And the second to the last symptom, right between *Indigestion* and *Nagging cough or hoarseness,* was what was worrying me now: *Obvious change in wart or mole.*

I held my compact and aimed the little mirror at my ass, twisting around to look at the reflection in the bathroom mirror. From what I could see, the mole appeared reddened and irritated. The itching was new—I couldn't remember the last time I had scratched my ass. This represented a definite change. There were times when I could resolve my medical issues by myself, and there were times I needed my doctor. This was one of those times. Hopefully I could get in to see him this afternoon. But how was I going to get through the rest of the school day without the threat of skin cancer totally consuming me? And then I remembered the mole on my right foot. I could scratch that and see if it looked the same as my ass mole!

I zipped up my pants and directed my attention to the little mole on my ankle. It wasn't quite as big as my butt mole, but it would have to suffice. I dug at it, wincing, and blood appeared. I dabbed it with a wet paper towel and waited. It looked red, and irritated—much like the other one. So the "obvious change" in my ass mole was maybe because I'd scratched it. A bit of relief.

And then panic. I hadn't washed my hands before scratching the mole on my ankle! What if I'd somehow introduced bacteria into it? What if I had just given myself a staph infection? How could I have been so damned careless? I started to breathe more heavily. *Calm down,* I told myself. Should I need my foot amputated, they were doing marvelous things with prosthetics these days. I could do some research, maybe find some pictures on the inter—

Jess. Waiting for me. Shit.

I checked to make sure my ankle mole had stopped bleeding. It had. At least I wasn't a hemophiliac. Another quick look in the mirror to check for any residual facial blotchiness, and then I hustled my butt and the mole on it to Jess's classroom. I would probably have my doctor check me out. Just to be sure.

"Well, it's about time!"

"Sorry. I was just...putting on makeup." I stared down at Jess's computer screen. A checkerboard of faces. Faces of men.

"What is this?" I asked.

"What does it look like?"

"I KNOW what it looks like, it looks like an online dating service. But those sites are supposed to be blocked."

"I have the administrator password," Jess smiled. "One of the perks of being buds with the technology coordinator."

"But you have to pay to join," I said. "I don't have my credit card with me."

"Good thing I do. It's my gift to you."

"And a gift for you and Fitzy, right?" I knew they were getting tired of hearing how horny I was.

"Exactly." She pointed to one of the men. "Check *him* out. If I wasn't with Scott, I'd be all over him."

I leaned over her shoulder to scrutinize the photo. Light brown hair, blue eyes, dazzling smile, and quite buff in his white tank top. And then I read his user name: *Haulinassss*.

"Very classy," I said.

Jess waved her hand at me. "Forget classy, just think *sex*. You're not ready for anything serious. You need to get your feet wet, so to speak, and take the plunge with someone more substantial later."

My ass mole began to itch again. I watched her scroll down the pictures of potential sexmates. Some were in t-shirts, others wore jackets and ties, the twenty-five-and-under crowd mainly in sleeveless wife-beater shirts. I squinted to read the usernames, which could tell you a lot about a person. The 30ish, bespectacled, rather scrawny guy was *Aimstoplease*. *Hikeandbike* leaned up against a tree, unsmiling in his fleece vest, and my personal favorite was a grinning, bearded, ZZ-top lookalike in black, otherwise known as *696969*.

I cleared my throat. "So what was she wearing? Was she showing cleavage?"

"Who?"

"Richard's masseuse slash new girlfriend."

She shook her head, her ponytail sweeping across her back. "Nope. We are not going to talk about this anymore. I am not going to feed your anger."

I sighed.

"Here's one!" Jess pointed at a square containing a man with a young girl on either side of him. "He looks quite normal. And he has kids."

"Or he's a child molester, and those are his victims." I checked the clock. "I need to make a phone call to my doctor."

"Just look at this guy, will you? He seems harmless. And he sounds like he has a great outlook on life."

I decided I'd just get it over with. I gave an

annoyed sigh and read the headline to his profile: *Life's short, be happy!* And further down: *I don't let the little things get to me.* I had to admit that his username, *BetterDaysAhead,* was optimistic. Not to mention I was horny as hell. I was aching to touch someone, to be touched. The custodians were even beginning to look good to me. I knew I had to act fast. I could hear my mother's warning: *Christine, you need to stop thinking of yourself and your sexual wants. If you join the church, you can direct your energies into pure endeavors.*

"Move over," I told Jess. "I'm going to email him."

*****

"So you have a mole on your buttock," said my doctor.

"Yes. Thank you for seeing me on such short notice." I was sitting on the examining table in a johnny. My cheeks (both sets) were flaming. I had been a patient of Dr. Jordan's for the last twenty-five years. He had to be over sixty, with sparse, neatly-trimmed white hair and kind, gray-blue eyes that crinkled up when he smiled. He wore plaid button-down shirts, tan pants and bow ties. Whenever I looked at him, the word *impeccable* came to mind. I was probably like a daughter to him. He didn't want to look at my ass! Of all the things I could have come to him with.

"If we can put your mind at ease, we want to do that. But I think I might be able to diagnose you better if I actually saw it," he smiled.

"Oh! I'm sorry. I'll show you," I said, turning around and cringing as he lifted up my johnny.

"How are things going, Christine? The last

time I saw you it was right after you and your husband separated."

That time, I had come in for a throat culture, and ended up walking out with a negative strep test and a prescription for Lunesta. "I'm doing better, thanks."

"Sleeping okay?"

"Yes." I struggled to keep from breathing shallowly as I always did when I was anticipating a diagnosis. *Christine, this does look suspicious. I think I'm going to refer you to a dermatol—*

"Nothing to worry about, Christine. It's a very straightforward, benign common nevus."

Relief rushed into my every cell, crowding out the fear, until I felt weak. I cast my gaze to the ceiling in a silent thank you!

"It looks a little irritated. Have you been scratching it?"

More embarrassment. *Yes, Doctor, I HAVE been scratching my ass!*

"You probably have some dry skin there. Eucerin or Lubriderm should take care of it."

I wrapped my johnny around me as Dr. Jordan typed some notes into the computer. "What are you doing to relieve your stress?"

"Um, a little jogging, and some yoga." (Lies.) "And I'm...I'm going to start dating." There, I'd said it.

He nodded. "Sounds good." He reached for my hand and shook it. "Nice to see you. Take care." As I watched Dr. Jordan leave, I found myself itching again—itching to get home and check my email to see if BetterDaysAhead had responded. There had to be other men who might enjoy seeing my ass.

CHAPTER FIFTEEN: *Toilet Trouble*

"You're going to think this is weird," said my date from across the table.

"No, I won't!" I insisted, stretching my mouth in a smile. It was kind of like when someone says, "No offense, but..." and then they slam you with an insult. So I braced myself.

We were sitting in the cafe at Books-A-Million (my suggestion). I figured #1, it was a cheap date, #2, it was very public and therefore safe, and #3, if the date bombed, I wouldn't have to sit through an entire meal making small talk. Background music was provided by a John Mayer clone playing acoustic guitar, and the books and chocolate pastries in such close proximity comforted me. So the stage was set for a romantic comedy, or tragedy, or whatever was going to happen. I just hoped it wouldn't be a murder mystery.

I had taken much too long getting ready. Lily and Carli had watched me rushing from bathroom to bedroom. Carli regarded me with solemn curiosity, but Lily was disapproving. I tried to act like my date was no big deal, because I didn't want my daughters to grow up thinking life depended on just the right belt to make a person look hip but not hippy—although tonight, of course, it did.

Steve (a/k/a *BetterDaysAhead*) and I had exchanged several emails and had spoken by phone, but this was our first meeting in person. Steve was a bit nervous, and this somehow made me feel more at ease. He kept twirling his straw in his fruit smoothie (the selection of which, for some reason, embarrassed me).

"I probably shouldn't be telling you this on our first date."

If you don't think you should be telling me, then you probably shouldn't be telling me. Please, please don't be wacked. I picked a moth's asshole for a husband; please don't let me have picked a freak for a date.

I studied him carefully. He looked normal enough: average height and weight, dark wavy hair flecked with gray, brown eyes, a short, straight nose, a small scar on his left cheekbone, but I wasn't born yesterday. I knew that oftentimes, the most disturbed people could look—well, just like Steve.

I flashed him my most winning smile. If he was going to turn out crazy, I supposed I'd better find out now. "What is it?"

"You know how I told you I'm renovating that old house?"

I nodded. Steve had told me all about the farmhouse he was working on—the sloped pumpkin pine floors that needed refinishing, the layers of ancient wallpaper he'd stripped. He'd even emailed me photos of his work. Right or wrong, his carpentry skills factored into my decision to date him. My ex-husband hadn't known a hammer from a handsaw. But he could sure pick out a hoe.

"Well...I was in the bathroom the other night—the one with the cracked tole-it I need to replace—and I saw this strange *face* in the mirror behind me, only it wasn't really a face, it was more like just *eyes*...and then when I turned around, I felt this *chill* go through me."

I stared at him. His eyebrows looked messy. I hadn't noticed that before. "What did you just say?"

"I said I saw this face in the..."

114

"No," I interrupted. "Not that."

"The chill that went through me?"

"No. The part about something being cracked."

"Oh," he said, nodding. "The tole-it."

The *tole*-it? We were in a bookstore, surrounded by the works of authors like Yeats and Thoreau, for God's sake, not in some trailer out in East Bumfuck! I could picture the scene: Steve, in a flannel shirt with a pack of Marlboros thrust in the pocket, squatting on the bathroom floor with a few inches of ass-crack grinning at me over the top of his jeans. *Woman! Bring me a goddamn beeyah, for Chrissake! I need some alchy-hol before I work on the tole-it!*

I fought the urge to run to the reference section and shove Steve's head into a dictionary for the correct pronunciation. "So do you think it was a ghost?" I said casually, like I was asking if he thought it might rain later.

He shrugged. "I don't know. I'm gonna look into the history of the house—you know, see if anyone died there or somethin'."

All right, enough about the spooks. I needed to change the subject to something safe. "Have you been to that new Italian restaurant by the mall?"

His face darkened. "Yeah, but I wouldn't bother going there if I was you. They gave me the wrong goddamned salad dressing, and marinara instead of meat sauce. I told the waitress right where to shove it."

I slid my chair the teensiest bit backwards as I contemplated what he'd written in his profile: *I don't let the little things get to me.* Thank God the girl at the cafe counter got his smoothie right.

Steve inched his chair forward. "Want to see

115

some pictures?"

Finally, some normalcy. Photos of his children, undoubtedly.

"You'll probably think this is weird, too," Steve grinned, reaching behind him to where his windbreaker hung on the chair.

Oh, God.

He fumbled in his coat pocket. "I have this little garden out back, and every morning when I'd come out, the onion seedlings would be all uprooted. I was like, what the hell is eating my onions? My neighbor Eddie, he said it was birds pullin' 'em up. But I had this feeling it was somethin' else."

Perhaps the spook told him.

"So I took my camera and went out back one night, and I sat there and waited for the goddamned birds Eddie was so sure of. And THIS is what I found." He tossed an envelope on the table and folded his arms triumphantly.

Carefully, I picked up the envelope. The corners were bent and there were lots of creases as if someone had opened it again and again. There were three photos. Baby onions at the end of bright green shoots, uprooted and lying on their sides on top of soil. And long, brownish worms that looked like they were creeping toward the onions. I flipped over one photo. *Exhibit 1A* was written on the back. I did not allow myself to look at the back of the other photos. I returned them to the envelope and slid it back to Steve. It was then I decided to add the moniker *Creepy* to his name.

Clearing his throat, he leaned closer. He expected me to make some sort of comment. What did one say, in a situation such as this? *Good work!* Or, *You caught 'em!*

"They're...*worms,*" I said, finally.

"Nightcrawlers," he corrected.

My stomach tightened and began to gurgle. I clenched and unclenched my toes, but I knew it was only a matter of time before I had to use the tole— *TOY*-let.   Diarrhea.

"You should've seen Eddie's face when I showed him these photos."

"I can imagine," I said. A major cramp then, like someone had fastened a C-clamp to my intestine and twisted it really, really hard. First I would kill Dick for divorcing me, and then I would kill Jess for encouraging me to date. Both deaths would be slow and painful.

"Would you excuse me?" I stood up. "I need to use the bathroom."

"You're not going to take off on me now, are you?" A hint of unpleasantness to his voice.

"Oh, no!" I reassured him. "I just really need to use the bathroom. Or," I added, laughing, "I'll be sitting in it, and you'll be downwind. And I don't think either of us want that."

I could see the neon sign flashing in Creepy Steve's head, like the end of a video game: DATE OVER. His nostrils flared ever so slightly. "Right," he said, and remained seated as I left the table.

I prayed my bowels would wait to let loose until I was sitting on the toilet. I prayed that the women's bathroom would be empty so I wouldn't have to worry about the horrific noises resulting from the impending explosion. And I prayed that I did not have intestinal cancer, hepatitis, the ebola virus, or Crohn's disease. I would have welcomed colitis, gastritis or irritable bowel with open arms. I felt myself begin to sweat as I pushed open the door to the women's room.

It was full. Not just full, it was actually

*over*full. There were two stalls, but one was marked OUT OF ORDER. Two women were waiting in line. They were chatting in a relaxed manner, and I immediately hated them because they clearly just had to pee, whereas my excretory needs were more extensive.

I stood there for a few seconds until I realized I didn't have a few seconds to stand there. There was only one solution. The men's room.

My gut felt like a pressure cooker. I wanted to groan, or at the very least whimper, but I was unsure I'd be able to prevent myself from screaming. So I bit my lip as I opened the men's restroom door, and expelled a tiny sigh of relief. It was, as I had hoped, empty.

I scrambled into a stall, pulled down my pants, and detonated. The sudden absence of abdominal pain was almost humbling. I reached around to flush the toilet with the heel of my hand, my mother's voice a distant echo in my head: *Use your foot, Christine! Do you have any idea how many germs there are in a public bathroom?*

I did not care. This was Shangri-La. Every muscle in my body relaxed. I could have fallen asleep right there on the toilet. And would have, if it wasn't for a couple of things: one, Creepy Steve waiting for me in the cafe, and two, the very large Adidas sneakers which were now outside my bathroom stall.

My body went rigid again, because I knew there had to be a man on top of those sneakers. I prayed that he was a mutant without a nose or ears. A longshot, but I prayed for it anyway.

I decided I would sit on the toilet until he left. I could not bear to have him see me. And, I realized with a shock, I could not have him see me bare! My underwear and pants were down around my ankles. My God, he probably saw my leopard-spotted panties! *My date* hadn't even seen those (and wouldn't, by the way things had been going). I quickly yanked them up and zipped my skirt, fastening my belt with trembling fingers.

Silence, except for the sound of my shuddery breathing. And then, a voice. Deep, yet gentle.

"Hello-o?"

I said nothing.

"Hello? Are you all right?"

I had to answer him. "Yes."

"Oh." Brief silence. "Would you mind leaving so I could use the bathroom?"

Well. Wasn't that just like a man. Thinking of himself. This irritated me and gave me the courage to open the stall door.

I had to tip my head back to look at him. He was even taller than the Adidas had suggested: six foot four or better, with a pleasant-looking face, good skin, eyes the color of caramel and coppery tints in his light brown hair (which was noticeably sparse). Typical male pattern baldness, with a little hair around the sides and back of his head and a hopeful tuft at the front. A pity, because my dream man had to have a lot of thick dark hair. Except for his ass. That could be bald.

I did a quick inventory of his outfit. Ralph Lauren polo shirt, pale blue. Khaki tan shorts, with no wrinkles and an expensive-looking leather belt. So he knew how to dress himself. But still, the balding thing. I didn't do bald.

A slow smile spread across his face. His mouth was wide, his teeth very white. "So...do you come here often?"

I studied him warily. Was this a pick-up line,

119

or just polite conversation? Hard to imagine he would be flirting with me in such a malodorous setting, but he *had* seen my leopard panties. "Yes, for the books, of course, but I enjoy the music on Friday nights."

The skin around his eyes crinkled. "By *here*, I actually meant the men's bathroom."

I bristled. "There was a stall out of order in the women's room. And there was a line. I couldn't wait." I straightened my back and raised my chin. This princess was determined to maintain some modicum of dignity, even in her palace of toilets and tile.

"I understand. I'm just teasing you."

"Well...all right."

"So...would you mind...?" He tilted his head in the direction of the bathroom stall.

"Oh! Of course. I'm sorry." In addition to giving him his privacy, I also needed to come up with an excuse to ditch Creepy Steve. If he was even still out there.

"Maybe I'll see you here on another night," Tall Adidas was saying.

I shrugged and forced a smile, but inside I was cringing. My first night of dating had ended in the tole-it.

CHAPTER SIXTEEN: *Small Lumps*

It was a triple threat: three major stressors in quick succession. One, I had a date tonight with Fitzy's coaching buddy who'd been recently divorced. Two, I confronted Slick about Lily not enjoying weekends with him. And three, I would have my yearly mammogram tomorrow—or, as Jess called it, getting the girls' pictures taken. Fitzy had once asked us what a mammogram felt like. Jess had told him to picture himself lying on his side on the garage floor with one of his testicles against the cold concrete. "I would then run over it with a truck," she explained. "After that, I'd tell you to switch sides and we'd do it again." Fitzy did not ask us any more questions for a while.

Since I hadn't done my self-exam in a few months, I was convinced a lump would show up on the films. I would be extra-friendly to the x-ray technician, as if she could somehow control the development of cancerous cells. I would watch her expression as she studied the computer screen and would listen for a hint of sympathy in her voice when she told me I was "all set." Then I would go home to wait for the inevitable phone call from my doctor's office where the nurse would tell me they found something suspicious. She would be nonchalant about it, because she made these kind of phone calls all the time. "Your mammogram showed an abnormality," she'd say, and then she'd cover the mouthpiece and whisper to her coworker that she'd like a Boston Kreme and a French vanilla coffee for their daily Dunkin Donuts run. I would then be left to battle the malignancy in my body while she looked forward to noshing on a donut. I hated her.

Although I had emailed Slick regarding Lily's displeasure, he had insisted that any time spent with him was beneficial to her, and that she needed to be more willing to do things *he* was interested in. I viewed this as a viable excuse to remind him he was an asshole. He had pulled in the driveway at 4:29 (maddeningly punctual, as usual, but the huge zit on his nose cheered me), and I repeated Lily's concerns. I did not raise my voice, or, in the spirit of Lorena Bobbitt, pull out his penis and slice it into attractive wedges with my Pampered Chef Crinkle Cutter (although the latter idea was intriguing). I couldn't wait to tell Jess the progress I'd made with my anger; I'd only called him a fucking bastard twice.

I was in the midst of contemplating my wardrobe when the phone rang. Hank, giving me the latest on Stella who was now a week past her due date and willing to give her OB-GYN a blow job if he would induce her. I told Hank about my impending date.

"What are you going to wear?"

"Working on that right now. Jeans, probably, and something black."

He gave an irritated sigh. "You always wear black."

"It's sexy," I retorted.

"A hearse isn't sexy. And it's almost summer. Wear something bright and young. You know...*hopeful.*"

I did have a white lacy tank top, and I could steal Lily's short pink jacket. The tank top fit snugly and managed to suggest I had breasts. *Breasts.* The mammogram. I had to do a quick self-exam to prepare myself for the inevitable phone call from my doctor's office. I scrunched up my shoulder, cradling the phone against my right ear. It fell to the floor with a loud bang. I picked it up hastily.

"What was that?" Hank asked.

I cringed. "Sorry, just dropped the phone."

"Oh. So are you going to Riley's for dessert, or someplace nice?"

With my left hand, I poked at my breast around the nipple area, the dread thick in my veins. This was how I always began my breast exam. If I didn't feel any raging tumor, I'd allow myself to relax the tiniest bit and slow down the jabbing until I would palpate like I was supposed to. After I was done, I'd get down on my knees, look up at the ceiling and mouth, *thank you, God!* Then I would be just *scared* for the results of my mammogram. And scared was a hell of a lot better than terrified.

The phone dropped to the floor. *Shit.*

"I am now officially deaf in my right ear. What ARE you doing?"

I hesitated.

"Poking at yourself again, hmmm? Let me guess...lymph nodes? Ovary? Abdominal mass?"

I sighed.

"Jesus, will you stop? If you're looking for something, you're going to find it. You should know that by now."

"I know," I said meekly. "I have a mammogram tomorrow."

Hank sighed. "It's days like these that I wonder why the hell I became a doctor."

"I'm probably just stressed about the date."

"Well, it's not like it's a blind date, like Creepy. Fitzy knows this guy, right?"

"They're not best friends or anything, but yeah."

"Then you shouldn't have to worry about him being a total loser."

"You're probably right."

"So give yourself one less thing to stress about. Just concentrate on the breast cancer, and you'll be fine."

"Okay." *That* I could do.

*****

My mother called the moment I hung up with Hank. She got right to the point. "Two things, Christine. First, we think we've found a house. You know how I despise ranches, but we figured a one-story would be best for our later years. Your father likes the yard, and the best part is we'll only be ten minutes away! What do you think of that?"

Ten minutes away. "Wow. I can't believe it."

"Yes, it's wonderful, isn't it? And the second thing...Carli mentioned to me that you had a date with a man the other night."

The adult in me folded in on itself so I could become twelve again. It was an unspoken reality that I remain suspended in perpetual prepubescence when my mother was displeased.

My hesitation in answering was all the proof she needed. "That is very disappointing."

"Well, I...."

"How often do you need to be reminded? You shouldn't be dating yet."

"It was just one date," I told her. "It didn't go anywhere."

"This isn't your time. This is the KIDS' time. You're quite a few years away from *your* time."

I took a moment to process what she was saying. "So even though I'm living my life right now, this isn't my time?"

"That's right." Her voice had that *you get a gold star!* tone. I could see her oversized silver earrings trembling as she nodded her head in approval.

I knew my place. I would not question her. "I guess I could wait a little longer. You're probably right," I said. The folded-up adult in me stirred.

My mother gave a little laugh. "Have I ever not been?"

*****

So I waited a little longer to date. Two hours, to be exact. Had I known that my breasts were going to be so thoroughly groped, tweaked and squeezed, I would have skipped the self-exam. After sharing an obscenely huge dessert aptly named Chocolate Explosion, Manch (short for Mancharo, his last name) and I hastily climbed in his Jeep Cherokee to find the perfect spot for night moves by the dashboard light—the darkened rear parking lot of Goodwill. Lily would probably be mortified to hear it, but I liked Goodwill, liked being able to heap my shopping cart with name-brand shirts and dresses. I drew the line at pants, however. The idea of being in such close proximity to the remnants of someone else's crotch just didn't appeal to me. Although right now, in this car, I was full of good will being close to a crotch.

Manch rolled down his window and threw his gum onto the tar. I arranged my lips into a smile. Within minutes Lily's hopeful-colored jacket was in a crumpled heap on the car floor, my tank top was pushed up over my breasts and my bra was off. Manch had optimistically unbuckled his belt, but he had yet to see any action below it.

He was a good kisser. He took my lower lip and pulled just a bit of it into his mouth, sucking on it gently, which sent little shock waves all through my belly. He pecked around my mouth and then attacked it with hard, open-mouthed kisses and generous tongue until I was literally breathless. "Whoa," I said, "can we come up for air?"

He pulled back, grinning sheepishly. "Sorry...it's been a while," he said, his chest heaving. He reached out, and with his index finger dabbed the corners of my wet mouth. I returned the favor. We both laughed. It felt like we were teenagers. He certainly was attractive: thick brown hair, great cheekbones, a rugged athletic build. I put my hands on his shoulders and squeezed. Very buff. He grabbed my buttocks with both hands and returned his attention to my chest, cupping my left breast and leaning forward to pull my nipple into his mouth.

"Sorry they're so small," I whispered.

"It's okay," he mumbled around my nipple. "It's your ass I really like."

Was that a compliment? He was sucking a little too hard. I didn't want to insult him, so I squirmed a bit to see if he'd get the hint. This seemed to excite him and he sucked harder, even sinking his teeth into me. "OUCH," I said. He looked up at me and grinned. In the dim glow of the streetlight, his eyes sparkled. He was damned good-looking. I forgave him. He released my nipple and began kissing me in a straight line down my belly. My God, I hoped he wasn't thinking what I knew he was thinking.

I grabbed him by the ears. He looked up, startled.

"What are you doing?" I asked.

"What do you think?"

My cheeks were burning. "It's just...I'm not ready for that."

Undeterred, he resumed kissing my stomach. "You're a lot more ready than you think you are," he said. His tongue circled my belly button. "I know you'll love it. It's one of my favorite things to do. Once, when my wife and I rented a movie, I went down on her and stayed there for the whole thing."

Wha-a-at?! I felt myself weakening. My entire lower half melting, melding into him. "Did that include previews and credits?" I whispered.

He chuckled gently. "Mm-hmm. At the end, she was practically begging me to stop." He was kissing me along the top of my pants, darting his tongue below my pant line. I was gasping. *Breast cancer! Think of the tumor that could be found!*

"I want to make love to you so bad," he murmured. He sat up, fumbled with his zipper and then took my hand and pushed it inside his pants. I was now touching another man's penis. A real live penis. Of a man who was not my husband.

He looked down at me as he slid off his jeans. It seemed to excite him even more to watch me holding him. His breathing quickened. He was rock-hard. He slid his briefs down, and his penis sprung forward and waved at me. *Waved.*

I had a wild urge to laugh. I ran my tongue around my upper teeth to unstick them from my lip. What was I going to do? A blow job was out of the question; I was not about to munch on Manch. And sex...I had just met him. I needed to find out about his sexual history, have him take a few HIV tests, and then insist upon a condom...maybe even use two, like how they sometimes double-bag your groceries.

This was moving much too quickly. Manch was a little too...*eager*. Pawing at me in his car like a sixteen-year-old. I should have known any friend of Fitzy's would be a concoction of two parts Fritos, three parts beer and filled to the brim with testosterone.

"Listen," Manch said huskily, *and suddenly, I am back with Richard in our bedroom, thirteen years ago. We are lying in bed, our bodies curved crescent-like around our new baby daughter. I am nursing her and am still at the stage of incredulity that my breasts, once merely a man's playthings, are now vessels of nourishment for this miracle in terrycloth. Lily is making tiny contented sighs in between gulps of milk. "<u>Listen</u> to her," Richard breathes, and I know at that very moment he GETS IT. This is the stuff of oil paintings. If someone had been looking in our window, I know they would have seen a golden light bathing all of us in that bed. And given that moment, I never, ever would have imagined my husband would go from that kind of awe and enchantment to* walking out on the mother of that precious baby.

And then I became aware of a man's fingers in my panties. "I know you want me," he was saying. "You want me inside of you. You're ready."

That was what did it. *No, I was not. I was not ready.*

I pushed him away. "I'm sorry," I said. "I thought I was ready for this, but I'm not."

Manch stared at me for a moment, and then sighed, cast his gaze at the roof of the Jeep and raked a hand through his hair. "You really know how to hurt a guy." He shook his head, laughing softly as he pulled up his jeans. "And Fitzy said you were horny as hell."

"I am," I said, and the tears started flowing then. "I really am. But it's about more than that for me." I knew that my mascara was probably making its way down to my ankles, but I was filled with gratitude that I had not given my virginity (the second time over) to a virtual stranger who slobbered over my (bite-sized) breasts but wasn't crazy about them. I needed to find someone who wanted to be not only in my pants, but inside my head and my heart. But who would that be? And when?

Suddenly, I was filled with an almost panicky urge to be at home, where things were settled and familiar. Where there were solid things, like drooling dogs and humming refrigerators and rumpled beds, where there were calming answers rather than anxious questions.

"I'm sorry," I whispered, and when Manch answered it was all right, I let him think I'd been talking to him.

CHAPTER SEVENTEEN: *Stagnant*

Fitzy came over the following week to help me get my swimming pool inhabitable by something other than amphibians. I had seen him in the grocery store the day after my first and last date with Manch. He felt a little guilty about having set me up, but added I should have relaxed and just enjoyed the ride, so to speak. I told him he never should have fixed me up with someone hornier than I was, and that he could make it up to me by helping me with the pool. Then Fitzy offered me his own "services," and I punched him in the arm. It was so nice to be able to hit a man.

Lily came into the kitchen where I was waiting. "So Fitzy knows about pools?"

"Supposedly, yes."

She snorted. "The neighbors will appreciate it."

I had to agree. For the past two weeks, the frogs of the town (and very likely, the county) had made our chlorine-starved pool their new pad. In the early days, I found the sounds they made quite charming. "Oh, listen!" I'd tell the girls. "It's just like living on a lake!" And then these few charming frogs told their friends, and those frogs told THEIR friends, and so on, and so on, and so on. I would walk Winston down the street at dusk to see just how loud it was to other neighbors, and was horrified to hear the volume of the *trilling: brrrrrrripppp! BRRRRRRIIPP! BRRRRRRIIIPPPP!*, punctuated by the banshee frog who had to one-up his peers with *kkkkk-KAI-KAI-KAI!* My next door neighbor, an old widower who smoked cigars on his porch, was hopping mad and would glare at me as I passed. I always gave him an *I'm doing the best I can* smile, but he wasn't buying it.

The doorbell rang. Winston huffed and barked, his nails clicking on the kitchen tile as he trotted to the door.

I opened the door. Fitzy bent down to pat him. "Hey, big guy. Are you taking good care of your mom?"

I smiled. That, at least, hadn't changed.

Fitzy leaned closer to me and winked. "Of course, there are some things a dog just can't take care of."

I ignored that statement as I went to the pantry to get Winston a cookie. "So are you going to help me with the pool?"

"Call me the Frog Whisperer. Bet you didn't know that was one of my many talents."

"No, I was just thinking slimy, and you immediately came to mind."

Carli appeared beside me, linking her arm with mine, and regarded Fitzy solemnly. "Are you going to fix our pool?"

"Sure, after I convince the frogs to leave."

"Good," Carli said, tipping her head back to look up at me. "Because Mom doesn't know what she's doing."

How very true, on several counts. We walked into the backyard, Carli in the lead. Winston raced off to the edge of the woods in search of a tennis ball, undoubtedly encrusted with mud and seasoned with slugs, just the way he liked it. In the good old days, Richard would throw the ball for Winston off the deck. I knew Winston must have missed that, but I was grateful he kept it to himself.

Soft croaking punctuated the stillness. They always started out this way, lulling you into thinking this would be a peaceful symphony of nature. By now, I knew better.

"Holy cow!" Fitzy exclaimed as he approached the pool. "You weren't kidding when you said you needed help. This is impressive as hell. The frogs must think they've found paradise."

Carli giggled. I smiled politely.

"I don't know as I've ever seen water this color before," he continued. "What would you call it? Kind of a muddy green?"

"Puce," I said, lacing my words with frostiness. "I'd call it puce."

He caught on quickly. "Well, it's nothing that can't be fixed. I brought some bags of shock. We'll sneak up on it after I take care of the frogs."

I found an empty drywall pail in the garage. Fitzy took it, scooped up some of the puce water and then handed the pail to Carli to hold. There was silence. The pop-eyed sons-of-whores must have known what we were up to. I started to say something and Fitzy held his fingers to his lips. Seconds later, a tentative *brrrrrrrt*. Fitzy moved to the source of the sound and grimaced as he dunked his hand into the pool.

"Do you want some rubber gloves?" It was a courtesy question, really, since I didn't have any. I hoped he'd say no. Plus, only a wimpy man would say yes. It would be a good test.

"No, thanks." He pulled his hand out of the water and raised his arm in triumph. "First one, right here." He brought his hand back down to study the frog closely. "He's just a little guy."

"With a big mouth." Lily had come out to stand on the deck. She waved at Fitzy and looked over at me. I could feel the eyes of my mother in her gaze. What was she thinking?

Hesitantly, I stepped closer to the pail where Fitzy had just deposited the frog. I had never been too keen on jumpy things like frogs or crickets or grasshoppers, but it was a bit rude to let Fitzy do this all by himself. The least I could do is act like I wanted to help.

A brief silence, and then another *brrrrrrrrt* from the other side of the pool. With Carli at his heels, Fitzy moved quickly, found the noisemaker tucked under the pool rim, and soon frog number one had company in the pail.

As the dusk deepened, we all began swatting mosquitoes. I got a bottle of bug spray from the house and asked Fitzy how many frogs he'd caught. I was beginning to feel a bit guilty I'd asked him over in the first place.

"If I haven't lost count, this makes twelve," he announced. I moved closer to peer into the pail and as he plopped the frog in, a few stray water droplets splashed against my face. "I think we're getting there. The Kermit chorus isn't so loud anymore."

Carli slapped at her arm and flicked off a dead mosquito. "I'm going in, Mumma."

Fitzy nodded his approval. "Good idea, kid. You sure have a skeeter breeder out here. I think I'm down about a quart of blood."

I hated to admit it (because this was Fitzy, after all), but I was enjoying the scent of his deodorant mingled with the smell of his sweat. Despite my resistance, my netherlands began to tingle. And then I froze thinking of a comment he'd made.

"Fitz," I said. "I'll be right back. Okay?"

"Yeah. I'm almost done, and then I'll drive

'em to the pond at the cemetery. At least the people there won't be bothered." He grinned, but I couldn't smile back. I had to get on the internet. He had mentioned mosquitoes. I would start there.

Lily was sitting at the bar with a plate of apple wedges and a jar of peanut butter. "Don't double dip," I muttered, heading for the computer.

"Why don't you just go out with him?"

I came back into the kitchen. "What did you say?"

She bit off the end of her apple and swiped at the peanut butter. "Fitzy. You should go out with him."

I knew it was important that I remain calm and pleasant. "Why would I do that?"

She gave that little sigh that mothers will give their children when there's a lesson to be learned, but the kids just aren't getting it. "Because you need somebody, and he's pretty cool."

Indignation flamed in my cheeks. How dare she tell me I needed somebody? And how the hell would she know that? I had been careful to cry mainly into my pillow, to purge the dating websites from the search history each night. Did she not hear the times when I'd sing I WILL SURVIVE? Was she oblivious to the miraculous transformation when I would metamorphose overnight from a restless sleep as the former Mrs. Bacon, to wake up as Christine Kellen, Supermom/ Superteacher, ready to face the day?

I resented Lily even more from delaying my internet search. "I am not going to date my coworker," I said stiffly. "And I don't need anyone. I'm doing fine by myself."

"Okaaayy," she said, sighing again, and I could have sworn I saw a smirk.

"Stop double-dipping," I snapped. I passed Carli watching TV in the family room as I hurried to my computer for a google search on mosquito-borne illnesses. Within seconds, I had some possibilities. *Malaria, yellow fever, dengue fever, West Nile, lymphatic filariasis*...now that last one was intriguing. I clicked on it. *A disease caused by nematodes in the blood or tissues causing blockage of lymphatic vessels.* I didn't know what nematodes were, but they sounded serious. I would have to research that later. With such limited time, I needed to hit the symptoms.

Some of the symptoms of Lymphatic Filariasis include...**No symptoms.** I froze. I had that.

I read on. *Lymphedema, swollen armpit and groin lymph nodes, arm swelling, breast swelling* (I could live with that one; that is, if I could actually *live* with that one), and *leg swelling.* I squirmed in my chair. I was starting to feel bloated. I kept reading: ...*a parasitic infection of the lymphatic circulation system which can lead to the disfiguring disease known as elephantiasis.* Elephantiasis?! Not only did it end in "iasis," which was never good, but it sounded dangerously similar to *Elephant Man.*

My heart thudding wildly, I clicked on the term. *Severe swelling of body areas often caused by worms...a syndrome characterized by the thickening of the skin and underlying tissues, especially in the legs and genitals.* This just kept getting worse and worse. I was already worried about my vagina drying up from lack of use, and now I was reading it could also thicken. My netherlands were well on their way to becoming Never-never land.

I was jerked from my bulging genitalia

reverie by Fitzy calling to me from the backyard. "Hey, Christine? Are you coming out?"

"Yes, in a minute," I called back, as pleasant as one could be with potentially puffy private parts. I returned to the text on the computer screen for further investigation. Naegleria (nuh-GLEER-e-uh) is an amoeba commonly found in the environment, in soil and stagnant bodies of fresh water and in swimming pools lacking chlorination. I gasped. *Infections are rare* (I gave a little sigh of relief) *and occur when the amoeba enters the body through the nostrils or mouth, then traveling to the brain or spinal cord as the person swims.* Obviously, I hadn't been swimming in our backyard cesspool, but droplets of the pool water had splashed on my face. Some of the water could have easily entered my nostrils. My eyes darted across the screen. *Headache, fever, loss of balance and bodily control...most cases are fatal without immediate treatment.*

"Chris? Are you all right?"

I put my hand over my mouth to stifle my cry. Fitzy shouldn't be dealing with this. *Dick* was the one who should have been out back getting the pool ready for his daughters, not to mention handling his wife's neuroses. Although when we were married, he hadn't done either very successfully.

Larval tendencies. I had to keep reminding myself of how Hank had labeled Dick. But the continued splitting of everything—our lives chopped up and shoved into separate little containers of *this is my weekend, this is your weekend,* and *at the kids' events, I will sit here, you will sit way over **there**—*felt even worse than the empty whole I fought so hard to keep during the last few months of our marriage. My life right now, to coin a favorite middle school verb, sucked. Sucked *bogwater*.

And here came those feelings again, sliding in thick and dark and sludgy. Would I ever learn to just let it *be,* this getting to know someone else? I hadn't wanted macho Manch, but there had to be other men in the world whose penises didn't wave. There had to be men out there who would not violate their wives' trust. And I had to keep looking.

God knows, I'd had my fill of frogs.

CHAPTER EIGHTEEN: *Attention Deficit Disorder*

I always felt sorry for myself on trash night. This was compounded by my playing the role of martyr and refusing to ask my children for help. Thanks to the divorce, I believed they had exceeded their crap quota; they should not have been expected to haul it, too. Yet I still resented them for not helping. I made a production of whipping the trash bag through the air to open it, slapping and banging the kitchen and bathroom wastebaskets to dislodge anything stuck to the bottom. I hoped I'd find chewed gum clinging to the side of the can so I could yell. I would heave the stained and reeking trash barrels to the end of the driveway, scraping the tar if they were particularly heavy. I prayed that people were watching and feeling as sorry for me as I was. Everyone on this street was married, complete, and therefore blissfully happy. I imagined them peeking at me from behind their curtains, whispering things like, *oh, look at her! She's taking the trash out by herself!* This gave me comfort: the thought that I was not only *seen,* but pitied.

Even the thought of street sympathy could not lift my rank mood. Dick had taken a reluctant Carli to dinner (it felt somewhat like a kidnapping), Lily was at the mall with a friend, and I was stressing over how stressed I had been lately. This was summer, after all, where time was measured in ice cream trucks and crickets instead of whistles and school bells. However, I could not relax and had to be in constant motion. I was unable to concentrate on one thing for more than a few minutes at a time and even worried I might be coming down with a case of mid-life hyperactivity. I reminded myself of Cameron, one of my former students with classic ADHD symptoms. I had to speak Cam's name to redirect him about as often as I blinked. He would begin to do his work, and then his pencil would inevitably start tapping his desk. Then his legs would start jiggling, and he'd look around: at the ceiling lights, the classmate beside him, a paper clip on the floor. His parents had refused teachers' recommendations of testing and possible medication, so his tapping and jiggling and staring continued. I used to get annoyed, until the day I asked Cameron rather sharply to please *try* to focus. A troubled look had curtained his face, and he had said simply, "Mrs. Bacon, I just have too much going on."

Now I knew exactly what he meant. My daily routine went something like this: Start unloading the dishwasher. *Heart rate accelerates for no apparent reason...tachycardia? atrial fibrillation?* Notice the counters need to be wiped. Open the drawer for a dishcloth; none there. This reminds me I haven't washed towels in a while. Upstairs to the bathroom to get the hamper. *Left ankle feels weakish. Lou Gehrig's?* Spy splattered toothpaste on the faucet. Get the bottle of disinfectant spray; almost empty. *Pinging over left eye. Tumor has returned.* Head downstairs to add disinfectant to my grocery list. Groceries...dinner. What should I make? Realize there is no food in the house. Decide I should balance my checkbook to see if there are funds available for groceries. Sit down with laptop. *Tingle in my right hand. Carpal tunnel—no, no, that was for amateurs. More likely MS.* Realization that I haven't responded to my mother's latest email. Guilt. I needed some chocolate. Or a man. Or a chocolate-covered man.

As scattered as I was, Lily could not have been more focused. She had inherited my obsession with dying, only hers had an extra **e** chromosome. For the past several weeks, she had insisted on dyeing her hair pink. I feared that her desire to change herself would lead to even greater defiance. I was unfamiliar with this concept, as I, of course, had always been a good girl. My idea of rebellion as a teen had been pulling up to the McDonald's drive-thru with a few friends in the back seat, and upon hearing the greeting, "can I help you?" we'd yell, "NO THANK YOU" and drive off.

Garbage detail for tonight was over, and I had moped sufficiently. I contemplated how I was going to persuade Lily not to go through with her colorful scheme. I knew I needed something better than *because I don't want you to.* If worse came to worse, I could always sic Mimi on her.

It was so quiet in the house I had to walk from room to room to reassure myself that children did, in fact, live here. I needed music. I headed for the entertainment center in the family room, pushed the FM button on the tuner and clicked to my favorite radio station, WKIT: an "oldies" station, otherwise known as real music. I was not in an ipod kind of mood; I needed to hear a voice in this room. I would make a song request. Hadn't done that in about twenty years. It was high time.

I dialed the number to the radio station and prepared myself for the inevitable busy signal.

"WKIT classic hits."

"Hello?" My voice quavered. I felt like a teenager. I was talking to a real live D.J. And on the first try!

"Hi there. What can I do for you?" The voice was raspy and masculine at the same time. It was...*rasculine*. And it was talking to *me*.

"Hello, I'd like to make a request."

"Name it."

I plunged into the flirting pool with a big splash. "I'd like somebody to love."

A chuckle, deep and rich, as he dove in, too. "I'll be right over."

Tingles all over my skin. I smiled. "Nicely done."

"Thanks. So you're single, huh?"

He might as well know; everyone else did. "Yes. I'm divorced."

"You're in good company. What is it now, like fifty percent?"

"I think it's a little higher than that. My husband left me."

Rasculine was silent for a few seconds. "Well," he said, "let's see if Freddie can help."

He wanted to keep swimming with me. "Thank you, Freddie," I said. "But if you don't mind me saying so, that's not a very radio name."

He laughed again. "I was talking about Freddie *Mercury*. Lead singer of Queen."

I moved the receiver away from my head so he would not feel the heat from my flaming cheek across the phone line. "Oh," I said lightly. "Sorry about that. Thanks for taking my call."

"Hey, wait a minute," said Rasculine. "I'm getting off in a few minutes."

"Oh, and will you be done your shift, too?" The words were out of my mouth at the same time I decided I shouldn't say them. Hank and Stella would be proud, but what was I thinking?

More chuckling. Rasculine had a very sexy laugh. "Listen," he told me. "I'm going to call you back from my cell."

"Prison?"

"*Phone*. You're good, Queenie. I'll play your song, and I'll call you. Okay?"

"Okay." I gave him my number and started to tremble. This was starting to feel a bit dangerous. I had to remind myself of myself. *I am a good person. I get my flowers in by Memorial Day. I do not avert my gaze from the flag during the playing of the national anthem.*

I turned on my radio and waited. Furniture store ad, then a car ad and tomorrow's weather. And then...Freddie. I smiled. Rasculine had come through for me. He said he would play my song, and he played my song. Seconds later, the phone rang.

"Hello?"

"Are you tuned in to WKIT?"

"Of course. Always."

"Is it helping?" Rasculine asked. "The song?"

I closed my eyes and listened to the lyrics, let them slide inside the very core of me to the place where I was raw and scared and aching. Oh, *please. Please don't cry,* I begged myself. *You have a sexy D.J. on the phone and everything.*

I swallowed hard. "Yes," I answered. "It helps. Thank you."

"Good. I aim to please." The sound of a car engine starting.

All at once, I realized that I loved him. It was so easy, to love somebody again! I decided I should probably find out more about him. Age, for starters.

"So how old are you?" Wait, did I really want to know that? He could be any age I imagined. I would let that alone. "Never mind," I said hastily.

"You don't have to tell me that." It didn't matter how old he was. Or what he looked like. He could very well have belly button lint and nose hair; I did not want to know. What mattered was that he was talking to me, and I loved him.

"All right." He sounded amused. "So are you ready to find somebody to love?"

Now there was a question I'd asked myself a few thousand times. "I don't know. I think so."

"Breakups are hard," he said, as if he was talking about a failed high school romance. "But you should get out there. Have you been dating at all?"

I hesitated. Had I? I didn't know if you could call looking at photos of worms, making out in the Goodwill parking lot and meeting someone in a men's room *dating*.

"Any prospects?"

No on Creepy Steve, no on Manch, and probably not on Tall Adidas, as I hadn't seen him in the bookstore since that one night. "Not really."

"Well, don't give up. I'm sure you'll find somebody."

Oh, I already have. I sank into the sofa and stretched out. Winston looked up from the floor. "It's trash night," I told Rasculine. I could feel my throat start to tighten.

"What?"

I could hear the clicking of his car blinker. "I had to take the trash out by myself tonight. I just hate being alone," I whispered.

"I'm sorry about that, uh...hey, what's your name, anyway?"

The thought occurred to me to make one up, but I needed this to be real. "Christine."

"No one's with you right now?"

"No." Hence, the phrase *I just hate being*

alone. "How long of a drive do you have?"

"About twenty minutes."

My throat closed again. I tried not to ask, tried my *damndest* not to ask, but the question seeped out. "Will you keep talking to me?"

"Sure. I like the sound of your voice. Very sexy."

"Thank you," I said, and the tears came. Winston lifted his head and looked at me. I smiled to make him think I was fine.

Rasculine's voice softened. "Do you want me to be with you, sexy Christine?'"

I didn't know what to answer. Yes, I did, because I loved him, but there was also the issue of not actually *knowing* him. And I wasn't sure when the kids would be getting home.

"What are you doing right now?" he asked.

"Sitting on the couch."

"Lie down and close your eyes."

I did as I was told.

"I want you to pretend I am there with you, sexy Christine. Okay?"

"Yes."

"Take your shirt off," Rasculine said. His breathing had quickened, and hearing this made my heart beat faster.

I am a good girl. I come to a complete stop at stop signs. I return my grocery cart to the carriage corral. I am more wholesome than threesome. But I need to do this.

I took off my shirt and tossed it on the floor.

"And now take off your bra. I want you to feel your breasts."

I cradled the phone between my chin and shoulder and began groping myself tentatively.

"Take off your pants, sexy Christine."

I wriggled out of my shorts and panties and they joined my shirt on the floor. Winston glanced up again, and I caught his eye. I hoped he would not think less of me.

"Are you naked?"

"Yes," I whispered.

"I want you to touch yourself," he said huskily. "Touch yourself, and pretend it's me."

I squeezed my eyes shut as the tears trickled down the sides of my face and into my ears. I slid my hand between my legs.

"You're hot. And beautiful. And you are not alone. I am right there making love to you, sexy Christine."

He was whispering into my ear. I could hear the sharp intake of breath and then his forceful exhale. I could feel him on top of me. My own breathing came in deep, shuddery gasps.

From his car, miles away, he was holding me. And when it was over, I thanked him. I would not tell Hank or Stella or Jess. I was not ashamed, but it needed to belong to me. I got up off the couch, slipped back into my clothes and motherhood, and waited for my daughters to come home.

CHAPTER NINETEEN: *Off Balance*

"Details," Stella said, with happy expectation,. "I want details." Our phone conversation had just begun, and already she was after me. I could visualize her basking in the comfort of her own solid relationship, sinking into a cozy chair which was undoubtedly now baby-fied with a set of plastic keys and a pacifier tucked into the cushion.

"There isn't anything to report."

"Chris. Come on. I need some excitement."

"Well, so do I." What did she think this was, some game? This was my life, for God's sake.

"What about Mr. Sneakers from the men's room at BAM? You know, the night of your bowel blitzkrieg?"

"I've only been there a couple times since and haven't seen him."

"Oh. That's too bad. But I guess it's just as well."

I felt my hackles, usually reserved for Dick, begin to stand at attention. "What do you mean?"

"Maybe you've been putting too much pressure on yourself. There's really plenty of time for you to date." Stella pondered this. "You know, you shouldn't worry about it. You have enough on your plate taking care of your kids right now, anyway."

What was this, invasion of the body snatchers? I could have sworn my mother was speaking through Stella. I braced myself for the phrase *it's not your time*.

146

My silence prompted a half-apology. "Chris, I'm not trying to tell you what to do. I just want you to be okay. Maybe it's the new mother syndrome—me trying to look out for everybody."

Her know-it-all attitude had activated my bitch button. "So Landon's probably not sleeping through the night yet?"

"Ha! He's been sleeping through the night for the past month. I'm telling you, this motherhood thing is not nearly as stressful as I thought it would be. And Graham is so helpful. We even argue over who gets to diaper him!"

How very, very nice. Dream husband, dream baby, dream life.

"I have to go," I said. "Got to get ready for the date I don't have tonight."

Stella sighed. "I pissed you off, didn't I? I'm sorry."

"No problem!" I told her, in a tone that clearly indicated otherwise.

"I really am sorry, Chris. Call me later, okay?"

I hung up and walked to the window to check on Carli and her friend who were swimming in the backyard. They were both on inner tubes on their hands and knees, rocking back and forth and riding the frothy waves they'd created. At least one child of mine was happy. Lily was sulking in her room after yet another fight we'd had about her dyeing her hair. She said it was summer, and no one would care. I told her that pink was an unnatural color, and that it didn't even fit with her personality. She yelled that she was "different" now. I told her I was different too, but you didn't see me going and dyeing my hair. (Instead, I had phone sex with disc jockeys.) And then she told me to stop feeling sorry for myself. I had stood there, stunned, and she burst into tears, ran in her room and slammed the door hard enough to loosen the hinges. I screamed at her to STAY THERE until she learned to treat me with RESPECT and SENSITIVITY.

I watched Carli and her friend a bit longer, hoping that their fun might be contagious. Unfortunately, I didn't catch it. I left the window and headed into the kitchen to make some lemonade. But instead of walking, I *wobbled*. A wave of dizziness cascaded over me. I clutched the bar in panic and sat down unsteadily on one of the stools. What if I fainted? Lily wouldn't know how to help me. And given the recent fight we'd had, she probably wouldn't *want* to.

I sat for a few moments, shaking and queasy. I needed to call Hank for reassurance. He was at work, but he would understand. He always did.

"What's going on, pumpkin? Aren't you supposed to be outside getting melanoma or something?"

"I'm dizzy."

"You mean, more than usual?"

"Shut up, I'm serious. I really felt like I was going to faint."

Hank sighed. "Oh, my...well, here we go. Vertigo can have a number of causes. We've done this one before. Remember the inner ear conditions? Meniere's disease, benign positional vertigo, vestibular neuronitis?"

I loved when he talked like this. It sounded so *medical*. Still, I wasn't satisfied. "But there's nothing wrong with my ears. I think it's something else."

"Of course you do. How about atrial flutter, benign paroxysmal positional vertigo, or orthostatis hypotension? Do you like the sounds of those better?"

148

"I guess," I said. "Could it be a brain tumor?" I shivered in anticipation of his response.

"Sure it could," said Hank cheerfully.

He must have been in a good mood to be so generous with me. He had probably gotten laid last night.

"Maybe it's shallow breathing from hyperventilation syndrome." I sighed.

"Wow, you must be a bit off if you're settling for *that* one. What's up?"

"I don't know, I just feel out of it. I still keep dreaming about weird things. Like last night, I had this dream about seeing that tall Adidas guy I met at BAM, only he was in *my* bathroom. Then Dick pounded on the door and told him not to get involved with me...he said, "'Christ, you'll have to reassure her 24/7 she's not dying, and then you'll want to kill her yourself!'"

"Oh, dear. Nasty, nasty, nasty."

"I know. Plus, I haven't really done anything this summer, and it's now almost over. And Lily hates me, and Dick is being one. I can't believe he's the father of my children. I just wish I'd known how he really was before I married him. I would have saved myself all this *shit*."

"Stop blaming yourself. I've told you, people don't always turn out to be who you think they are. It's like the time I saw my veterinarian at the lake, remember? Throwing rocks at the ducks to get them off his boat."

I had forgotten about that.

"And besides, you wouldn't have your beautiful girls if it wasn't for Richard. So two wonderful things came out of that marriage."

"I know," I sighed. "I'm just sick of not feeling like myself."

"You *aren't* yourself, pumpkin. Not yet. You have to figure out who Christine Kellen is, and what she wants. Not what your mother wants for you, but what *you* want for you. The thing is, you have to allow yourself to make mistakes. Because learning who you're not can help you figure out who you are."

And then something clicked.

"I'm good, aren't I?" asked Hank.

"Yes," I said. "You are very good. I love you for that. I'll stop by this weekend if you're around, okay?"

"Yup. Just don't go making any HUGE mistakes, all right, kitten?"

"All right." I made a kissing noise into the phone before saying goodbye and got up from the barstool to walk upstairs. Steadily, this time.

Lily's door, as usual, was shut, her bedroom pulsing with the sounds of rap music and intense keyboarding. I knocked lightly and opened the door, half-expecting to feel the rush of teenage hormones escape her bedroom and enter me, like some youthful elixir. As expected, she was surly in her greeting. "WHAT."

"Can I talk to you?"

I could hear her disgusted sigh and the creaking of her bed. The door opened, and she stared at me. Thin trails of mascara had snaked their way down her cheeks.

"If you really want to dye your hair, then do it."

Her mouth dropped open.

"I mean it. Maybe you need to find out if that's really you. You know how I feel, but I guess the important thing is to find out how *you* feel about it. Can I come in for a second?"

Lily looked at me warily but stepped aside to

let me enter. "Why did you change your mind?"

I sat down on her bed and patted the spot beside me as an invitation. She remained standing, arms crossed. I continued, undeterred. "I'm sorry about us not getting along and about all the stress. I guess part of me didn't want you to dye your hair because I just didn't want any more change. I want things to be like...steady, and straightforward. Do you know what I mean?"

Lily nodded, looking down at the floor.

"Part of me admires you, you know."

Her eyes darted up to my face to see if I was serious.

"Because you're willing to shake things up a little. I've never been much of a risk-taker. Can you imagine how Mimi would have reacted, if I had come home with pink hair?"

Her mouth twitched with the effort of holding back a smile.

"Anyway, I just wanted to let you know I'll respect your decision. It's your hair, even though technically I *made* you—"

Lily huffed and rolled her eyes.

"—but I don't want to fight with you anymore. And I want to be a cool mom," I said. To my dismay, I started to cry. "I'm sorry that I've felt sorry for myself," I blubbered. "I'll try to be better."

In two quick steps Lily was at my side, wrapping her arms around me. I sat on her bed and bawled as she kissed the top of my head.

"You're doing a good job, Mumma," she said softly.

"Thank you," I sniffed. "That means a lot." I pulled her onto my lap and was grateful she pretended to be as little as I needed her to be. "Lil?"

"Yeah?"

"Strawberry-blonde might be nice."

"MOM!"

"Okay," I sighed. "Okay. But you're telling Mimi. She scares me."

Some things never change.

CHAPTER TWENTY: *Bitter Taste*

I was on my way to Lily's first soccer game of the season when my cell phone rang. From the back seat, Carli said, "it's Lily," without looking up from the book she was reading. I was inclined to agree with her. Lily had (thankfully) abandoned her obsession to color her hair and had instead become almost apathetic about things. This had mutated into forgetfulness: books from school, cleats, chores around the house (the latter perhaps being an intentional choice). I answered the phone.

"Mom?"

"Hi, Lil."

"I started my period. Can you bring me some pads?"

She was the only almost-fourteen year old I knew who didn't wear tampons, due to her fear of toxic shock syndrome. Couldn't imagine where she'd gotten *that* from. I began to lecture her on being better prepared and then stopped myself. An understanding mother would just let that go. Then again, I wasn't perfect. "Why didn't you pack any in your sports bag?"

"MOM. I started early. Will you just bring me some, like right now?"

"Yes. Lily?"

"What?"

"Is your father there?"

Silence. I cringed. I shouldn't have asked, and it shouldn't have mattered. His attendance at the kids' events this year had been sporadic at best. Not only had he lost interest in our marriage, it appeared he had become less enamored with fatherhood, too.

"Never mind," I said. "It doesn't matter. I'll see you in a few minutes." I was not opposed to stopping; I was feeling a new case of sharp-toothed heartburn gnawing at me and needed some antacid.

At the convenience store, Carli went immediately to the candy rack for her usual Reese's peanut butter cup. I picked up some Rolaids and a package of Always (with wings) and went to the counter. The cashier was a twenty-something blond guy who looked like he needed a cigarette. For some reason, even at forty-three, I always felt embarrassed buying feminine hygiene products from a male. I cast my gaze on the floor. It was then that I saw the Adidas out of the corner of my eye. And froze when I realized who was on top of them.

"Well, hello, stranger," the voice said, and the voice had a smile in it.

I looked up. His caramel-colored eyes were warm.

"Yes, hi," I said, very aware that Carli was standing beside me. I could feel her curiosity begin to spark and flicker.

Tall Adidas kept smiling. What did he expect me to say? I turned to the cashier, rustled in my purse for money, and thrust a ten at him.

"Do you want a bag?" the cashier asked.

I stared at him. He must have known that the alternative would be walking around *without* a bag, carrying the maxi-pads with wings. Tall Adidas was standing there next to me and Carli, and we were all staring down at the package of Always pads.

"Yes, I would like a bag. Thank you very much, " I replied coolly. I looked at Tall Adidas. "These are for my daughter." Had I really just said that?

Carli gave me a sharp poke in the side.

"My *other* daughter," I corrected. "She's playing in a soccer game."

"Oh," said Tall Adidas. He stood looking down at me and nodded to Carli, still smiling.

"Well. I have to get to her game. Nice seeing you again," I said, and took Carli by the hand.

"Yes, nice seeing you. What's it been, a few months?"

"Something like that."

"Well, maybe we'll run into each other again sometime."

"Maybe," I said. He had been witness to my bathroom explosion, and now he'd seen me buy maxi-pads. Perhaps I could invite him to my next Pap smear.

"On second thought, let's make that a more likely possibility. Why don't I give you my card...just in case you need an uplifting experience." Tall Adidas reached into his pocket for his wallet.

Uplifting experience? How presumptuous of him! I took the card without looking at him, and in doing so dropped the bag I was carrying. I bent down to pick it up and was face-to-feet with his Adidas. They were very large.

As we stepped outside, Carli tugged at my hand. "Who was that?"

"Just...someone I met in the spring," I said. "At Books-A-Million."

"Is he like your boyfriend?"

I looked down at her. Her eyes were wide, vulnerable. The sunlight was bright and I could see little flecks of green and gold in her irises. And beyond the color I saw the uncertainty and confusion, the grief and pain from the divorce that I believed still rattled inside her. My heartburn worsened. It could very well be Gastro-Esophageal Reflux Disease. *Severe long-standing GERD can lead to damage of the esophagus.* Which I knew could lead to scarring and narrowing. Which could lead to a condition called Barrett's Esophagus. Which was a risk factor for the development of esophageal cancer.

I was standing there developing cancer right in front of Carli in the parking lot of a convenience store. I ripped open the package of Rolaids and crammed four of them into my mouth. "No," I said firmly, crunching the tablets. Little fragments flew from my mouth. Carli blinked. "He is not my boyfriend. I don't have a boyfriend. Now let's get to your sister's game."

We drove, the car filled with the smell of peanut butter. It had been surprising running into Tall Adidas again. He had seemed genuinely glad to see me. He was truthfully quite good-looking, despite being follicularly-challenged. And those sneakers... bigger than I'd remembered.

Sneakers. I would need to start jogging. Keep my body in prime dating shape, and for when I'd have sex again. Dick was undoubtedly getting it on a regular basis. His sexual tastes probably had changed along with the rest of him. The heartburn jabbed at me again, red-hot. I gave myself a mental shake. Anger did not bring healing; I knew this. But sometimes I just liked it. I liked it a whole lot.

I could feel something burning in my throat and swallowed. The acrid taste remained. I swallowed again and gripped the steering wheel tighter. Once they operated on my esophagus, I wouldn't be able to eat. I would not know the pleasures of creamy-sweet Reese's peanut butter cups. I would be desperate for chocolate. Unable to

156

speak, I would write a note to the nurse begging her to put a taste on my tongue. She would be unsympathetic, and I would be left there to lie in a hospital bed until one of my kids visited and snuck me a piece.

Lily was running toward the car. We had made it to the school parking lot, and I didn't even remember driving. I twisted around to see if Carli was still with me. She looked at me, her brow wrinkled, a dot of chocolate on her upper lip.

I handed the bag to Lily.

"Thanks," she said breathlessly, and added, "Dad is here."

I waved my hand at her. I was not about to aggravate my esophageal cancer by more anger. "That's good," I answered generously. "He's your father. He should be at all of your games."

"And he brought his girlfriend."

The acid sizzled in my throat. I had known this moment was coming, when I would have to see her, but why at one of my kids' games? I shuddered at the anticipated awkwardness, at the rekindled feelings of vulnerability and shame from that night.

"Mom?"

"I'm okay. I wish—listen, just hurry up and use the bathroom before your coach wonders what you're doing."

Lily hesitated.

"Go," I said. "And good luck in your game."

I watched her run to the locker room, her ponytail swinging. I checked my face in the rearview mirror and smoothed the stray pieces of hair around my face. "Come on, Carl," I announced. "Let's go watch some soccer."

Together we got out of the car and walked toward the bleachers. I smiled and nodded at the other parents, my arm lightly across the back of Carli's shoulders. I could feel the apprehension from my scalp to my toenails. I hoped it wasn't visibly emanating from me, like when the air shimmers above the pavement on a searing hot day. I would need to remain cool, especially for my children's sake. I would tame my trepidation, stuff my stress, and act as though it was perfectly fine to be at my daughter's soccer game with my ex-husband and the woman we both made out with.

They were sitting in red and white canvas chairs across the field at the center line. I watched them applaud as Lily's team took the field to warm up.

"Carli, do you see Mimi and Poppa anywhere?" Now that they had officially moved, my parents never missed a game. They often brought the video camera, and my mother would do the play-by-play while my father filmed.

She scanned the field. "No, but I see Daddy. And Eleanor."

I felt myself go rigid. Carli knew her name. "You met her?"

"Yeah. She came over to Daddy's when I had dinner with him. She brought a funny dessert—jam roly-poly."

And did she roly-poly around with Daddy afterwards?

"It was good," Carli continued. "And she's really nice."

"She is?"

"Yeah, she even showed me how to do this cool braid in my hair, and gave me a bracelet."

She had touched my child's hair. That was a mother thing to do. Not a kinky slutty British massage therapist thing to do. "Carli, why didn't you tell me any of this?"

She shrugged. "I don't know, I forgot. Can I get some M & M's?"

"You already had a Reese's." I was still trying to process this new information. I decided I didn't have the stamina to argue with her. I needed to put all my energies into looking like everything was hunky-dory, peachy keen, roly-poly. "But yes, go ahead." I handed her a dollar bill and then pointed to the concession stand. "Look, there's Mimi and Poppa. Go find out where they're sitting, and I'll be over after I use the bathroom." I had forgotten to pee before I left the house.

"Thanks, Mumma!" She skipped off to see her grandparents.

Lily jogged past me as I headed into the school. Her forehead was creased in confusion. "What are you doing?"

"Needed to pee."

"Probably should have been better prepared," she smirked.

Touché.

Washing my hands in the bathroom, I felt my heartburn begin to subside. I took a long, deep breath. It would be all right. My mother would see to it that we sat as far away from the new couple as possible. I would just enjoy Lily's game, and I wouldn't need to even look at—

Her. Standing right in front of me.

"Hallow, Christine. How AHH you?" Eleanor was standing much too close to me, as in, within the same country. She was wearing her hair longer and her neckline lower. The twins were even bigger than I'd remembered. Had they grown?

"SPLENdid day for a futball game, don't you think?"

Football?

She corrected herself, laughing. "Oh, royt...you people call it soccah."

I stood there, unable to speak. What was it with me and awkward moments in bathrooms? I knew I needed to say something. "Yes. We do." My voice was shrill. I had so hoped it would not be shrill.

She took a step closer. I caught a scent of French vanilla, and every muscle in my body steeled. "I've been looking fo-wud to seeing Lily play. You ray-lee have such fahntastic kids."

I did not need to hear that from her. I knew they were fantastic, but she had no business discovering that for herself. I swallowed hard against the acidic taste in my throat. It felt surreal to be standing here with her, almost as if we were in two separate dimensions, and she was penetrating mine: this bathroom, Lily's game, my life. It felt as though there wasn't enough air for both of us.

"Christine, I hope we can oll be friends one day...put the pahst in the pahst where it belongs."

Friends? Like, let's go out for coffee and chat about the good old days, the memory of that time when we were all naked together and my husband took pictures...

"Are you out of your fucking mind?"

Her eyes widened, her full lips parted. I hadn't intended to drop the f-bomb, but something needed to puncture the unbearable balloon of tension.

"You and my husband—excuse me, EX-husband—humiliated me! I not only had to say goodbye to my marriage, I had to say goodbye to trust, to feeling safe, to my whole pathetic little naïve world. And I really liked my pathetic little

160

naïve world! I didn't want *any* of this—not the threesome, not the pictures, not the divorce. You and Richard don't seem to get that. He isn't even being the father he should be. My 'fahntastic' children deserve better. *I* deserve better. Now if you'll excuse me, I'm going to go watch a fucking FOOTBALL game!"

My entire chest felt engulfed in flames. I wanted to spit my acid indigestion at her, watch it drip down her forehead and splash onto her cheek, making lines in what was undoubtedly CoverGirl Simply Ageless foundation. Maybe it would even burn.

Two bright spots appeared on Eleanor's cheeks. She closed her mouth and walked into one of the bathroom stalls. I left before I had to hear her pee.

On the way out, I looked over at the elementary school down the hill, where a few kids were on the swingset. I filled my eyes with their innocence. I felt rubbery, boneless, very Gumby-like. If the children on the playground had known, they could have tugged on my limbs and stretched me across the jungle gym. A mother passed me, walking with her little boy. I fought the urge to grab him by the front of his shirt and tell him never to have a threesome and then take pictures of it. Ever!

It hadn't felt good, losing control like that. I needed to focus on Lily's game—her present, not my past, and hope that my future was going to taste sweeter.

CHAPTER TWENTY-ONE: *Hard to Swallow*

The kids and I are driving up the middle of a steep road, and suddenly there is Richard, slaloming downhill on a skateboard. We swerve, trying to avoid him. Or maybe we are trying to hit him. He keeps coming toward us, and it is as if we are in a life-sized video game. I can see the pockets of sweat on his t-shirt as he curves around our car. It is as though he doesn't even see us, or won't see us. He passes us and looks like he's having the time of his life on this skateboard. Within seconds, he is at the bottom of the hill, and I can't see him anymore.

My mother's phone call woke me up at 9:07 on Saturday morning. I was convinced she still enjoyed getting me out of bed. When I was young, she used to come into my bedroom and pull up my shade (the rudest of all awakenings), giving it a good strong tug so that it shot to the top of the window, rattling its cylinder, and my nerves.

"Christine? Are you still in bed?"

I covered the mouthpiece and cleared my throat to rid it of sleep. "No."

I could hear the frown in her voice. "What are the kids doing?"

A pang of guilt. I didn't know, since I'd been sleeping. "I think they're downstairs watching TV." I waited for the disapproving pause, which came.

"So what's been going on?"

I stretched my left arm over my head, wincing as my shoulder cracked. Winston yawned from the end of the bed. I smiled at him. *He* never minded

162

when I slept late. "Not much," I said.

This seemed to please her. "Well, you know your father and I are always available if you'd like some company. We'd be happy to take you or the girls out for dinner tonight. You need your family around you, Christine. I'm not saying you shouldn't have *urges,* even *sexual* ones, but I guarantee you'll be glad you waited to start dating."

When *would* it be acceptable for me to date, according to my mother...after the kids were grown? Carli wouldn't be an adult for eight more years. If I didn't date until Carli was out of the house, my vagina would practically be all shriveled up! And then what would be the point?

"Your children need you right now, Christine," my mother was saying. "They need *all* of you. No distractions."

I started to retort and then stopped myself. Arguing with my mother was fruitless. My father had once secretly told me about the two possible outcomes of arguing with my mother: either she will be right, or you will be wrong. I was determined not to let her get the best of me. This topic of dating was going to dry up like an unused vagina.

As my mother droned on (...*positive female role model... be strong within yourself... good example for your daughters... Maya Angelou...),* I reached for the water bottle on my nightstand, took a drink, and swallowed. Or tried to.

"Christine? What was that noise?"

I was choking. On *water.* This had never happened to me before. ***CAUTION!*** *Know Cancer's Seven Warning Signals! Indigestion or **difficulty in swallowing**.* Sweet Jesus, I had the second half of the letter **I**!

Spluttering, I opened my mouth and gagged.

163

Water and saliva ran down my chin and onto my nightgown. Winston cocked his head and looked at me curiously. I took a few long inhales and was horrified that these breaths had a sound. Like a donkey being tortured.

"Are you all right? Do you want me to call 9-1-1?" My mother's tone had turned almost frantic.

"EEEEEEaawwww," I groaned. Winston jumped off the bed and ran downstairs.

"Christine! I'm going to hang up and call an ambulance!"

"No—" I gasped. I could feel my breathing start to return to normal. "I'm...all...right." I took a few deep shuddering breaths and reached for the Kleenex box so I could wipe my mouth. I had to be brave with my mother, move beyond the vulnerable, helpless little girl I'd always been. *I was woman.* Hear me roar! But inside, I was whimpering, *I could have died! I could have choked to death on water and Dick wouldn't have been here to save me. The bastard!*

"Oh, Christine," my mother gasped, "you scared me. You have no idea how terrifying that was!"

Carli ran into my bedroom and pounced on my bed. "Hi, Mumma! FINALLY, you're awake!"

I covered the mouthpiece.

She snuggled up next to me, smelling of maple syrup with a dash of orange juice. "Who are you talking to?"

"Mimi."

"Let me say hi!" She tore the phone from my hands.

I swallowed to prove that I still could. It felt normal, but that certainly didn't mean anything. The choking incident could easily happen again. What had caused it? There was a plethora of possibilities. Yes, the water could have gone down the wrong way, the wrong "pipe" as some called it, but difficulty in swallowing was a symptom of many serious diseases, too, such as MS, ALS, larynx cancer, and Huntington's. The latter I had stumbled across during my internet research on my bothersome symptom of *difficulty concentrating*. I learned that Huntington's was a degenerative disease with a poor prognosis, affecting people in their 40's and 50's. I was at a prime age for this illness.

Carli's voice yanked me out of my self-diagnosing. "Mumma. Mimi wants to talk to you."

Reluctantly, I took back the phone. I did not want to hear any more of how this wasn't my time. I might not even have much time *left*. I wanted to cup it in my hands like a precious sparkling jewel. And my mother was trying to tell me it wasn't mine.

"Christine?"

"Yes."

"Are you sure you're all right?"

No. "I'm fine."

"Your father and I were thinking of taking the girls shopping with us. We could stay overnight in a hotel, and you could have a weekend to yourself." She emphasized the *yourself*, as in, no men.

I swallowed. Dick hadn't taken Lily or Carli overnight for the past month. Even though I felt he was shirking his responsibility, I was quite content to always have them in the house with me—dependent on it, even. It felt safe to know that just down the hall, there were two living, breathing people who loved me. Sometimes I'd let Carli sleep with me. Sometimes I would even ask her to.

"I'll think about it," I said.

"It would be good for the girls to get away.

You'd have time to be alone and perhaps try to *gather* yourself. Do some meditating—take it to the next level and *pray*, Christine. Work on making yourself a stronger person, so you can be a better mother. Think about it."

My throat tightened. "I have to go." I spoke pleasantly, because Carli was lying on the bed, and I thought it might be a bit alarming for her to see the telephone fly across the room and slam against the wall.

You're quite a few years away from your time. But these days belonged to me, too.

Walking downstairs and into the family room, I saw Lily clacking away on her laptop. I ruffled her hair as I passed. She grabbed my arm, and I stiffened when I realized she probably resented being treated like a little girl. I started to apologize, and then she kissed my hand and went back to her typing without looking up.

I could do this. I could be a good mother *and* have my time, too, even if my neurological disease was going to cause facial muscle spasms, apathy and progressive mental deterioration. Tall Adidas would have been a possibility, if he hadn't been so presumptuous. *Call me if you need an uplifting experience.* Did I still have his card? I didn't even know his name. I went to the closet for my purse, took out my wallet and found his card sandwiched between a wrinkled five dollar bill and a pack of Trident White.

In bold black letters was the company name EAST SHORE ELEVATORS. There were two phone numbers below this. At the bottom in red was *Gavin Treworgy, Sales Representative.*

I stood staring at his card. Call *me if you need an uplifting experience.* He sold elevators.

I felt something tugging at the corner of my mouth. Maybe it was a facial spasm.

But it could have been a smile.

CHAPTER TWENTY-TWO: *Hyper Tension*

So I decided that an uplifting experience was exactly what I needed. After leaving Lily and Carli with my parents (under the guise I'd be meeting Jess for dinner), after promising Carli I would be home to put her to bed, and after one wrong left turn and overshooting his driveway, I arrived at Gavin's. I hadn't been able to imagine what his house would look like, and yet this fit: a dormered white Cape with blue shutters, a black eagle over the front door, and silver-blue junipers flanking the steps. Unlike the neighbors' meticulous lawns, Gavin's grass was dotted here and there with a few vagabond patches of crabgrass, which somehow made me like him more. As I entered his walkway, I couldn't help but smile at the orange and yellow chrysanthemums in the black kettle planters. Sexist of me, perhaps, but still.

I was careful to keep my expectations for this evening in check. I had already determined that I would not sleep with him, no matter how much he begged, and no matter how much I liked thinking of how much he might beg. Granted, it had been a long time. Months on top of months. I hoped I would be able to control myself. And I hoped he would be able to control *him*self, especially since I was wearing my clingy white shirt with the rawhide ties across the bodice which whispered *wild, wild West*. I had even left the ties loose and dangling. An unpleasant thought occurred to me. He might think of *me* as loose and dangling. This was something I hadn't considered. What if he was a nymphomaniac? Or worse, a rapist? I didn't even *know* him, and here I was, ready to go in his house where he could do anything to me and no one would—

The door opened, and Gavin was standing there smiling with a towel in his hand, his hair tousled and damp. I put my palm against his and squeezed a little harder than usual, to let him know I was not to be taken lightly.

"You're early," he said. "I just got out of the shower." His gaze traveled down the front of my unzipped jacket and back up to my eyes. "You look nice. I like that shirt. You never told me you were a cowgirl."

Wild West! He was thinking wild West! I had to change the mood, and quickly. "My daughter bought this for me. For Mother's Day." A lie, but at least he'd be forced to think of me as maternal.

"Well, she has very good taste. Come in."

My heart was banging like an overloaded washing machine. I followed Gavin through the tiled foyer into the living room. Burgundy recliner, brass lamps, navy plaid sofa, oak coffee table. It all looked very normal. But that was what rapists wanted you to think.

"Can I get you a glass of white wine, or a Corona?"

So he wanted to get me drunk. He certainly wasn't wasting any time. My chest tightened; my breath came in short spurts. I hoped Gavin wouldn't notice. Rapists preyed on the weak and vulnerable.

"I also have some Diet Coke, if you'd rather have that."

And now he was insinuating I was fat. I asked for a glass of water. I settled myself on the sofa while Gavin went into the kitchen. My symptoms were beginning to worry me. I was sure my blood pressure was elevated. *Symptoms of hypertension include headache, dizziness, tinnitus, fast heartbeat, chest pain or pressure.*

Gavin appeared with my water, a lemon wedge perched on the rim of the glass. He sat beside me on the sofa and grinned. I smiled back, grateful that he couldn't see the health warnings flashing inside my head.

"Is this weird for you?" Gavin was asking me. His face had taken on an earnest expression.

I sipped at my water. "A little," I admitted. "It's hard getting back into the dating thing."

"Who says this is a date?"

Startled, I looked up at him and realized he was teasing. I liked the way the skin around his eyes crinkled when he smiled.

"So you were married," I said.

"Yes. Twelve years."

"But no children?"

"No. We couldn't have any. We tried for the last five years. In vitro and the whole works. She had two miscarriages. We thought of adopting, but she didn't want to go that route, and by then it was too late, anyway."

"Too late?"

"She'd moved on."

"To another man?"

"To another woman."

Oh. Now there was something I hadn't expected. "I'm sorry."

He waved a hand at me. "It's all right, I don't have any hard feelings. It wasn't her fault. She hid it for a long time. It wasn't like it was a choice for her. More like allowing herself to realize it."

I grew bolder. "Have you had any other relationships?"

"A couple, but nothing too serious. I hadn't met the right person."

He'd said *hadn't* instead of *haven't*.

"Are you finding it hard to trust again?"

I was taken aback. He sounded more like a therapist than an elevator salesman. "A little."

"My situation was different, I guess. It wasn't so much me that was lacking but my gender, whereas your husband picked another woman he thought met his needs. That must have really done a number on your self-concept."

And now he sounded like a man: cluelessly insensitive. My pulse throbbed. What were the other symptoms of high blood pressure? Edema was one. I would have to check my ankles for swelling. "May I use your bathroom?"

"Sure. Down the hall on the right. I'll put the finishing touches on the mashed potatoes and we'll eat."

Gavin's bathroom was surprisingly clean for a single man. I winced as I thought of the splotches of toothpaste on my own faucet. I fought the urge to look in his medicine cabinet, and lost. Generic ibuprofen, extra-strength Tylenol, contacts lens solution, Q-tips, two pairs of nail clippers (small and large), a thermometer, a prescription bottle...I got on my tiptoes to read the label: *Propecia* (finasteride 1 mg, taken daily with a full glass of water). So he did know he was balding. A sigh of relief as I scanned the rest of the shelves. Breathe Right strips for nasal congestion (size large), Vick's Vapo-rub (what was he, ten?), an Oral-B toothbrush still in the box, a half-empty bottle of mouthwash, a package of Sport-strip bandaids and a small jar of Eucerin cream. So he didn't seem to have any major medical issues. Which reminded me.

I lifted up my pant legs and pulled down my socks to check my ankles for swelling. They looked the same as they always did, but I could still feel the blood pounding in my ears.

Looking in the mirror, I tightened the rawhide ties of my shirt ever so slightly and headed for the kitchen. Immediately, I stiffened at the scent of the candle burning. French vanilla. I'd have to forgive him for that; he didn't know. Besides, there were other more palatable odors: something seafood-ish, and the scent of hot rolls.

Gavin was frowning as he opened the oven door. "The popovers are a little overdone. But the crabcakes should make up for it."

I looked at the potatoes in the cobalt blue bowl on the counter. "What's the orange stuff on top?"

"Paprika," he said, giving me a puzzled smile.

I blushed, and my mother's voice was hissing in my ear. *If you'd read* Real Simple, *you'd know about things like spices!*

Gavin leaned down to speak in my ear, as if to share a secret. "And the white stuff underneath is the potato."

We ate, sharing alma maters, on-the-job stories, where we'd spend Thanksgiving. The jazz music playing masked the awkward sounds of chewing. Given my current anxiety level, I found myself fighting to keep my gag reflex in check. The thought of choking in front of a prospective boyfriend took center stage. I took tiny, delicate bites of food, chewing carefully until each morsel turned to mush in my mouth. Consequently, it took me about forty-five minutes to clear half my plate. Gavin didn't seem to notice. I cursed myself for not bringing anything to the meal. I hadn't needed *Real*

Simple to tell me this was proper etiquette. But he had thought of everything, from the pats of butter on small white dishes, to the steaming popovers nestled in the cloth-lined basket, to the beautiful centerpiece vase of pink roses, fern and baby's breath.

"That's yours to take home," he said, watching me admire it.

"Oh, I can't do that!"

"I've never known a woman to refuse flowers." He smiled.

I smiled back, but inside I was wary. It sounded as though he had lots of experience buying women flowers. Which would mean he was a player. Which was exactly the wrong type of man for me. And what were his intentions for this date? Did he want something I wasn't ready to give him? I curled my toes inside my shoes. My chest felt constricted and heavy. Was that ringing in my ears? Ringing...telephone. I needed to check in with Lily and Carli. They would undoubtedly be anxious to talk to me. Carli, especially.

I put my fork and knife across the top of my plate. "Thank you for dinner," I said. "Everything was delicious."

Gavin stood up and began to clear the table. "I'm glad you liked it. But I hope you're not planning on leaving so soon."

Was that a question, or a threat in disguise? The blood thrummed in my ears. I had to remain calm, especially if he was up to something. "No," I said lightly. "I was just getting my phone to call my children." That statement would serve two purposes: to remind him again that I was a mother and therefore virtually sacred, and to let him know I could use my cell phone to call for help if needed.

I felt a bit more confident. I put my dishes in the sink and went into the living room to make my phone call. I let it ring four times, and the machine picked up. I hung up and tried again. This time, Carli answered, out of breath. "Hi, Mumma."

"Hello, sweet pea! How are you?"

"Fine. Are you still at that guy's house?"

I cringed. I had not wanted to lie to the girls and tell them I was going out with Jess when I wasn't. It felt wrong. My mother...she was a different story. I hoped she hadn't overheard Carli—*no*. I would not think that way. I was not twelve. I was a big girl, in the house of a person with a penis.

"Yes," I told her. "We just had dinner."

"Was it good?"

"Yes, very."

"When are you coming home?"

I smiled. She had missed me. "Probably pretty soon."

A pause. "Can you stay a little later? Mimi brought a movie, and she's going to make us root beer floats."

Stay a little later? As in, *we don't miss you one bit. Spend more time with a man you don't really know who could be a rapist.* While we have root beer floats.

"Sure!" I said. "I'm having a good time, too. I'll see you later."

"Christine?" My mother's voice. "Did I overhear Carli saying you were at a man's house?"

Deep breath. *Big girl, big girl.* I could do this. "Yes. I'm having dinner." My voice did not waver. Much.

"I was under the impression you were going out with Jess. Who is this man?"

"Someone I met at a bookstore." I trembled

with pride at having told her. At that moment I could have taken down Chuck Norris.

"Who is he? What does he do?"

I could have said he was the man behind Habitat for Humanity and it wouldn't have mattered. "His name is Gavin, and he sells elevators."

My mother laughed softly. "A *salesman.* You picked one of *those* again."

My heart leapt inside of me as I prepared to stand up for myself. "I think I am capable of choosing who I date."

"I don't care for that disrespectful tone of voice, Christine."

"Sorry."

"Again, that tone."

"I'm sorry, Mother."

"That's better," she said briskly. "You needed to think this through a bit more. Sometimes people need guidance with these sorts of things." The triumph in her voice was unmistakable. Triumph, because in her eyes, when I'd wandered away from her, I had picked another salesman. I had failed—just as she had known I would.

I trembled again. Chuck Norris folded his arms and shook his head at me, laughing. The retorts exploded inside my head, brilliantly colorful fireworks with no sound. I told her I'd be home to put the kids to bed.

Her tone was light and congenial because I had been defeated. "All right, Christine. See you soon."

Hanging up the phone, I walked back into the kitchen where Gavin was wiping the table. "Guess I don't have to leave just yet," I told him. "My kids are having too much fun with their grandmother."

He smiled broadly. "I'll have to personally thank her." He draped the dishcloth over the faucet and motioned for me to follow him into the living room. We sat on the couch. I could feel my carotid artery pulsing, and the tiniest ache taking hold in my lower back. The beginning of kidney disease.

"So," I began.

"So."

"You're a good cook."

"Thank you."

"And this is a really nice house."

"Thank you again."

A faint pounding in my temple. Either a headache starting, or he had slipped something in my drink. I'd heard about date rape drugs, but I never thought I'd have to worry about it, because after all, I had been married, and protected from bad things.

Gavin reached over and began stroking my hand. His fingers were long and beautiful. I swallowed, praying I would not choke on my own saliva.

"May I kiss you, Christine?"

I nodded and closed my eyes. And then I felt his lips on mine, soft and tentative. I parted my lips to receive his tongue, put my hands at the back of his head and pulled him closer. He tasted of Corona and peppermint. And I felt...nothing. I could have been kissing an anatomically-correct mannequin.

His arms went around me. I had to slow things down. I spoke against his lips. "The mashed potatoes were really good. How did you get them so creamy?"

"Mayonnaise," he mumbled, and continued to kiss me.

Did high blood pressure stifle one's libido? I

continued to feel nothing for him. What the hell was wrong with me? He was attractive, despite the balding thing. He was kind and funny, and he had chrysanthemums on his front steps. The throbbing in my temple intensified. I tensed, waiting for the vein to pop free from my forehead and flail around like a garden hose at full blast.

He sat back and looked at me. "Are you okay?" His voice sounded sincere, without the underlying *I hope so, because I want to get laid.*

"I don't know."

He leaned forward to kiss my forehead. I flinched.

"Let's just leave it like this for now," he said softly. "Okay?"

"Okay," I said. I didn't know if I was more relieved or insulted. Was I not worth the effort?

"Do you want me to put in a movie?"

I shook my head. "I think I'll get going."

"Would you mind if I emailed you tonight?"

That sounded safe enough. We walked into the kitchen, and I wrote my email address on the back of an envelope.

He helped me into my jacket, I thanked him again and we hugged, my face pressing into his chest. I smelled the clean cotton of his shirt, a hint of deodorant. But I felt nothing. I clenched my fists, and my nails dug tiny half circles into my palms. I was relieved that it hurt a little. At least I could feel *that.*

Gavin waved from the doorstep and stood watching me as I drove down his street. I saw him in my rearview mirror, still standing until I turned the corner.

Later, after the kids were in bed, I checked my email. There were two messages. The first, from

Dick:

I'm going to be out of town next weekend and won't be able to take the kids. I'll plan on having them next week.

I hit reply, wrote "PRIORITIES...!" and smacked the send button.

The second email was from Gavin. *Christine, I had a nice time tonight and hope you did, too. There is something I want to say to you: don't expect so much on the first meeting with someone. It is nice to think when you meet someone for the first time, sparks fly, rockets explode and you fall in love. That mostly happens in the movies. A relationship takes time, and love takes time. There has to be chemistry, but even that has to be wanted. You are at a point in your life where you are afraid of relationships, because you have been hurt very deeply by someone you loved. You are not quite ready to move on emotionally, and that is understandable. It takes time to put the past in the past. It is hard to start a fire with wet wood, and your wood is still too wet. I don't know if you've considered counseling, but it may be helpful.*

I enjoy talking to you and hope that we will remain friends. If we can't, so be it, but I think we do have at least that kind of connection. Feel free to call me if you ever need to hear a friendly voice. Take care, Gavin.

I sat a moment, contemplating his words, and decided, finally, that most of it was bullshit. He didn't even know me, yet he felt justified in telling me what to do. I already had a mother, thank you very much. Wet wood, my ass. I could start a damn fire any time I wanted, with whomever I wanted. I didn't need him, or his know-it-all advice.

My phone rang. Gavin. I hesitated, then

answered. It would probably be best to just end it tonight.

"Hello, Christine." His voice was rich and warm, like a cup of cocoa. I felt a tiny stirring in my belly. No. I would not take a sip.

"Hi. I got your email, and—"

"I was just calling to see if you were all right."

"Oh. Well, thanks. I'm fine. I got your email, and I—"

"I hope you don't think I was presumptuous. I just didn't want you to be frustrated that there was no fireworks display tonight."

"I wasn't frustrated."

"You were clenching your fists when I hugged you."

He had known this?

"I felt them against my back. I thought for a second you were going to punch me." His tone was teasing, but gentle.

"No."

"Well, good. I just want you to know I'd like to wait in the wings for you, if that's all right. For when you're ready."

I may never be ready. Sometimes as I'm waking up, before I open my eyes, I reach out to touch Richard. And I still expect him to be there.

"I won't pressure you, Christine. I can't really explain it, but I don't want to let this go. I don't want to let you go."

I could not speak.

"Besides," he added gently. "You forgot your flowers."

End it. It hasn't even really begun, so it should be easy. He is a nice man. He deserves better than a hypochondriac with trust issues.

I opened my mouth, and deep inside my

chest, a warm spreading feeling. But not a heart attack. "Okay," I said. "Maybe we can wait for me together."

CHAPTER TWENTY-THREE: S.O.B.

You might say the ear-nose-and-throat doctor examining Carli was bland. But that would have been an understatement. He had the personality of duct tape, only slightly less engaging. He was vanilla pudding, white rice and the eggshell paint landlords use for apartments, all rolled into a fifty-ish, brown-haired, dull-eyed, bespectacled, pale-skinned male. But he was a doctor, and therefore deserving of respect.

Carli had been dealing with laryngitis for the past two weeks. Her pediatrician wanted her vocal cords checked by an ENT for nodules (code word: tumors) or inflammation. So we were referred to Dr. Bland.

Carli sat in the exam chair clutching the arm rests, flashing me smile after smile, as the doctor stood silently flipping through her file. Doctors' offices always made me nervous, and I tried to concentrate on my breathing, which made me even more uneasy, because this made me concentrate on my breathing. And I was having shortness of breath. Lately, I'd been taking quick, shallow breaths followed by a few deep ones, which only seemed to make matters worse. I worried about my lungs, or my heart, or on bad days, my entire cardiovascular system. To make matters worse, the holidays were almost upon us, and I anticipated Dick demanding the kids to share both Thanksgiving and Christmas with him and his tacky ornament.

Dr. Bland moved his eyes over toward me in what looked like a tremendous effort. "Has she ever had a laryngoscopy?"

Her name is Carli. Why wasn't he looking at her? "No," I said, and gave Carli a wink. She smiled again.

"Laryngitis can be caused by a number of things. Excessive use of the voice, infections, inhaled irritants, or gastroesophageal reflux."

"Well, she does talk a lot," I grinned. There, that ought to get at least a facial twitch out of him.

Nothing.

"I'm going to start with an indirect laryngoscopy," he continued. "This involves looking down her throat with a long-handled mirror to check her vocal cords." He addressed Carli. "Do you think you can handle that?"

She stopped smiling. "I guess so," she said slowly. "Does it hurt?"

"It is a painless procedure, although you might feel like gagging. But you will need to suppress that urge so that I am able to get a good look down your throat."

Carli looked over at me. Her face had paled. I smiled brightly and made myself breathe slowly and evenly. Her stress was contagious.

"That will be all right, won't it, honey? The doctor's going to take a peek down your throat, but it isn't going to hurt. So you'll just need to sit very still. Okay?"

Dr. Bland looked over at the table and frowned. "Excuse me. The nurse forgot to get my headgear." He left the room.

Carli waited for a few seconds and then whispered, "Mumma. He's not very nice."

"I know, sweetheart," I whispered back. "But he's supposed to be good. And this won't take very long. Just try to sit very still and it will be over with."

The doctor returned, wearing a light at the front of his head. He looked like he was ready to head into a coal mine. He picked up a strip of gauze from a silver tray on the table. "This is to wrap around your tongue to keep it out of my way."

Carli looked over at me, wide-eyed. The chair seemed to swallow her up. Dr. Bland stepped toward her and told her to stick out her tongue. I wanted to follow his instructions, only not for medical reasons.

The effect of Carli's tongue sticking out of her mouth would have been comical, had she not looked so vulnerable. I wanted to lunge at him. *Look* at her, I wanted to yell. This was my baby! Did he not understand? Did he not see the subtle rise and fall of her chest, the dilation of her pupils, the flaring of her nostrils? Did he not see what he was doing to her?

He picked up a tongue depressor, inserted it into her mouth and reached for his long-handled mirror. I began to feel lightheaded.

Carli gagged and grabbed his hand. The tongue depressor fell to the floor. The doctor's face hardened.

"I-I'm sorry," I blurted, and got out of my chair to pick up the oversized popsicle stick. "She didn't mean to." I smiled encouragement at Carli, but it was not convincing. Her eyes began to brim with tears.

You son-of-a-bitch! How dare you do this to her!

"Let's try that again," Dr. Bland said. "You'll need to sit still. If you keep gagging, I'll have to spray some anesthetic on your throat and up your nose. It doesn't taste very good."

His last words had an edge to them. I did not appreciate that edge. He leaned in with another tongue depressor, and I watched as the tears began to roll down Carli's cheeks. She gagged again.

It was the sigh and the face that did it. Dr. Bland expelled a long blast of air *(he* had no issues with shortness of breath) and tightened his lips. He looked over at me, like, *can't you control her?*

"Can I see you in the hallway?" I found myself saying sharply. It was the tone I'd used many times with misbehaving students.

Dr. Bland's expression turned to one of surprise. He put down his instruments and followed me out of the room. I was glad he didn't close the door; I wanted my daughter to hear this.

I tried to lengthen each breath that I took. I couldn't afford to pass out in front of him. Something told me he'd enjoy that.

"Do you have children?" I asked.

His cheek muscles tightened. "Yes."

"Well, I'm surprised to hear that. Because you certainly don't act like a father."

He blinked rapidly behind his glasses.

"You have absolutely no bedside manner," I continued. The voice coming out of my mouth was calm and cool. This amazed me. "You could have put her at ease, but you made her uncomfortable, and you didn't talk to her. Do you even know her name?"

He opened and closed his mouth three, four times. I could hear the air whistling through his nose.

"It's Carli," I said. "And I'll plan to find another specialist. This appointment is over."

*****

"I did a good thing," I told Gavin on the phone that night.

184

"Tell me."

"I told off a doctor. Except I didn't get mad. That was the best part."

"Explain, please."

"Carli had an appointment with an ENT because she's been really hoarse. He was such an ass, really arrogant and insensitive. He didn't even treat her like a little girl. She was just a...a *file*, or something. He made her so uncomfortable she started to cry."

"I'm sorry. If you tell me where he works, I'll go beat him up."

"I handled it, thanks. I asked to talk to him in the hall, and I told him I didn't like the way he treated her, and we left."

"I'm really sorry you had to deal with that."

"You know something? I'm not! This felt so good, Gavin. I felt...*empowered*. And Carli was able to see that. I think she was proud of me."

"Well, that's great. I know I wouldn't want to mess with you."

"Oh, you might, under certain circumstances," I said playfully.

"Wet wood, remember?"

I sighed. "Yes. You keep reminding me. Anyway, can I call you right back? I feel like I'm on a roll, and there's something I want to do."

I hung up with Gavin and hesitated. Was I ready for this? Probably not. But I'd give it a try. I'd call his cell phone, because I knew I wasn't ready to call the home number. I still didn't like thinking of that as his home.

Four rings. And then, his voice. A surly *hello*.

"Hi. I'm calling about the kids."

"What about them?"

"I think you should be spending more time

with them. Not because I want you to, but because I know they want you to."

Silence. He hadn't expected this.

"I want what's best for them. And I think you do, too. I know you have other...things you like to do, but the girls are growing up so fast, Richard, and you need to make time for them. I just don't want you to separate yourself from your children. They deserve more than that from you."

"Don't tell me how to be a father," he snapped.

I gritted my teeth. *Be authoritative, but calm! Not confrontational. Like talking to Dr. Bland.*

"Look, I'm working on accepting what you did...what happened between us. I'm still angry with you, but I can push that aside to tell you that your daughters need you."

He was silent. And then, angrily: "Fine. I'll have them over for dinner this week. I'll let you know which day." He hung up before I could say thank you. Which was a good thing, because I wasn't ready to say that to him. I doubted I ever would be.

So he had listened. This time, there had been no shouting, no cursing. I breathed slowly, steadily, as I dialed Gavin's number.

"Hey," I said. "I did another good thing."

CHAPTER TWENTY-FOUR: *Tongue in Cheek*

My English 9's and I were discussing how the characters evolved throughout *To Kill A Mockingbird* when the conversation suddenly veered off course.

"I was just wondering," Robbie said, "who invented ears?"

We looked at him to see if he was serious. He was.

Dan was the first to respond. "I'm guessing it'd be the same person who came up with eyes."

"Wouldn't that be, uh, *God?*" Madison chewed on her fingernail as her eyes darted from classmate to classmate. She always looked afraid someone was going to punch her. It was probably a safe bet.

"Do *you* believe in God, Ms. Kellen?" Robbie asked.

I regarded his mop of tousled blond curls and his earnest expression. I could feel the nineteen pairs of eyes upon me. Did I? My beliefs in significant things—love, protection, trust—had failed me. But there were miracles, big and small. The beauty and fury of the ocean, the poetry of a tree laced with snow, the digestive system. And the fact that despite everything, I still believed.

"Yes," I said slowly. "I do."

"But how do you know God exists?"

I couldn't tell if Robbie sincerely wanted to know, or if this was a ploy to delay the book discussion. Probably a little bit of both. I would need to handle this delicately. "I can't really explain it," I answered honestly. "It's just a feeling. That, and because of everything around us. I mean, how could there *not* be a God?"

Mariah nodded in agreement. "And I believe in life after death. My uncle had this near-death experience when he ran his snowmobile into a tree, and he said he had a glimpse into the other side. He wasn't wearing a helmet."

Of course he wasn't.

"Cool," said Robbie.

I was beginning to get caught up in the discussion. "Isn't it weird we are all going to die someday? Every single one of us. And we don't know how, or when. Doesn't that freak you out?"

Silence. They looked at me, and then at each other. Perhaps I had gone a bit too far. Literature would save us. I smiled at them and looked back down at my book, running my tongue around my bottom teeth and to the inside of my cheek. And thus began my own near-death experience. I discovered what felt like a bump with a small indentation in the center. The average person might assume canker, but I knew better. Cankers were painful. This was not.

I had eight minutes to go before my free period. Eight torturous minutes. Every cell in my body quivered with the effort of holding back from running out of the room in search of a mirror and a flashlight. I knew I had to distract myself. "So, can anyone tell me how one of these characters evolved?

Robbie spoke up. "You mean like, going through puberty?"

I opened my mouth, but Jerry beat me to it. I was grateful, because this would give me another second to probe my oral cancer with my tongue. "Characters don't have to develop pubic hair to *evolve,* you freaking moron."

Robbie shrugged. "I was just guessing. I'm not even reading the book."

This was going well. I would most likely have part of my cheek carved out to get rid of the tumor, and my teaching expertise apparently had a few holes in it as well.

"Stop," I said. "I can't stand this anymore. Let's just silent read till the end of class."

They looked at each other and opened their books. I went to my desk and sat down at my computer to check my email. I wanted to give the illusion of normalcy so my students didn't suspect anything. I discreetly poked my tongue at my cheek. It was still there. The minute the period ended, I would find Jess and make her look at it, have her try to reassure me, and then I'd call my dentist. I didn't want to let this go too long.

Stella had emailed me. Landon could roll from his back to his belly and was close to sitting without support. She had attached a picture of him propped up on the couch with pillows. Did she know how I envied her? To be completely wrapped up in your baby so that nothing else mattered. Who cared that there were bills to pay, or snow to shovel, or that someday we would all cease to exist. There was only precious, burgeoning life, to kiss, caress, and hold in your arms. This was bliss. This was peace.

The period ended. I reminded the kids of the chapters they needed to read for tomorrow, listened to the groans of protest, and hurried out of the room to Jess's classroom. I knocked on her door, mouthing *I'm sorry* when I saw she was in the middle of a lesson. But this was important.

She clicked off the overhead projector and came to the door, telling her students she'd be right back. "Hey. What's going on?"

"Can you look at something for me?"

"Right now?"

I stared at her. She knew better than to ask that.

Jess sighed and followed me to the nearest bathroom.

"It's this little thing inside my cheek. It might be hard to see, but I want you to tell me what it looks like." I hooked a finger in my mouth and pulled it open.

Jess leaned in close, peering. "I can't really see anything."

I fought the urge to roll my eyes. "Here, let me get under the light."

"Oh, now I see it...that little canker?"

"I don't think it's a canker. It doesn't hurt."

"Well, it's probably some abrasion from you biting your cheek or something. By the way, how's Gavin?"

"He's fine. Stop trying to change the subject. You know that doesn't work with me."

We headed into the hall. I decided she was not going to be of much help. "I think I should call the dentist."

"You do what you need to do. Hey, have you and Gavin...you know...done anything?"

I looked at her. What were we, in high school? "No. My wood's too wet."

"What?"

"My wood. It's just an expression. Gavin said I'm not quite ready emotionally to be with anyone right now. But we're friends."

She smiled knowingly.

"I know what you're thinking. But we're really just friends right now."

"Mm-hmm."

I leaned in closer to her and lowered my voice. "I'm not saying I'm not horny. He's attractive, and something *might* happen. Just not right now." And then realization. "You bitch, you got me to stop thinking of the thing in my cheek!"

Jess grinned. "I'm getting better, aren't I?"

*****

It was a little after 10 p.m. when the phone rang. Gavin, calling from his sales meeting.

"Hi. I hope I'm not calling too late."

"No, you're fine. I was just...*[staring into my mouth with a flashlight? looking up pictures of oral cancer on the internet?]*...sitting here." I winced as I spoke; my tongue muscles were sore from all the prodding.

"How was your day?"

"It was good." I hesitated. Did I dare to tell him? Maybe I could just ease into it. It was something he was going to find out anyway, and if he couldn't handle it, we both might as well know now. "I've been a little worried."

"About what?"

"I found this little spot inside my cheek, and I'm kind of concerned about it." *Kind of* didn't quite cover thinking about oral surgery, biopsies and planning my funeral, but I didn't want to overwhelm him.

"Is it like a canker?"

Why did everyone always point to that? "I don't think so. I mean, it *looks* like a canker, so I suppose it could be, but it doesn't hurt."

"Then maybe it's healing. I've had those before, where you don't notice them until they're

191

almost gone. I'd give it a week or so to see if it clears up on its own, and then maybe you could call your dentist."

He meant well. But like everyone else, he didn't seem to realize that a week was an eternity. "I already called."

"What did they say?"

"They said I could wait a while longer and see if it clears up on its own."

"Well, there you go."

"It's just that...I worry about my health sometimes. Okay, more than sometimes. More like, all the time."

A pause. "Are you saying you're a hypochondriac?"

How I loathed that label. But I had to be honest with him. "Yes."

"Oh. I'm sorry. For you, I mean. That must be really hard."

I hadn't known what I wanted him to say, but his response was comforting. He wasn't making an excuse to stop talking to me (at least not yet), and he didn't seem to be alarmed. Plus, he was sympathetic.

"It is hard. When I get stressed, I seem to get a lot of symptoms."

"You must be having symptoms all the time, then." I could hear the smile in his voice.

"Pretty much."

"Have you ever tried taking something?"

I had to forgive him for that one. He was new to this, couldn't see how a hypochondriac would have researched the side effects, potential complications and horror stories of anti-anxiety drugs. Nausea, weight gain, vivid dreams, drowsiness, and loss of libido (in a few cases, permanently). Also depression, and ironically, an increase in nervousness. No thank you.

"I don't want to take anything. I guess I'd rather live with being scared." My hypochondria was a part of me, like my eye color and the few freckles sprinkled across my nose.

"I can understand that. Maybe you could work on thinking differently...you know, more positively?"

"Maybe." I needed to change the subject. "So how's Chicago?"

"Cold and windy. And boring. We haven't really left the hotel. If I have to listen to another rep give his forecasting presentation, I'll scream like a little girl. But I'm coming home tomorrow."

A small feeling of pleasure uncurled inside of me. "Would you want to help chaperone a party my daughter's having on Saturday night? I don't really want to do that to you, but I'd like the company."

"Well, sure." He sounded pleased. "Do you think your kids are ready for that?"

"I think so. They know about us being...you know, friends, and Lily's asked when she's going to meet you."

"Sounds like fun."

I laughed. "No. Fifteen high school freshmen in my basement is not going to be fun. We'll have to keep a lid on the kissing."

"Really? I would have thought they'd be a little too self-conscious for that."

"I was talking about you and me." The flirt in me couldn't help it. A warm flush crept up my neck and into my cheeks.

A pause from Gavin. "Wet wood, remember?"

"I've been working on drying it out. I don't think I'm as keyed up about my ex. I'm not dreaming about him like I had been. The last dream

I had was about a month ago when I kept poking him over and over. He was just standing there, looking absolutely indifferent."

"Kind of symbolic, don't you think?"

"Of my anger?"

"Maybe, but also how you told me you've been urging him to be more of a father."

Oh. Yes. That was very true.

"I'd say that's really good, only one dream in the past month."

He sounded proud of me. I liked that. "So you think I'll be ready to start a fire soon?"

"We'll see. But if not, we can wait. Listen, I'm going to get ready to hit the sack. We have a breakfast meeting at 7 a.m."

"Okay. Talk to you tomorrow?"

"Sure. Sleep tight, Chris."

I hung up the phone and my tongue went back to the side of my cheek. I poked the bump again. I couldn't be totally sure, but it felt like it had gotten smaller.

CHAPTER TWENTY-FIVE: *Susceptible*

I was watching Lily fry her hair with the straightener before her party. She caught my eye in the mirror. "So when's this man coming over?"

I didn't like her tone. It was something about how she said the words *this man*. It reminded me of her grandmother. "Probably about a half hour after the party gets going. You okay with that?"

"Yeah. Why wouldn't I be? I told you I wanted to meet him." She studied her reflection in the mirror. I drew in my breath. When I hadn't been paying attention, my baby daughter had metamorphosed into a woman. She had soft curves—and breasts larger than mine, I noted with fleeting envy. She ran her hands through her honey-colored hair (natural, not chemically-enhanced) and it slipped through her fingers like silk. This pleased her, so she did it again, coaxing her bangs to fall across her forehead and over her right eye just so. Although my hair had never been as pretty as Lily's, I used to spend a lot of time on it, too, using the curling iron to create soft tendrils on either side of my face. It was important that the tendrils looked as though they had curled naturally, as from a walk on the beach of a steamy tropical island. So I would work for about a half hour to achieve this effect. The mirror was both fan and critic. There were times when I would be surprised—shocked, really—at how good I could look, and there were times when all I could see was a glaring pimple, or a cluster of blackheads, or my stick-straight eyelashes. But when I was Lily's age, I mostly remember staring at my reflection and thinking, *who ARE you, anyway?* Little did I know at age forty-three, I'd be asking myself the same thing.

There was an episode of an old family TV show in which a daughter asked her mother, "Do you think I'm pretty?" and the mother had answered, "No." After a brief pause, she added, "I think you're beautiful." I loved that scene. So much so, that after watching it, I'd asked my own mother the same thing. However, she had stopped at No. Perhaps she and I were just in the middle of a very long pause.

With Lily, I didn't wait for the question. "You look beautiful."

She beamed at me in the mirror. "Hopefully, Matt will think so and ask me out."

"Wasn't he supposed to by now?"

"Yeah, but yesterday he told Julia he was going to wait a little bit longer. So that I'd like him more."

Arrogant little bastard. "Well, he better not wait too long, or someone else will beat him to it."

She smiled again. "Speaking of boyfriends, are you and Gavin like a legit couple?"

"No. We're just dating." My temple began a slow, steady throb. I had been feeling draggy for the past couple of days, with a hint of a sore throat and swollen glands. Last week, it had been a yeast infection. The week before that, a cold with a persistent nighttime cough. If my malaise continued, I would have to get my blood drawn and wait for the phone to ring with the results, the doctor's somber voice saying—

"I didn't mean it would be a *bad* thing to be legit," continued Lily. "I was just wondering."

"Understood," I said. "I'm going to get some

Tylenol and break open the bag of Fritos. Just to see if they're okay for you kids."

"Don't eat a lot of them, Mumma."

She knew me well. I waved at her as I left her room. Carli was at the foot of the stairs holding my phone. I hadn't heard it ring. "Hey," I said. "Shouldn't you be getting ready for your sleepover? They're going to be picking you up soon."

"I am ready. And Daddy wants to talk to you."

I steeled myself. Why did he have to call on a night like this, when I should instead be focusing on a fun event like Lil's party? Maybe he had found out and was calling on purpose. Or maybe it was about the holidays, and some excuse why he wasn't going to take the kids.

I took the phone, went to my room and closed the door. Deep breath. "Hello."

"I'm calling about Lily's eye doctor bill. She's getting contacts?"

Calm and authoritative. "Yes...she's at the point where she needs her vision corrected."

"Well, if you're thinking I'm going to pay for them, I'm calling to tell you I'm not."

"What?"

"I think you heard me.

I was stunned. "But they're for Lily's eyesight."

"I realize that. But she can get glasses instead. Contact lenses are an ongoing expense. I don't want to make that kind of long-term commitment."

You mean, as in marriage? I clenched my jaw. Lily's party...a special night. I would not let him get to me. "Richard—this is your daughter we're talking about. She's in high school now. Girls don't want to wear glasses after a certain age. You have an obligation to your children. We've been over this."

"No, *you've* been over this, Christine. Don't tell me what I should and shouldn't do. If you want to pay for her contacts, go ahead. But I'm not going to."

I shoved over calm and authoritative to make room for loud and livid. "You selfish son-of-a-bitch! You don't give a shit about anyone except yourself! You may not be a husband anymore, but you're still a father. Start acting like one!"

"In the future, I suggest you save your childish rants and realize that I will fulfill my obligation as I see fit." *Click.*

In the future, I suggest you go f— Little shoots of anger, green and glistening, sprouting from all my secret gardens. I needed to stop nourishing my animosity; it would never wither and dry up otherwise. But I still couldn't. It was so damned easy being green.

The phone rang again. Hank. "Hello, my little figgy pudding! Happy fucking holidays."

"My sentiments exactly."

"How's it going?"

"Oh, wonderfully. I'm getting ready for Lily's party, and I just had a nice conversation with Richard who's refusing to pay for her contacts."

"1-800-hitman, sweetheart."

"I wish. Listen, do you think it's normal that I've been feeling run down, and picking up colds and stuff?"

"Considering you're exposed to everything with teaching, yeah, I think it makes sense."

"But I never used to get sick. I've built up immunities to things at school."

"Well, your stress level is certainly higher than it has been, right?"

"I guess."

"You slept with that bald guy yet?"

"BaldING. No, I haven't."

"What are you waiting for? That would be a good boost for the old immune system."

"I'll think about it."

"Good. Is Lily all excited for her big shindig?"

"Oh, yes. It should be fun. Gavin's coming over to help chaperone."

"Ooh, could be dangerous! All those adolescent hormones floating around. Better be careful you don't catch *those.*"

I could hear Carli yelling to me. "I've got to run. I'll let you know how everything goes."

"All right, kitten. I hope Gavin enjoys coming. And I hope he likes going to your house, too."

I went to Carli's room to help roll up her sleeping bag. I could feel her eyes on me, even before she spoke. "What did Dad want?"

"Mostly just to tick me off." Instantly, a twinge of regret. But it was true, and the bastard didn't deserve to be protected. "So are you all set for the sleepover?"

"Yup. We might go to the mall to see the Christmas decorations. And speaking of Christmas, can you get me a digital camera?"

"We'll see. They're not cheap."

Carli clasped her hands to her chest. "But the look on my face when I get it will be *priceless.*"

I rolled my eyes and discovered my headache had worsened. I realized I hadn't taken Tylenol. Or Fritos. I headed downstairs to the kitchen to rectify this.

I soon discovered that corn chips weren't exactly soothing to a sore throat. Maybe I would need to get a throat culture. Maybe it would turn out to be mono. What was it I'd read about the Epstein-

Barr virus? Something about it can cause Hodgkin's disease. So if I had mono, that could be the first step toward developing cancer. Or, since I already had swollen glands, I could skip the Epstein-Barr and head straight for Hodgkin's. I contemplated this.

The doorbell rang. Lily and her perfume flew by me. Breathless, she opened the door, and I could hear the sweet sounds of teenspeak: *oh my GODDD, I love your HAIRRR! Is Brady coming? Yes, yes, and so is Collin!* Squeal of approval.

Lily ushered in Ava, her best friend of the week. I wrinkled my nose at their competing scents.

"Hey, Mrs. Bay—I mean, hi, Ms. Kellen."

I smiled at her. If freshman girls were animals, which of course everyone knew they were, then Ava was a mink. Sleek and dark, with slinky-smooth movements like water rippling over rocks. Beautiful, but watch out for the teeth and claws.

The doorbell rang again. Winston woofed and trotted to the door with Lily and Ava at his heels. I watched Lily's face, saw the flush of excitement and anticipation, and my throat closed. It was hard standing here, alone in my love for her and trying to be enough. I so wanted to be enough.

"Hi, Mrs. Bacon." It was Ben, one of Lily's earlier crushes. He was the spitting image of Fred Savage in *The Wonder Years* so I could forgive him for not getting my name right.

He spied the Fritos on the bar and flashed a grin at me as he reached for the bowl on his way to the basement. He was so endearing, this not-yet-man. And suddenly, an image of Richard (the boy, not the cheap, selfish son-of-a-bitch) unfurled in my mind, like a piece of wadded paper slowly uncrumpling. Richard had been about Ben's age when we'd met, with an intriguing dual personality.

200

Shy in jeans and a t-shirt, but put a guitar in his hands, and he was transformed into an enticing concoction of bold and brash with a splash of arrogance. I let my mind linger on this memory and slipped into something shockingly close to enjoyment.

The doorbell. More sagging jeans, untied sneakers. The smell of hairspray, spearmint gum and too much cologne. And then, someone for me.

A rogue gust of wind lifted Gavin's tuft of hair and set it back down in disarray. BaldING, I told myself firmly. Not bald. There was a difference.

"Hey," he said, smiling. "I heard there was a party."

"You heard right."

"It's freezing out here. Are you going to let me in?"

"Yes," I said, "I am," and shivered as I opened the door.

CHAPTER TWENTY-SIX: *Flutters*

I told Gavin about allowing myself a nostalgic Richard moment as I frosted cupcakes for the party crew. I loathed making cupcakes. Searching the cupboards for the mixer which never seemed to be in the same spot, injuring my tongue licking the beaters for a woefully inadequate taste of chocolate, slopping the batter into bent and wobbly cupcake liners—but I did it because of Ava's mother. About five years ago, as room parent for Lily's class, I had called Ava's mother to contribute to a Valentine's party. She had sighed then, clearly irritated, and said, "well, I suppose so. But it's *not* going to be cupcakes. I *hate* making cupcakes." After meekly agreeing to her offer to bring a bottle of Hawaiian punch, I vowed I would never be that kind of mother. And so I made cupcakes. Even though I hated it as much as Ava's mother did.

The meeting between Gavin and Lily had gone well. They both had smiled, shaken hands, and she had made me proud and grateful by adding, "nice to meet you." And then she had gone downstairs with her friends, like her mother having a new boyfriend was not a major event.

I gave Gavin the spatula to lick. It was a generous move on my part, because the only good thing about cupcake-making was this little reward. But then again, I *could* watch his tongue.

He licked the spatula unabashedly, as if there was nothing sexual about it. "Well, I'd say that's a pretty big step, thinking of your ex in a positive light, especially with how he's been."

"I suppose, but I still have a long ways to go."
I hesitated. "I know this is probably wrong, but it's like I'm not complete without someone else to share things with. Sometimes I feel like I'm half of a whole. Do you think that's needy?"

"Probably a little bit." He smiled, and something in his eyes warmed me from my scalp to my soles. "But it's also natural. You had someone with you for a long time. It's understandable you'd want that again." He paused. "You deserve that again."

Sometimes I wondered. Had I been a good wife? Were there things I could have done differently?

I recalled a scene in this very kitchen: Richard and I, making grilled cheese sandwiches for the kids. I'd been watching him slather on the butter. Sensing my gaze upon him, he'd looked up at me and asked me what was the matter.

Oh, nothing, really. I was just thinking I don't butter the bread that way.

He snorted. "I didn't realize there was a right way to do it."

"I'm not saying that. But you're using too much. You really only need a few dabs."

He had paused a moment, and then shook his head, throwing the knife down on the counter and walking away. "Do it your way, Chris," he had snarled. "Everything has to be your way."

Christ. Could marriages disintegrate over a sandwich?

"Hey." Gavin touched me lightly on the shoulder. "Where are you?"

"Oh...sorry. Just remembering some minor thing with my ex. That maybe wasn't so minor."

He regarded me solemnly. "What do you miss

the most?"

I'd had plenty of time to think about this, and I didn't hesitate sharing it with Gavin. The unbroken family. The security and comfort of being married. Turning over to look at his face on the pillow and seeing his messy morning hair, and knowing we could look our worst with each other and still want to have sex later. Going to the grocery store, and looking at the rings on other people's hands and thinking, *I'm one of those people, too.*

Gavin nodded slowly. "But what about *him?*"

A couple of the girls and their scents came upstairs and sat down at the bar. "Could we please have some more soda?"

I swallowed, hoping my throat would feel a bit better. It did not. The Hodgkin's again. "Of course!" I smiled at them as though I would live a long life and went to the refrigerator.

"How are things going down there?" Gavin asked.

Julia shrugged. "Pretty good. But somebody threw an air hockey puck at Mari, and it cut her nose. I don't think she'll need stitches, though."

Oh, *God.* Good parental supervision on my part. "Does she need a bandaid?"

"Nah," Julia said. "She's fine. Ooh, cupcakes!"

I pushed the plate toward her and the rather mousy-looking girl whom I did not know. Collin bounded into the kitchen, his black hair disheveled to perfection. "Do you have anything cold, Ms. K? It's getting kind of hot down there."

I gestured toward the bottle of Sunkist.

He shook his head. "No. I mean *really* cold. As in, frozen." He went to the freezer and whooped in delight. "Hey, how about these freeze pops?"

I hesitated. "I don't think you'd want those,

Collin. They're kind of...old." *Kind of old* meaning at least a couple of years. I felt a twinge of embarrassment, but they *were* in the way back of the freezer.

"That's okay! These things don't spoil. They're frozen."

I watched uneasily as he grabbed the scissors from my counter and snipped off the end of the freeze pop. "I really don't think you should..."

"MMM," he said. "Grape is my favorite."

I looked with raised eyebrows at Gavin who shrugged and smiled. "He's a teenage boy," he reassured me. "Their stomachs can take anything."

Collin went to the basement door and hollered down. "Hey, you guys. There's freeze pops up here!"

Feet, thundering up the stairs, and then fifteen or so teenagers milling about the kitchen. *I want one of those freezy things! Is there an orange? Give me the scissors. Rip it off with your teeth, you pansy!*

"Stop...please," I begged. "Those things are about two years old. Three, maybe."

They did not hear me. The floor was soon littered with little plastic snips. And then the crowd was gone.

Gavin shook his head in awe. "They're like...*buffalo*. Only more destructive."

The basement door opened again, and Candice appeared. She swaggered toward us and hoisted herself on one of the stools, sighing loudly.

I did not care for Candice. "Did you get a freeze pop?" I asked hopefully.

"No," she said. "I'm really not in the mood to eat."

This was a surprising statement, given that

Candice was rather large. There were certain heavy girls who invited the comment, if *she lost weight, she'd be really pretty.* Candice was not one of them. I tried not to look at the space where her belly shirt had ridden up, exposing her ample gut, but it was impossible. Gavin was staring, too.

Candice's gaze rested on the plate of cupcakes. "Well, maybe I'll just have one of those."

I pushed the plate toward her. I felt like I knew her from what Lily had told me: Candice's brother had to go to jail for beating someone up; Candice's mom was an alcoholic; Candice had to visit the guidance counselor *and* a therapist outside school on a regular basis. The kids were fascinated by her misfortunes, and even though Candice looked perfectly capable of protecting herself, her friends wanted to do it.

I supposed I could feel a little sorry for her. "I heard it was your birthday tomorrow. Are you doing anything special?"

She rolled her eyes as she bit into her cupcake. A few crumbs tumbled from her mouth and onto the bar. I watched as she smeared them into the formica. Her fingernails were glossy purple with tiny gold stars in the center.

"I'm going to the hospital to visit my cousin. He got stabbed last night and he's in a coma."

Well, happy birthday! "Is it a medically-induced coma?"

Gavin and Candice stared at me. I continued, undaunted. "It's just that sometimes, doctors do that to let the person...you know, rest and heal. So a coma can be a *good* thing."

As I spoke, I felt something deep within my chest: a fluttery feeling that skittered from one end of me to the other, like when you run your hand along piano keys. I had to catch my breath. How was I going to get through this? Survive, as a single mother, my heart palpitations *and* the teenage years, with my children's questionable friends, and parties where there would be more to worry about than ancient freeze pops?

The basement door opened. Someone yelling for Candice to come play air hockey. Clearly pleased, she brushed the remaining cupcake crumbs onto the floor, heaved herself off the bar stool and headed downstairs.

My phone rang. First Dick, now my mother. It just kept getting better.

"Christine? You didn't tell us about Lily having her first high school party tonight."

Shit. Shit, shit, shiiiiiiit. "Oh...well, I've just been really busy. How did you—"

"Carli told me when I called yesterday. I've been out shopping and thought I'd stop by. I wouldn't miss this for the world."

"Mom, you don't—" I was speaking to dead air. I put down the phone and turned to Gavin. "Is your car in my driveway?"

"Uh, ye-e-s...where else would it be?" He appeared amused.

"I need you to move it into my garage."

"What? Why?"

I tugged at his arm. "Quick. Please. I can explain later."

Gavin looked bewildered but went to the door. Cold and clammy dread seeped through my armpits as I bolted to the garage and waited for him to drive in. He entered much too cautiously; he didn't understand this was not the time to be careful! I motioned for him to *hurry*, smacked the garage door opener to close the door and raced to his car, scrambling inside and breathing hard. "Thank God. That was close."

He leaned across the passenger seat and whispered. "Why did we just do that?"

Well, Gavin, it's like this...I know I'm in my 40's, but...

"Are you really divorced?"

I looked at him, incredulous.

"I'm sorry, Christine, but I have to ask. Are we hiding from your husband?"

"No! I'm divorced, I swear to you." I hesitated. "It's actually...my mother."

His eyes widened, brows arched in puzzlement.

I asked him to stay in his car for a little while. It won't be long, I told him. Just a few minutes. The arch in his eyebrows crept farther north, as in, *are you serious?* I was. A few minutes, I repeated. I flashed him an apologetic grin as I went back into the house.

My mother blew in moments later, laden with party supplies and importance. Her L. L. Bean bag was crammed with Tupperware containers of carrots, celery, cucumbers, red and yellow peppers, two kinds of dip, and a Twister game.

I followed her into the basement. "I don't think the kids really need any more food. I bought quite a bit."

Ava met us at the bottom of the stairs. My mother immediately pulled out the containers of carrots and dip and handed them to her.

"Oh, thanks!" Ava's smile was dazzling. "I was hoping we'd have something nutritious. We've had soo much junk food tonight!"

Mom beamed at her. She leaned closer to me and spoke under her breath, as if we were in on this together. "Wait till they see the game I brought."

I didn't want to dash her hopes. I wanted to crush them. "That game is really old, Mom. Kids these days are into high tech stuff. I really don't think—"

Brady appeared and checked out the bag. "Is that *Twister?* Man, I love that game!"

Lily came over to hug her grandmother. "Thanks, Mimi. The party was starting to get kinda lame. Hey, Matt, come help me set this up."

My mother reached out and patted me on the arm. "These parties do get easier, Christine. You'll get the hang of it. I was more than happy to help." She blew a kiss to Lily. "I'm leaving, sweetheart. I told Poppa I'd stop in for just a few minutes."

A few minutes. Gavin! I followed my mother up the stairs and headed straight for the door. She waved at me on the way to her car. I squared my shoulders, waved back and went to the garage for Gavin.

"Everything under control?"

"Oh yes, thanks to my mother." What did Gavin think of me? What did *I* think of me? The flutters returned, a thousand wild birds on Vivarin.

"Are you okay?"

"Not exactly, no. I'm sorry about making you hide. I know it's ridiculous, having it be this way."

"So you really are still married. To your mother, I mean." Gavin's eyes were smiling.

"That's one way of putting it. I need to work on at least a separation, but I feel like I used up all my courage in my real divorce."

"You're stronger than you think."

I sat down at the bar and sighed. "I've heard that before. But sometimes I just want to run away from everything."

"And where would you go?"

I answered without hesitation. "A horse stable."

"Really."

"Yes. I had a little Morgan mare named Lyric for eight years. I sold her when I went into college. I didn't have enough time for her, but I hated to give her up. And she didn't want to leave. She wouldn't get on the trailer when her new owner came to get her."

I had pushed her, pulled her, pleaded with her, gotten angry with her. She would not budge. I stopped for a moment, and she pressed her head against my chest, her nostrils pink and flaring. I smoothed her ruffled forelock and kissed the few white hairs between her eyes that wanted to be a star. I'd promised myself I wouldn't cry, but my tears made a slow path down the length of her nose. I whispered, "you will always be mine," and she followed me onto the trailer.

My eyes filled. Gavin took my hand. Turned it over to kiss my palm once, twice. There was the scent of fresh cupcakes and his cologne. And floating in the air like pixie dust, those damned teenage hormones. I opened my mouth to speak, and he saw his chance. Soon we were kissing like kids in the basement of an improperly-chaperoned party.

"My throat is sore," I whispered. "And I don't want you to catch it."

"I'll take my chances," he murmured against my mouth. His arms went around my waist, gently pulling me off the barstool and into the V his legs made.

I was very aware of what was in the middle of that V. "I might even have Hodgkin's disease," I informed him. I didn't want any secrets between us.

That shuddery piano-key feeling surfaced again, compounded by my Hodgkin's disease, multiplied by the risk of starting over with someone else, rivaled by the fear of being alone.

Gavin put one hand under my hair and began stroking the back of my neck in small circles. "Then we'd better make the most of the time you have left." He put his other arm around my waist, pressing me against him. I could not breathe. I could have died. But that was a possibility I could live with.

One last attempt. "I have this fluttery feeling inside my chest. It might be some sort of heart condition."

He drew back and looked at me.

"But flutters aren't *always* a bad thing," I conceded. "Just sometimes."

"Come here," he said. I laid my head against him, on the shoulder I had just begun to know—and for that moment, there was no Epstein-Barr, or Hodgkin's, or heart disease. There was just Gavin, me, and fifteen teenagers downstairs, who were blissfully unaware that mothers were about as solid as dust.

CHAPTER TWENTY-SEVEN: Rash

It was a few days after New Year's, and one of my resolutions had already come true: *be brave; take more risks.* Which in this case meant having sex with Gavin. Presented with unfamiliar male genitalia (and this time being ready), I found myself feeling very much like a schoolgirl. Sex had been so automatic with Dick's dick, although the first time I ever touched him had been painful for both of us. I had been in the back seat of his '74 Chevy Vega at the height of our grope-fest, and I had mustered up enough courage to start stroking him. At least I thought that's what I was doing. But he took my hand and mumbled that the "pull technique" wasn't going to work. Then he showed me how to touch him, and I'd sat there, both mesmerized and horrified, watching him masturbate until we were both sprayed with droplets of ejaculate. Thinking back, it must have hurt him, all that penis yanking. If only I'd had that to do over again. I would have tugged even harder.

I knew the sex was inevitable, so in preparation, I'd had Gavin take two HIV tests, both in December. I said the proof he was HIV-free could be his Christmas present to me. He said he'd been thinking more along the lines of a book or CD rather than blood, but he liked the idea of being able to skip the gift-wrap. He went to his doctor for the first test, had labwork and presented me with a letter detailing the results. The only abnormal finding was slightly elevated cholesterol. His second test was using the Home Access kit, which involved pricking your finger, placing drops of blood on a specially-treated card, and mailing in the card for testing at a licensed laboratory. He gave me his fourteen-digit identification number to phone in for the results (available in only three business days). I called, my heart thundering, and listened to the recorded message. *Your tests results were negative.* Never had five words sounded so sweet. I called again, and listened to the woman repeat the message. And again, just to be sure I had entered his ID number correctly. I grew to love that woman. Since the Home Access test had FDA approval and was supposedly as reliable as HIV tests used by medical professionals, and since his doctor had stated in his letter that Gavin was HIV-negative, I had dropped from extreme panic to mild terror on the fear scale for contracting this illness.

However, death was the furthest thing from my mind when Gavin led me into his bedroom. His room looked similar to what I'd imagined: solid oak bureau and nightstand, a small television, a bed with a navy comforter and an arched, tastefully-simple headboard of honey-colored slats.

I tipped my head back to look at him. He brushed a stray piece of hair from my face as he spoke. "We have been very good, waiting like this."

"Yes."

"Richard was a fool," Gavin said softly. "An absolute fool."

"Yes," I said again, and began to cry. He took my face in his hands. We started to kiss. And then we were on his bed. He lowered himself gently on top of me. Lying there fully clothed heightened the anticipation and desire. He reached his hand inside my shirt.

I flashed back to Manch. "Sorry about the

small breasts."

"They're perfect," Gavin said. "And stop it."

"Stop what?"

"Fishing. You are beautiful and you know it."

"Okay," I said meekly. I felt the sincerity of his appreciation for me through his jeans, and the reality of the situation hit me. I was going to have sex again. After all this waiting, after the multiple close encounters of the Waterpik kind, I was going to have sex with a real live man. A real live, big, beautiful, balding man. Everything in the room became sharper, clearer, brighter. Undoubtedly, deer in a nearby forest glen raised their heads to ponder this monumental event.

I unbuckled Gavin's belt. He slid down his pants. And I saw him. All of him. I couldn't be sure how long it was. But I knew small, and this wasn't small.

He reached for the condom on his nightstand. I had to fight the urge to ask him to use two. And then it was almost as if I was making love with two men. Gavin's arms were wrapped around me, and his kisses were soft and slow, as if we could take all night, but his lower half was urgent and insistent. The combination of the two was erotic with a capital EROTIC. I was with Gavin, and I let myself love the moment. The glory of both of these was overwhelming.

I felt the shudder of him climaxing. And as his penis waned, so did my glory.

What if Gavin was lying to me about being free of STD's? What if the condom had some sort of defect—a microscopic hole where his infected semen could have seeped out? Nothing was 100% effective. What if he'd sent in *someone else's blood* to be tested? I'd never actually seen him prick his finger.

Or, the likelier possibility, what if he'd somehow forged the letter from his doctor? With a computer, people could make anything look official.

How could I have been so foolhardy? I had been so busy enjoying myself during the sex, I'd lost all sensibility. I could feel my (perhaps now tainted) blood pounding in my ears.

Gavin carefully rolled onto his side and kissed my cheek. "Wow. That was wonderful. Did you...you know...get there?"

"Yes," I lied.

He began kissing my neck.

"Listen," I said, "about that HIV test. Did you really get one?"

He took my earlobe between his lips and nibbled on it. "I had two of them."

"Was it your own blood?"

I felt him stiffen, but not in the good penile sense. "Of course."

"Oh. All right."

He put his arm around me, drawing me close. I did not move. His breathing was slow and even. I hoped he couldn't feel how fast my heart was beating.

He spoke softly into my hair. "You don't believe me, do you?"

"Of course I do. I was just...checking." I propped myself up on my elbow to see the clock on his nightstand. "I didn't realize it was this late. I've got to get home and make the kids dinner."

Gavin sat up on the bed and smiled at me ruefully. "Well, at least you were there for a little bit...in the moment. That's my goal for you. To not dwell on the past, or worry about the future."

"Really."

"Yes. You need to learn to live in the *now*."

Who did he think he was? I wasn't about to take any psychological advice from an elevator salesman, thank you. Especially an elevator salesman who forged letters and falsified medical results.

I stood up and began to put on my clothes. "I'd better go."

"Chris, don't get irritated with me. I just want you to enjoy your life."

What there was left of it, anyway. It was hard knowing how much longer I had. Some people with HIV lived years and years, while others developed AIDS soon after. What would happen to my children? They needed me! Gavin stood silently watching as I dressed and left him.

*****

Jess and I were in the teachers' room just before lunch. She looked up from correcting quizzes. "So a couple days ago, you get up your nerve to finally have sex with him."

"That's right."

"And the sex was good."

"Quite."

"But now you think you have the AIDS virus."

"Well, not AIDS yet."

"Okay then, HIV. Even though he took two tests and wore a condom."

"Yes."

"What are you going to do about this?

"I don't know. Call my OB-GYN, probably. I think I might have some sort of infection."

"Chris."

"Seriously. It's all red down there. Kind of rashy."

216

"Well, you might have a yeast infection. Does it itch?"

"Yes, but STD's can itch, too.

She put down her pen and looked at me. One side of her mouth was twitching.

Was she *laughing* at me? "Jess?"

"I'm sorry, I can't help it. You're just so cute."

"This is not funny. I could be *dying* right now." I glared at her. From inside my pocket, my cell phone began to vibrate. I reached inside and looked at the number. It was Gavin. I glanced at Jess.

She stood up. "I'm going to go see what's for hot lunch. I'll be back. Try not to worry." She reached out and squeezed my arm. "Everyone's not out to get you, you know."

My irritation with her was deluged by fresh terror. What if Gavin was calling to tell me the truth—that he was, in fact, HIV positive? I answered the phone breathlessly.

"Chris, hi." He sounded relieved. "I was going to leave you a message. I was just calling to see how you were doing."

"I'm fine."

"Good. I was getting a little worried since you didn't respond to my texts last night." A cough, and he cleared his throat. "Would you and the girls like to come over for lasagna tonight?"

Why was he being so nice? Could it be he had something to hide? "Thanks, but I have progress reports, and a pile of papers to grade."

"Well, maybe we can get together later this week." He coughed again. "Chris, are you sure you're all right?

I could have asked him the same thing. "Yes. Do you have a cold?"

"No, just a cough, for some reason."

An unexplained cough. Lung cancer. Or maybe...something even worse.

The internet beckoned. "Listen, I have a class coming in. I'll talk to you after school." I hung up the phone, opened my laptop and placed my fingers tenderly on the keys.

*When clinical evaluation, spirometry and chest radiography are normal, the cause of persistent dry cough may be elusive... Diagnoses include abnormal intraepithelial airway nerves, temporal arteritis...*I skipped over the more common triggers such as allergies, acid reflux and environmental irritants. Gavin had coughed twice in the thirty seconds I'd talked to him. I wasn't sure how long he'd had the cough, but it was bound to continue. I added the word "persistent." I read through more search results and found the term persistent dry cough. And then I read the heading above one of the results. *ACQUIRED IMMUNODEFICIENCY VIRUS.*

Oh...my...*God.* My eyes bulged in their sockets as if I had Graves disease. Cartoon-character eyes, *WAA-**OOOOOOH**-GAH,* focusing on that grave disease. I began to feel lightheaded. I clicked on the heading and forced myself to read on. *Symptoms of later disease include enlarged lymph nodes, persistent fever or night sweats, sudden unexplained weight loss* (he had been looking a bit thin to me lately), *persistent diarrhea, **persistent dry cough**, and persistent oral (thrush) or vaginal yeast infections.*

My fear bloomed, great purple chrysanthemums of horror. Not only did Gavin apparently have AIDS, but my possible yeast infection was heading me in the same direction.

How could he have done this to me? I had trusted him!

The door to the conference room swung open. Fitzy came in, grinned at me and went to the refrigerator to get his bag lunch, as if one could just eat a sandwich without a care in the world.

"I need to go make a phone call," I said faintly. He wouldn't appreciate hearing me describing my vulva. Then again, we *were* talking about Fitzy.

I walked down the hallway to my classroom. The kids were in the gym for an assembly, and my next class didn't start for another fifteen minutes. This would be a good time to call my gynecologist. After checking the hallway, I closed the door to ensure my privacy and entered the number on my cell phone with trembling fingers.

"Dr. Carter's office."

"Hello...could I speak to a nurse?"

"Speaking."

"Oh! Well, that's good." I laughed nervously. "I think I may have some sort of vaginal infection."

A brisk, matter-of-fact tone. "What are your symptoms?"

My use of medical terminology was sure to impress her. "My labia minora is red and blotchy, and sort of itchy. And I have some vaginal discharge."

"What's the discharge like?"

"Um, it's kind of whitish. I'm worried I may have been exposed to an STD."

"Does your partner have a known STD?"

"Well, no, but...I'm just worried. I had sex a couple of days ago with him, and now I'm just scared I have something. Do you think I should make an appointment?"

"One of the nurse practitioners could see you around 4:00."

Although I always preferred seeing a doctor, I took the appointment and hung up the phone. There. I would be tested for STD's, and this time I could be confident in the results. I would take care of things myself, and there would be no risk of a man deceiving me. Everything would be—

I froze. Not froze in the sense of *I'm tiptoeing past the crib and the baby is stirring so I need to freeze* froze, but froze in the sense of *every cell in my being is at minus kajillion Fahrenheit with a minus infinity windchill.*

Oh. My. CHRIST. I was not alone in this room. I had made a phone call to my gynecologist, described the conditions of my vulva, and unbeknownst to me, there were two human beings in my classroom. Not human beings, exactly, but freshman boys—lying on the couch in the reading corner.

It was Luke and Jacob. They were, curiously, lying almost entangled with one another as kittens will do, and appeared to be sleeping. I rushed at them and screamed.

They both sat up with a start. Bleary-eyed, Luke was the first to speak. "Wh-what is it?"

Jacob was slower to respond. "God, Ms. Kellen, you scared the crap out of me."

Was he talking about my shriek, or my use of the term *vaginal infection?* Still, there was a shred of hope. These boys were masterful at tuning me out; sweet Jesus, please, let them not have heard me speak of my genitalia.

I was practically squealing. "What are you doing in my classroom? Did you hear anything? I was making a personal phone call! Were you

220

listening?"

The boys looked at each other in puzzlement. "Listening to what? We were sleeping."

Sleeping? And therefore oblivious to my phone call? This sounded too good to be true. I glared at them. They stared blankly back at me.

"I didn't give you permission to come in here. You were supposed to be in the gym."

"We were tired from the concert last night. We just wanted a little nap." Jacob looked like he could use a few more hours of shut-eye.

"We didn't think you'd mind." Luke's face was earnest.

I softened a bit. They were just boys, after all. They had meant me no harm. "So you didn't...hear anything?" I asked. "Nothing at all?"

They shook their heads.

Were they telling the truth? Or could they be simply blocking the memory of my phone conversation? Freshman boys didn't even want to think of their teacher having a vagina, let alone a red and itchy one. But I had to believe them, more for my sake than theirs. I sighed and motioned for them to leave. If only I had checked the room thoroughly before I'd made the phone call. A colossally stupid, careless mistake! Hopefully, my decision to sleep with Gavin would not be another one.

CHAPTER TWENTY-EIGHT: *Pregnant Pause*

Once my pelvic region cleared up after a few applications of Monistat, it resumed its role of taking over for my brain. Gavin had endured yet another HIV test at my request, although he complained of becoming anemic. That, coupled with the fact his nagging cough turned out to be from acid reflux, put me a bit more at ease. My parents had Lily and Carli for the weekend to go outlet shopping, which allowed me to find my own outlet: sex. Not only pleasurable, but free.

As I approached Gavin's house, I could see a white piece of paper taped to the front door with the words, FOLLOW THE TRAIL. I opened the door to find a path of Hershey kisses curving through the living room and down the hallway. I was a chocolate slut, and he knew it. At the end of the trail was Gavin, smiling and shirtless, in his bed. The soft glow of candles on his nightstand cast dancing shadows on his wall.

I folded my arms. "A bit presumptuous, don't you think?"

"I was simply kissing the ground you walk on."

I was not used to romance. When Richard proposed to me, he had asked me at a stop sign on the way to my birthday dinner. His words were, "I was wondering if you wouldn't mind marrying me." This put me in a difficult position. Answering "no" when a man proposing marriage expected an affirmative response seemed to constitute a refusal, yet the answer made sense here: as in "No, I wouldn't mind!" After a bit of hesitation, I answered, "I accept your proposal." But oh, how I had later minded marrying him.

After a rather vigorous lovemaking session, Gavin and I snuggled together. If I had not been so relaxed and drowsy, I would have been shocked at how relaxed and drowsy I was. It was as though all the stress over the past year was draining out of me and pulling me deeper into the bed.

We slept until dawn. As I awoke, Gavin drew me closer, nestling his nose against the back of my neck. "I hate to tell you this, but you just had sexual intercourse out of wedlock. What would your mother say?"

I covered my face with my hands. "Please. No references to her. I'd like to at least keep my mother out of the bedroom."

"Well, that's a good place to start." He tugged gently at my hands. "Holy Hannah, woman. These are ice cold."

"I'm sorry," I murmured sleepily. "They've always been that way."

"If you were a corpse, this is what it would feel like. In fact, I think death would be warmer."

I yawned. "Next time I'll wear gloves."

"But the rest of you feels quite warm." Gavin poked me playfully. "What's *that* a symptom of?"

A woman's temperature, which usually begins to decrease as she approaches the beginning of her menstrual cycle, will remain higher if she becomes pregnant.

I was out of that bed faster than you could say *mentally unstable*. All these recurrent thoughts of death had prevented me from being terrified of life: as in, new life. As in, a baby. Holy Mother of God.

"Chris? What's the matter?"

*zygote-->fetus-->morningsickness--
>nosleep-->sorenipples...*

"Christine, please tell me what's going on."

*...terribletwos--> orthodontistappointments-
-> canIborrowthecar?--> thirdcollegetuition...* I did
some quick mental calculations. The last time we'd
had sex was right around the time I would have
ovulated. I was due to start my period any day now.
But that didn't mean I would.

My eyes darted to Gavin's puzzled face. I was
going to have a baby with a man who was not the
father of my other children. A man to whom I was
not even engaged. I was a schoolteacher, and I was
going to have a bastard child. Who, with my luck,
would probably turn out to be a little bastard.

*rubberbabybuggybumpers...
rubberbabybuggybumpers...*

"Hey. Talk to me." Gavin was gripping my
shoulders.

The other early symptoms of pregnancy were
fatigue and nausea. I hadn't had those. But swollen
breasts...that could be a possibility. I would have to
find out. I stepped away from Gavin and pulled off
my pale pink J.C. Penney nightgown, which I now
wanted to burn because it had encouraged lust. I
pointed at my breasts and shrilled. *"Do these look
bigger to you?"*

His mouth opened slightly, the creases of
confusion in his forehead deepening. "No," he said,
slowly, and put his hands out on the air as if he were
going to cup my breasts.

I took a giant step backward.

"No," he repeated, in a calm, gentle tone.
"They look exactly the same size."

Seeing as I couldn't trust him, I raced to the
bathroom to check myself out in the mirror. They

looked like they could be a little swollen. That son of a bitch! He had lied to me. And I was sure this wasn't the first time.

Gavin appeared in the mirror. He was bleary-eyed, and his hair was rumpled. I might have felt sorry for him, if I hadn't wanted to kill him.

"We need to go get some pregnancy tests," I snapped. "And yes, I said *some*."

"Chris, you can't be pregnant. We used a condom. And I have a very low sperm count."

I whirled around and shoved my index finger in his face. "It only takes *one*. I'm getting dressed, and you can come with me or not. I want to use the first morning's urine so I can be sure."

Ten minutes later, at 6 a.m., Gavin, my full bladder and I pulled into the Shaw's parking lot. We headed straight for the feminine hygiene aisle. I could hear Gavin behind me, breathing hard to keep up. I grabbed a First Response, an EPT, and a Clearblue Easy. That would do for now.

The checkout girl beamed at us. I knew what she was thinking: oh, *how cute! They can't wait to find out!* I wanted to kill her, too, almost as much as I wanted to kill the father of my unborn bastard. In the car on the way back to his house, Gavin took my hand. After a few seconds, I pulled it away. We did not speak.

It proved challenging to pee just a little on the stick and then hold the rest for the other two tests, but I did it. After each test, I got on my knees, looked toward the ceiling and prayed with every fiber of my being and every ounce of my soul that I was not pregnant. I tried not to think about how, about fifteen years ago, I had prayed so hard for the opposite. I came into the living room, flushed with triumph but weak with relief, and told Gavin the good news.

"I'm not pregnant."

He glanced up at me from the couch where he'd been flipping through the channels. "I knew you wouldn't be."

I had thought he would be in more of a celebratory mood, like how I'd be whenever I'd get welcome results from medical tests.

"You shouldn't do this to yourself, Chris. It's not good for you. Worrying about health problems could actually cause you health problems."

And I had just started to not hate him. "Do you think I *like* doing this to myself?"

"No. But you should get at the root of why you do it, and work on trying to control your fear. In about three seconds flat, you go from symptom to diagnosis to coffin. Or in this case, symptom to diagnosis to cradle."

I stood without speaking.

"You don't have to go it alone, you know. I'd be glad to help you. I just don't want to see you waste so many precious moments on this. A life worrying about dying is not much of a life."

I could not listen to any more. He had very possibly forged his HIV test and had practically gotten me pregnant. And now he was telling me I had no life. "Maybe you shouldn't be with me," I told him.

He shook his head and looked at the ceiling. "That's not at all what I'm saying."

"Well, that's what *I'm* saying." I went into his bedroom for my overnight bag and headed for the front door. In an instant, Gavin was behind me, trying to wrap his arms around my waist.

I struggled against him, fresh panic filling the place where the baby would have been. "Stop it!

Don't touch me. Just go away!"

His words were crisp. "If that's what you want, fine. This is more aggravation than I need, anyway."

I felt his hands leave me. I would not look at him. I opened the door and stepped out into the cold.

There was something on the seat of my car. A square-shaped package, wrapped in green foil paper. I looked to see if Gavin was in the window. He was not. What would he be giving me? I didn't want anything from him, not from someone unjustifiably confident in thinking he knew what was best for me. But curiosity overwhelmed me.

I tore at the paper to reveal the back side of a picture frame with an inscription in Gavin's handwriting. *For Christine - because you said you loved them.*

I turned the frame over. It was a photograph of the pasture a couple miles away, with three horses, two bays and one paint, all looking into the camera, their manes and backs frosted with snow.

I paused.

CHAPTER TWENTY-NINE: *Seeing Red*

I was having stress and a chocolate donut for breakfast when the phone rang. Hope and dread rippled through me. Could it be Gavin? We'd had no contact since the pregnancy scare. He had apparently taken me seriously when I'd asked him to leave me alone.

It was Hank, calling from his office. "Hey there, chicky-boom."

"Hey."

"Happy fucking Valentine's Day."

"Same to you. How come you're at work on a Saturday?"

"I'm on call. And they called me."

"Fun."

"I was thinking of you this morning. Did you see the article in the paper about the Swedish study that said people who eat a lot of sugar are more likely to develop pancreatic cancer?"

I put down my donut. "No, I hadn't seen that, but thanks for the heads up."

His voice was sing-songy. "Just thought you could add that one to your repertoire. It's a pretty significant finding."

"Nice of you. Again, thanks."

"Sweetheart, don't mention it! So, any special plans for a big V.D. date tonight? You buy a lacy red teddy to wear for the big boy?"

"Not exactly."

"Oh, so he's a leather man."

I sighed. "No. I mean, I don't know. We haven't gotten that far. We're kind of...on hold."

"Really? Hmmm. Well, I'm surprised to hear that. I thought things were going well."

"They were, I guess." I heard the call waiting beep. My heart beat faster. Maybe this time it was Gavin. I checked the number. My mother. Not that I wanted to talk to her, but at least it would save me from explaining to Hank why Gavin and I were taking a break. Especially when I didn't know. "Listen, I've got to go. I have a call."

"Oh, come ON, honey. Inquiring minds want to know."

"You have work to do." I clicked in to take the call. "Hello."

"What's the matter? I can hear in your voice that something's wrong."

"Nothing's wrong. I'm just sitting here eating a donut." And growing some pancreatic cancer.

"A donut? That's loaded with fat and sugar. And did you hear that doctors have discovered that sugar causes—"

"Yes, actually, I did," I interrupted. "So what's going on?"

"Well." I could hear her voice bristling. "I'm calling to invite you and the kids out for dinner, since it's Valentine's Day. I picked up a couple of red jerseys for the girls, and a little something for you."

Perhaps it was a dildo. Although I'd prefer that to be a *big* something.

"Your father and I were planning on coming by around six, if you don't have any other...plans with the salesman."

She was fishing, dangling a question mark in the air. *You win, Ma. I'll bite.* "No, I don't have any plans."

"Are you still seeing each other?"

"I don't know."

"Oh! Well, it would be very sensible of you to end it. Those salesmen types...you, of all people, should know you really can't trust them."

Now it was my turn to bristle. It was one thing for me to badmouth Gavin, but it sounded so much worse coming from my mother. And despite my best efforts, it was damned hard badmouthing him.

"Ending the relationship is a smart move," my mother continued. "It was much, much too early for you to be thinking about yourself."

"I'm not ending the relationship. We're just taking a little break. And it's kind of hard not to think about myself since I *am* myself."

My mother snorted. "What do you think I did when you were a child? I certainly wasn't thinking of myself! *I always* put you first. I didn't go gallivanting around with your father, or out on the town with my friends...I didn't have *time* for friends. And it wasn't a picnic raising you, you know. I sacrificed a great deal. But now I'm free to do what I want."

Like continue to raise me?

"And being alone doesn't have to be all doom and gloom, Christine. I've come up with a list of spontaneous things for you to do. I'll bring it tonight. So, we'll pick you up at six?"

I racked my brain for an excuse and suddenly remembered an unpleasant but legitimate one. Dick was supposed to take the kids for dinner, to meet Eleanor's parents and brother who were visiting. He had seemed to take great pleasure in telling me this. It had taken every ounce of restraint I had to refrain from making a snide remark (something along the lines of, *will this dinner include sharing photos?*), but I had remained calm. At least outwardly.

I turned my attention back to my mother. "Tonight isn't going to work. Richard is planning to take Lily and Carli to meet his girlfriend's family."

A deep and lengthy sigh. "Oh, those poor girls! Having to deal with that. And apparently, there's nothing I can do. You don't know how hard it is for me to feel this helpless!"

"I have to go. I need to use the bathroom." I was getting better ending conversations with my mother, and this time I didn't have to lie. I'd had two cups of coffee this morning, and my bladder was protesting. I hung up and hurried upstairs, passing Carli's door. She had decorated it with hearts of all different sizes, some of them curling at the edges where the marker had dried, others lightly shaded with pink crayon. A few had sayings on them, such as BE MINE! and KISS ME. It was nice she still believed in love.

I entered the bathroom, closed the door and sat on the toilet. With Lily and Carli gone tonight, I would use the time alone to take stock of my life. Did I want to pursue a relationship with Gavin, or should I risk losing him and be on my own for a while? And if I was on my own, would I listen to my mother and not think of myself? Or—and here was a radical concept—would I listen to myself and not think of my mother?

I stood up to wipe. When my daughters came downstairs, I would put on my happiest Valentine's Day face and act as though the world really was made of hearts and flowers. Tonight, when Richard drove in to pick up the girls, I vowed to remain calm and would try my hardest not to think of sticking Cupid's arrow in my ex-husband's chocolate highway. No, I would think pleasant Valentine thoughts, like romantic candlelight dinners, truffles wrapped in pink foil, and red—*urine??!!*

Oh. My. God. ohmyGod, ohmyGod, ohmyGOOODDD, my pee was *red.* Red, red, **red!**

Deep breath, deep breath...there had to be a logical explanation, such as menstrual blood. But no, that was not the reason; I'd just had my period less than two weeks ago. Therefore, it had to be bladder cancer.

I stood and looked into the toilet bowl, chest heaving. My pee was red. Red like the lipstick Dick's masseuse was probably putting on this morning; red like the lingerie she would undoubtedly wear tonight. And to think I had been worried about being *pregnant!* At this point, I would have embraced triplets.

I needed to call my doctor, *stat.* And I would do so before Lily and Carli woke up, so they wouldn't hear the fear in my voice. I would spare them from knowing about my impending death for as long as I could, until the chemotherapy took its toll.

I flushed the toilet and hustled into my bedroom to make the call. Started to dial, and then realized it was Saturday. Which would mean an answering service. I had called after-hours before and always seemed to get the same woman, who acted like she was doing her nails or looking at a catalog while she took your message. This phone call was no different. Three rings, and then a sigh as she answered the phone. A *sigh,* and here I was bleeding from my urethra.

"Hi," I said. "I'd like to leave a message for the doctor."

"Your name?"

"Christine Bay—Christine Kellen. At least I think you have me as Kellen now. I'm divorced."

"Nature of your problem."

"I—there's blood in the toilet. From me, I mean. Blood in my urine."

"Phone number where you can be reached."

I told her.

"All right, I'll give them the message." As she was hanging up, I could have sworn I heard her yawn. Had she no heart? This was fucking Valentine's Day, after all.

I sat at the kitchen table and stared at the phone in front of me, Mr. Bean curling himself around my legs. Twenty-two agonizing minutes later, it rang. Although it almost killed me to wait, I picked it up on the third ring. I didn't want to appear too anxious.

"Christine?"

"Yes."

"Gabrielle from Dr. Jordan's office."

"Oh, hi!" Like it was a surprise to hear from her.

"So you had blood in your urine?"

"Yes. I'm sorry to call on a weekend, but I didn't think this could wait till Monday."

"I understand. Do you have any burning when you urinate?"

"No."

"Any lower back pain?"

She must have been thinking tumor. "No."

"Okay, so probably not kidney stones. Let's go down a different path. What did you have to eat last night?"

"Chicken, sweet potatoes, beets, corn..." Surely, she would be impressed with the nutritional value of that meal. We'd had Lucky Charms the night before, but she didn't need to know that. And then as I heard Nurse Gabrielle chuckle, I knew.

Relief washed over me, leaving me weak and rubbery. Beets. I'd had two servings. I should have known.

"I think we've found our cause. But if it continues, or if you have any other symptoms, give us a call."

I apologized, thanked her and hung up the phone. I did not have bladder cancer. But Little Red Riding Hood still had the big bad wolf to contend with later tonight.

*****

Winston barked and then waved his tail when he saw who was approaching the house. I opened the door to Dick and his stony expression. It continued to amaze me that over time, he was looking different to me—something about the edges of his face. Harder, maybe, and his eyes looked colder. He asked me if the girls were ready.

"They'll be right down. But I think Lily wanted to go out with her boyfriend instead."

The muscle in his jaw flickered. "She's too young for a boyfriend. And Eleanor's family takes one trip here a year. Lily is going to dinner with us."

Calm, authoritative. I noticed he had an impressive booger in his left nostril. I reveled in it. "Richard. Just listen to her. This boy wants to take her to dinner, for Valentine's Day. It's important to her."

Lily appeared then, followed by Carli. I stepped back so that Lily could get in front of me, although I wanted to protect her, act as her shield tonight. Forever, in fact.

"Hi, Dad."

Dick answered with false joviality. "Happy

Valentine's Day. Ready to go?"

"Matt asked me to dinner, and I wanted to go with him instead. Okay?"

His face tightened. "Eleanor wants you to meet her family. She's told them about both you and Carli. They're going back to England in just a couple of days."

"But Dad, I really want to go out with Matt. It's Valentine's Day."

The hardness in his face seeped its way into his words. "Yes, which is why I need you with me. I'm planning to propose to Eleanor tonight, and I want you and Carli to be there to celebrate with us."

Happy. Fucking. Valentine's Day. We all stared, open-mouthed, as Dick reached into his coat pocket and pulled out a small box. *Don't be stupid and insensitive enough to fucking open it!* I thought. *I don't want to see it!*

He opened it. The diamond was pear-sized and had to be a full carat. About double what mine had been. He appeared to be almost gloating as he looked at each of us, like *there, take THAT!*

I had absolutely no idea what to say. Carli's eyes were dark and luminous as she took in the sight of the ring. Lily's expression was a mixture of disbelief and horror, similar to mine when I'd be on the computer reading about symptoms.

"You're getting *engaged?* Tonight?" Lily's words were faint.

He nodded, his lips stretching into a wide smile. "Yes. I think she'll be very surprised."

Lily's voice grew stronger. "But you haven't even said anything to us about this! We don't even really know her. Don't you care what we think?"

Dick's smile faded. "Of course I do. But this is an adult decision, and I didn't need to consult with my children about it. Now let's go. We have reservations."

Lily shook her head, her eyes brimming with tears. "I don't want to be there. This is so *awkward*. I'm not going."

"Get in the car."

Carli's eyes were very round. She squeezed past Lily and headed for the driveway. I called after her that I loved her. Dick put his finger in my face. "Don't interfere."

I spat at him. "Don't try and prevent me from talking to my daughter!"

He focused his attention on Lily. "Let's go."

She folded her arms across her chest. "No."

"I am your father, and I demand it!"

Lily exploded. "You have not been any kind of fucking father! You don't care about us anymore!"

And then, everything slowed. Motions became big, fluid. I watched in utter amazement, as Richard grabbed Lily's arm, his voice gritty and cold. *"You are not to use that kind of language with me! And you will do as I say!"* Her anguished face, turning to me. The sound of Winston's tags jingling as he hurried out of the kitchen. I reached for Richard's arm, the first time I'd touched him since the divorce...the arm that used to hold me at night, pulling at his oldest child, as Lily screamed, *"Stop it! I hate you!"*

Incredulous, Richard and I stared at each other over the child we had created. For that sacred moment, we understood each other perfectly. I saw, then, sheer misery. It trembled on the surface for a few seconds, and then the muscles in his face became taut in an unyielding, impenetrable mask. But I had seen what was beneath, and it pierced me to my core.

Sobbing, Lily wrenched herself away from her father and ran upstairs. I looked over Richard's shoulder at the shadow in the car that was Carli. I was glad I could not see her face.

Richard turned and walked away. *Please,* I begged him silently. *Please, let's not ever have that happen again.* This was most likely something we could agree on. I closed the door and went to try and convince Lily that broken hearts would heal. Although I still had my doubts.

*****

"So how are things now?" Gavin wanted to know. I had called him tonight, just as I had known I would.

"They're all right, I guess. Carli came home with some chocolates and a red teddy bear. I asked how dinner was, and she said Richard had asked Eleanor to marry him. She didn't say any more, and I didn't ask."

"That's probably a good thing."

"I had a talk with Lily and told her that I was sure her father felt badly about what had happened."

"Nice of you to say."

"Well, it's the truth. He may be a bastard a lot of the time, but I do believe he loves his children."

"And how are *you* doing?"

"I don't know. I think tonight might have been a breakthrough for me. I saw what anger can do, and I don't want it for me. I need to concentrate on other things in my life."

"Like fatal diseases?"

"Very funny. But since you mentioned it, today I had bladder cancer because my pee was red, only it turned out to be from beets."

Gavin laughed gently. "You know, there's an expression that goes, 'when you hear the sound of hooves in the distance, assume it's a herd of horses.' Every time you get some symptom, you always think in terms of an exotic cause, like it's a herd of zebras. It's not likely that it's zebras, Chris. You just have to convince yourself."

"Easier said than done." I paused. "Do you think that sometimes I feel too sorry for myself?"

"Yes."

Well, then.

"It's understandable. It's just that whenever you do, or whenever you're angry, you're keeping alive what he did to you. If you can find a way to let it die, you'll be better off. What's that expression? The best revenge is..."

"...living well," I finished. I'd heard that before but hadn't paid much attention.

"You should get some sleep."

"Okay.

"Call me tonight if you need anything."

"I will. Thank you for the talk." I looked out at the night sky, at the snowflakes kissing my window. "Gavin."

"Yes?"

"Happy Valentine's Day."

CHAPTER THIRTY: *Growth*

The zebras visited me again after fifth period. I was sitting at my desk listening to Arnold, or at least pretending to. Arnold liked to talk, and he didn't like to bathe. Those two characteristics made him possibly the least endearing student I'd ever had. And he was strange. When writing on the board, teachers had to be careful not to make the letter **W** too rounded, because **W's** reminded Arnold of breasts. I always cringed when I'd have to write a **W,** because anything I might say after that would be punctuated with the sounds of Arnold snickering, *heh!heh!heh!*

Today, Arnold was sharing with me his free choice writing piece on four-wheeling. He could not come up with an engaging lead to save his life, but his run-on sentences were nothing short of masterful. His stories always had the same three elements: a mode of transportation, violence, and no punctuation. He was in the midst of reading aloud his latest narrative, and had just gotten to the part where his vehicle slammed into a cow. My years of teaching experience afforded me the beneficial skill of appearing to listen when I was so not, but today I was particularly distracted.

"...and then the cow exploded, and the guts sprayed all over me..."

I arranged my face to look attentive. *Please look like I care...please let me convey just the slightest bit of interest.*

I felt an itch in my ear, and scratched it. And that's when the zebras galloped up to greet me.

239

There was a tiny bump. It felt hard, and my pulse accelerated until I thought my heart might burst (much like the unfortunate bovine in Arnold's story).

Mercifully, the bell rang, and I looked at Arnold apologetically. "Guess we'll have to finish that up the next class." I told the students they had the night off from homework, heard a few cheers, and hurried into the conference room for the five minutes between classes.

Fitzy came in to grab a Diet Coke. "What's up?"

"Where's Jess?"

"Dentist appointment. Root canal or something."

Shit. That meant the only person I could turn to was Fitzy. I didn't want to call Gavin, especially when I was supposed to be thinking horses.

Inhale, exhale. The zebras stomped and snorted. "Have you ever heard of anyone having...ear cancer?"

Fitzy paused in mid-sip, the can at his lips. "Air cancer?" he asked tentatively.

I became impatient. "No," I said. "EAR cancer. E - A - R."

He swallowed, contemplating. "I've never heard of that. Why, do you have something in your ear?"

I nodded.

"What does it feel like?"

"It's a little growth."

"It's probably a zit. People get zits just about anywhere." He burped loudly as he tossed his can in the trash and headed into the hallway.

He was going about this all wrong. Much too dismissive. He hadn't even *seen* it. Clearly, he didn't understand the ramifications of this. If it was in fact ear cancer, it was very near my *brain*, for God's sake. I stuck my finger in my ear again and rubbed. I had to admit, it *did* feel a little like a pimple. Damn Fitzy and his common sense.

*****

Lily was finishing setting the table when Carli bounded into the kitchen. "Mumma," she said, her eyes shining, "can we do a Sabbath dinner?"

I looked at her. Perhaps she had forgotten. "We're not Jewish, sweetheart."

"But it's so *coool*. When I was at Amanda's Friday night, they had one. They sing and say little prayers, and they go around the table and say what they're grateful for, and what they did that day or one thing they learned. Can we please just do it?"

I stole a glance at Lily, who was placing silverware on the table a little too forcefully, and looked back at Carli's earnest face. "Well, I suppose we could. As long as we don't have to sing."

Lily snorted in exasperation. "Are we seriously going to do it? That is so *lame*."

Carli ignored her. "Do we have any bread? We have to break bread."

I found a rather stale bagel in the breadbox and handed it to Carli. We sat down, and thus began our Sabbath dinner.

Carli ripped off a chunk of the bagel and passed it to me. I took a piece and handed the bagel to Lily. Lily complained that she didn't think we all had to *touch* it, because that wasn't very sanitary. I said it would be fine because we had washed our hands. Carli said she'd actually forgotten to, and Lily put down her piece of bagel and smirked at me.

241

"So," Carli announced. "I'll go first so you'll know how to do it, and then you can go, Mumma. God, thank you for this meal we are about to eat, and thank you for my mother who made it."

I beamed at her. Lily rolled her eyes.

"Now I'll do the second part. In school, we're learning about the body, and today we talked about the male reproductive system, and—"

"Oh, like the penis and testicles?" Lily interrupted.

I glared at Lily. Carli blushed fiercely. "Yes. But I don't really get why we need to learn all about a boy's...private parts, since we don't even have them."

"I'll bet you'll have 'em someday," grinned Lily, ignoring my steely gaze. "I guess this Sabbath dinner *was* a good idea, after all."

"Shut up, Lily!"

I raised an eyebrow in warning.

"ANYWAY," continued Carli, "we also learned about birth. The pictures of the newborn babies were so cute."

"I'm never having kids," Lily announced. "We watched this childbirth video in health, and all you could see was tons of HAIR down there. It was so gross."

I had to step in. "I think there's just a bit more to the miracle of life and creating a new human being than someone's pubic hair."

"Well, *I'm* having kids," Carli said. "I'm going to name my baby Lindsay, even if it's a boy, and I'm going to spoil it rotten."

My phone rang. Carli pouted. I excused myself and held up one finger to tell her I'd be right back. It was Gavin calling me from the road.

"Hi, Chris." He sounded slightly irritated, or

tired, or both.

"What's the matter?"

"Oh, a customer with an elevator issue. No up-start, which means the elevator stays at the floor. He's had problems with a solenoid valve in the past, and I thought we'd fixed it. He's not taking it too well. I'm the guy who always has to put out the fire."

"I'm sorry."

"No big deal. What are you up to? Any major diseases today?"

I remembered the pimple/tumor in my ear. Even I had a tough time convincing myself there was such a thing as ear cancer. "Nope."

"Good girl. What else is going on?"

"Well, we're in the middle of our Sabbath dinner."

"Whaat?"

"I can't really explain it, but I wish you were here. You'd enjoy it. Can you call me later? Carli's having us share things, and it's my turn."

"Okay. Shalom."

I'd heard that word before but couldn't remember what it meant. I hung up and went back to the table. Carli looked at me expectantly. What would I say? All of a sudden, it occurred to me what today was. And I knew what I needed to say.

"First of all, I want to say I am so very grateful for the two wonderful children sitting here with me tonight, and I hope *both* of you have babies someday, because it would be a shame not to give a part of you to the world. And as for what I've learned...I've been doing a lot of thinking lately." I took a second to make a silent prayer that I would do this right. "Did you know that today is one year since your dad and I were divorced?"

Lily looked down at her plate. Carli shifted in

her chair. "It's no secret I've been mad about your father leaving, and you've seen that, which I guess is pretty understandable. And honestly, sometimes I didn't mind if you saw it. I just feel like now it's time I move on, because it gets pretty crazy when I get so caught up in being angry. Sometimes I feel like..."

I paused. How could I explain it to them so they would understand? I looked from Lily to Carli and then around the kitchen, the heart of the home. My gaze rested on an appliance. And there was my explanation.

"It's like I'm in a blender. Sometimes that's exactly what it feels like. It might be just the first button, you know, the 'stir' one, when something a little irritating happens, like..." I searched for an example.

"Like when you have to clean the litterbox?" Carli offered.

"Yes, perfect. And then sometimes the blender will be on *puree.*"

"Like when Mimi tells you what to do?" Carli smiled proudly. She was getting the hang of this.

"Exactly. If it's on *chop,* that's when I feel really sorry for myself. Once in a while, I even feel like the blender's set on *liquefy.*"

Carli's eyes widened.

"That's when things are really bad, like last month when Dad got upset with Lily. Luckily," I reassured them, "that button doesn't get pushed too often."

I took a deep breath. "I guess what I'm saying is, I don't want you in the blender. You don't belong there. I want you to be calm and happy and at peace with everything."

Carli reached out and put a cool hand on my arm. "But when will you get out of the blender?"

"When I'm ready."

Lily looked out the window, staring hard.

"I hope you're ready soon," said Carli.

"You know," I replied, "I really think I'm getting there." I smiled at her and remembered what Gavin had said to me before I'd hung up. *Shalom*...it meant, *peace*.

CHAPTER THIRTY-ONE: *Sniffles*

We were in the midst of our teacher inservice day, aligning standards with our curriculum, when Fitzy looked up from his laptop. "Do you know," he asked, leaning back in his chair, "the three best things about teaching?"

"June, July and August," I answered.

Fitzy high-fived me. "Abso-fucking-lutely."

Jess sighed. "You people are awful. What about the joy of witnessing a student grasping a concept for the first time?"

Fitzy reached down between his legs. "Grasp this." Jess reached across the table to smack him.

"You know," I said, "At this point in my career, I'm inclined to agree with him. There have been times I've thought of finding another profession."

"You're damned lucky to have this job," Jess said. "You could be working at a makeup counter, talking to women about their pores. I don't think I'd really want to do anything else. Except maybe be a restaurant critic. You'd actually get *paid* to eat."

"I'd like to invent something," Fitzy declared. "Make some big bucks. Like come up with a way to make semen chocolate-flavored. Talk about a win-win situation."

We looked at him. I sneezed—my third time this morning. My throat was a bit scratchy, and I felt the early stages of congestion.

Jess passed me a box of Kleenex. "Allergies, huh?"

"You'd better rest up this weekend," Fitzy

said. "It might be a spring cold."

I shrugged as I blew my nose. "I don't know. Maybe." A cold was a sign of a compromised immune system, which could mean...I struggled to retrieve the sound of Gavin's voice saying *herd of horses.* I cleared my throat, tried to lighten my tone. "Have either of you had a cold recently?"

They shook their heads. I thought about all of my students and could not think of one person who'd been sneezing.

Gavin's voice again, rich and warm. *Stop thinking zebras, Christine.*

Okay, I answered him. *I will think horses. Galloping towards me in a meadow full of buttercups and Queen Anne's lace...here a palomino; there a dappled grey; that one a shining ebony, muscles rippling, his tail held out like a banner...they are horses, not zebras. They are not deadly. They are good.*

I sneezed again. And again, and again.

"Jeee-zus," Fitzy said. "Are you going to live?"

I reached for another Kleenex. To my surprise, I told him, *probably.*

*****

I took Fitzy's advice and went right to bed that night. With Gavin. He studied me seriously, his gaze traveling all over my face. I blushed. I was not used to this much eye contact. "I'm very proud of you," he said, as he ruffled my hair. "So you imagined me talking to you when you were trying to convince yourself of this cold?"

"I did. It helps that you have a very sexy voice."

"That's a very big step for you, girlfriend."

Girlfriend. It had been about twenty-five years since anyone had called me that. It sounded fresh and sweet, conjuring up images of walking along the beach holding hands and sharing buttered popcorn in a darkened movie theater. I was someone's girlfriend. Gavin's girlfriend.

I had to be honest. "It wasn't that big of a deal, because sneezing isn't as scary as some other symptoms I've had. And I'm not saying I didn't have some doubt."

"I understand."

"Because I did. I did have doubt. My throat was kind of scratchy, so I started worrying about swollen glands, and what that could mean..."

"You're not a doctor. Remember that."

"No, but I play one on the internet. And I look kind of pale, too, so that made me a little worried I might be anemic. Do you think I look pale?"

"Christine. Please."

I sighed. This was so damned difficult.

"Just focus on the fact that you made a conscious effort not to think death."

"I will." It was springtime, after all, and spring was about life. I put my arm around Gavin. He felt warm, so I pulled the blanket off him. Gavin pulled it back up, chiding me. "I'd like to regulate my own body temperature, thank you." He gathered me into the curve of his body, and I rolled over and shifted so that my buttocks were pressing into his pelvis. I smiled when I felt him stir. I so loved spooning.

I began to drowse. A rare and delicious feeling, with no worries of coffins or cradles. I had arranged for Lily and Carli to stay overnight at my parents' house, so there would be no interruptions...just Gavin and me. And then my cell phone rang.

He spoke into the nape of my neck. "Make it stop."

It was my mother. Piano key feeling, up and down my spine. Not unlike the fear of death. I braced myself. *Calm and authoritative.* "Hello?"

"Christine. What are you doing?"

"I was sleeping."

A pause on her end. I could almost envision icicles forming on the phone line. "I guess the question would be, sleeping with *whom?*"

Gavin held me tight, flooding me with reassurance. "Mother," I said, "I am not going to answer that."

Her voice became shrill. "You asked your father and I to watch your children so that you could have *intercourse* with some virtual stranger? Have you not heard *anything* I've been trying to tell you?"

I took a deep breath.

"You have two young, impressionable daughters to think about! Not only are you not ready to date, there is the moral issue of casual sexual relations. I knew I should have started you in counseling with my minister. We are going to discuss this later, Christine! Mark my words, we'll discuss this—"

"No, Mom," I interrupted. "We won't." I hung up the phone.

Gavin kissed my shoulder. "You're shaking. Are you all right?"

"I don't know. I've never been like that with her before."

"Another first for you. I hate to tell you this, Ms. Kellen, but I think you're growing up."

"Yes, approaching adulthood at forty-three. Real impressive."

"Better late than never, right?"

"Mmm."

"We should get some rest so you can fight off this cold. I worry about how you're sleeping."

"You do?"

"I woke up in the middle of the night last night wondering if you were asleep, and I hoped that you were, so you wouldn't be worrying about anything."

Unexpectedly, the tears began a slow, straight line down the sides of my face and dripped into my pillow. I sniffled.

"Why are you crying?"

"Because no one's ever said anything like that to me." I rolled over and hugged and hugged him, pressing my wet face into his chest, breathing in the big clean smell of him, the smell of soap and comfort.

"I was also thinking about your hypochondria, and what that could mean."

"Besides the fact that I'm wacked?"

"Yes, besides that. Your pattern is really quite intriguing. You put all your energy into worrying about an imagined illness, which keeps you too busy to focus on the stress in your life, and then you seek reassurance until you find it. I'm no psychologist, but it might be the relief you get from the reassurance that's addictive. Maybe it's your way of telling yourself that everything is all right, and you need to keep hearing it over and over."

I lay motionless. It was as though someone had sliced me down the middle, peeled back my sides and laid me out for all to see.

"*We* have to figure out a way for you to think things are okay, without scaring the bejesus out of yourself."

He had said we.

"I'm here for you, girlfriend, and I'll keep telling you that you're all right."

The tears would not stop. "But how many times are you going to tell me?"

He took my face in his hands. "Until you believe it."

Then, I knew.

CHAPTER THIRTY-TWO: Anti-dote

If I had to choose between standing in a room with a couple of rabid wolverines who'd gone without food for three days, and standing in a room with my mother after I'd blatantly defied her, of course I would have chosen my mother to go stand in the room with the rabid wolverines. And then I would have run away really, really fast.

When I picked up Lily and Carli at my parents' house on Sunday, I tried to ignore the wrath emanating from their Mimi like a nuclear mushroom cloud. Since I had never confronted her before, neither one of us knew how to act. She stood in the doorway, her earrings trembling with the effort of holding in her fury. I thanked her for taking care of the kids, waved to my father who stood stiff and silent in the back of the room, and hustled my daughters into the car.

As Carli detailed what they had done with Mimi and Poppa the night before, I thought about the elevator salesman's psychological assessment of me. If Gavin was right—that I was distracting myself from the stress in my life by my hypochondria—then I needed to first and foremost look at what was causing me stress. I had just left one of the primary sites. But I would need to put more than just physical distance between us.

And then there was my anger toward Richard, which at times still smoldered and flared. He had never understood the humiliation I had endured after he had shared those photographs, how horrifically exposed and vulnerable I had felt.

Did I want revenge? Probably. Would I get it? Doubtful. I still wanted him to realize what he had done: feel it so deeply that every atom in every cell of his body would tremble with empathy. I had seen a glimpse of his innermost self that night when he'd gotten so angry at Lily—the unhappiness he'd been hiding. Perhaps that would have to be enough. I needed to find a way to shed the rest of my anger. It was springtime, and this was too heavy a coat.

I dropped off the kids at home to spare them the trip to the grocery store. I wanted to prepare a fine spaghetti dinner for them, and for Gavin: my homemade sauce with lots of mushrooms and garlic, a spinach and walnut salad, Italian bread.

I wheeled my cart toward the produce section. As expected, all of the cut watermelons were pale. A source of irritation, but strangely, a source of comfort as well, that some things never changed. I smiled at a gray-haired woman checking the cantaloupes and headed toward the Vidalia onions. That was when I felt it. A zinging in my left hand as I gripped the cart. As many symptoms as I'd had, I'd never felt anything quite like this before. It hurt and tingled at the same time. Signs may include brief pain, tingling or electric-shock sensations. Multiple sclerosis again. Panic slithered in.

Herd of horses, Christine. Inhale, exhale. *Horses, not zebras. You are doing this because you are stressed. You want reassurance that everything is all right. You do not have anything serious or deadly. It's a tingling in your hand, and that's all. Herd of horses.* This time, a familiar voice, but not Gavin's. Mine.

I began to breathe slowly, deeply. The tingling in my hand faded. My fear was slowly replaced by euphoria. I had talked myself out of thinking I had an awful disease. And this time, I had listened.

Tears rushed into my eyes. If other shoppers noticed, at least I had the Vidalias for an excuse. I needed to end my love affair with the search for reassurance. Breakups were hard; maybe I would die trying, but I hoped not. I knew I had a long way to go, mainly because of the mental red flags springing up at the *brain tu—correction, pain in my head—*I just felt. But this was a start.

I needed to celebrate. I would stop on the way home and get an ice cream. And I would bring one to Gavin, a huge mint chocolate chip sundae with hot fudge and marshmallow and whipped cream. He would be proud of me.

The line at the ice cream window was long for a Sunday afternoon, but I didn't mind, still glowing from my recent victory. As I walked away carrying my sundaes, I wanted to smile at everyone: the solemn little boy in front of me standing on his dad's shoes, the elderly man and woman leaving the counter with their pistachio cones, and the forty-ish couple to my right in their matching gray athletic shorts...

I froze.

It was them. Richard, and his British masseuse.

This was unexpected. The scene was similar to the one with my mother earlier today, with neither party knowing what to do. I looked first at Richard, observed the wariness in his eyes, and then at Eleanor. Sunlight glinted off the diamond on her finger.

I felt the cold drip of ice cream on my hand. The blood was pounding in my ears. My thoughts catapulted back in time...*I need a change...I want to blindfold you. It's part of my fantasy...it isn't so much about wanting someone else as it is not wanting* **this***...he..doesn't LOVE YOU...he doesn't CARE...*the events of the past, like ingredients in some colossal blender, tumbling and whirling around until suddenly I punched the off button with two simple words.

"Thank you."

They stared at me. I drew in my breath. This was truly unexpected, for all of us.

I looked steadily into Richard's eyes. *Thank you for showing me who you really are, so that I could find out who I really am. Thank you for releasing me so I could meet someone who would teach me what tenderness feels like. Thank you for giving me my new life.*

"I mean it. Thank you," I said, and turned toward the car. The best revenge was living well. I would go home, share ice cream with Gavin, tell him all about this, and do my best to live well.

But there was one more thing I had to do, because after all, revenge was also sweet. I would give Richard his just desserts. I set the sundaes in the cupholders in my car, wiped my hand on a napkin and walked briskly back to my ex-husband and his fiancée, who were about to order. "Excuse me," I said to the man behind them as I cut in line. "I just have to do this."

Richard turned from the counter just as I yanked down his shorts. I looked at the small crowd gaping at the sight of my ex-husband's buttocks. *Exposed. Vulnerable.*

"He has a hairy ass," I said. "And I'm glad to be finished with it."

As I walked back to the car to head home, I realized I'd never felt so healthy. There were bound to be recurrences, but for now, for this moment, I was done. And really, quite delicious.

31871801R00145

Made in the USA
Lexington, KY
28 April 2014